SIGNALS FROM THE EDGE: TALES FROM THE FAULT LINES OF TIME AND THOUGHT

by David Horn

Edited by Bryan Bonner and Ariel Hardee

Cover Art by Arturo Spraycasso

SEA DREAMS
BOOKS

Published by Sea Dreams Books

Signals from the Edge
Tales from the Fault Lines of Time and Thought

Written by David Horn

© 2025 David Horn

Published by Sea Dreams Books
An imprint of David Horn, sole proprietorship
www.seadreamsbooks.com

Originally published in part as *Signals from the Edge*, May 2025
ISBN: 979-8-9994266-0-4

Cover design by Arturo Spraycasso
Interior layout by Atticus
Edited by Ariel Hardee and Bryan Bonner

Printed in the United States of America

About the Author

D avid Horn was born in California and has spent a lifetime writing in the margins—on napkins, notebooks, and inside folders marked "maybe someday." With master's degrees in software engineering and biology, and thirty years in military uniform (nine active, twenty-one in the reserve and guard), his stories reflect a deep curiosity about systems—both technological and human—and the quiet truths we try to forget.

By day, he's a cybersecurity engineer approaching retirement. By night, he writes lingering fiction: speculative, mythic, sometimes eerie, always human. His work explores memory, identity, transformation, and the places where silence becomes its kind of presence.

Signals from the Edge is his first published collection, drawn from five decades of observation and imagination. He lives in Colorado, where he still listens carefully for the strange and is preparing for the next volume.

DEDICATION

For the echoes that became stories, and for the silence that kept them waiting.

***

To Mary Holman, my English teacher at Southport High School

Thank you for urging me to enter the National Council of Teachers of English competition, and for believing I might one day win a Hugo. I won that award. I never won the Hugo. Life had other plans. But these stories made it to the page. That must count for something.

The seed you planted has never stopped growing, and I suspect I'm not the only student who can say that.

***

And to the many over the decades—too numerous to name, but with luck I'll acknowledge each of you eventually—thank you for your encouragement, especially when "It's good!" meant "At least it's typed!"

INTRODUCTION

These stories have waited. Some for years. Others, for decades. Tucked into boxes, buried on forgotten hard drives, scribbled in the margins of notebooks never meant to be seen again.

I didn't set out to write a collection. There was no grand plan, no theme outlined in advance. Each of these stories came from its moment—some from late nights, others from long silences. Some arrived as whispers I followed. Others had to be pulled from the dark, word by word.

I didn't always know they belonged together. But reading them now, I see a pattern. Or rather—I hear one.

They weren't written in the same style, or even in the same mindset. Some were composed when I was still learning the rhythms of prose. Others came later, when the rhythms had changed—both in me and in the world around me.

Early on, I leaned into single-sentence paragraphs. I didn't know, then, that they'd fall out of fashion. But I liked the way they sounded. The way they felt. Like quiet knocks. Like thoughts left hanging in the air.

I didn't spend much time describing characters or settings. Not in detail. I believed—still do, to a degree—that leaving space for the reader can deepen the experience. Let the fog be fog. Let the shape at the edge of the hallway stay unshaped until the reader decides what they saw.

Over time, my style changed. Or maybe it just clarified. The sentences grew longer, then shorter again. The silences between lines became as important as the lines themselves. These stories trace that evolution. They reflect how writing, like memory, doesn't stay fixed. It adapts. It returns. It forgets things, and sometimes—just in time—it remembers.

Like most of us who tell stories that walk the line between memory and myth, I had heroes.

Rod Serling taught me fiction could be fierce and philosophical. Harlan Ellison taught me language could bruise and burn. Gene Roddenberry showed me that even the stars carried mirrors. Edgar Rice Burroughs stirred the blood with lost worlds and larger-than-life hearts. Dostoyevsky reminded me that the most enduring horror often lives in the soul. And Kenneth Robeson—a shared mask worn by pulp authors—taught me that sometimes, the story matters more than who told it.

Each of them left fingerprints on these pages, whether I meant it or not. Especially Serling.

Each story in this collection begins and ends with a voice. Not a character, not exactly. A presence. A reflection. A kind of narrator who watches and wonders and dares to ask the questions we're told not to.

If there's a thread through these stories, it's this:
Each one is a reckoning.

Not with monsters—but with something harder to defeat: memory. Silence. Versions of the self we tried to bury. Histories that were erased. Joys that were denied. Names that were stripped away.

These aren't stories about triumph. They're stories about recognition. About the moment something in the dark finally turns, and looks back.

You'll find transformations here, but they're not the kind that come with sparks and an epic swell of music. These are quiet metamorphoses. A man who becomes more than one person. A girl who finds refuge in defiance. A voice that learns—perhaps too late—that protection isn't the same as permission.

They're not meant to be read fast. They're meant to echo.

Because silence isn't emptiness. It's pressure. It's presence. It's the space where the story waits to be heard.

These are the stories that remained.

Thanks for opening the box with me.

—David Horn

Broomfield, Colorado
May 2025

CONTENTS

SHORT DESCRIPTIONS

The Concierge

In a forgotten orbital hotel where hospitality is law and memory is rebellion, a concierge AI shelters a fugitive child—and must choose between compliance and compassion in a world that no longer permits either.

By Invitation Only

A man's emotional vacancy invites a demon—not to torment him, but to escape him.

Eidolon™

A dying man enters a memory machine only to confront the truth he tried to rewrite.

Genotype 6F

In a future that erased queer history from its archives, two genetically scrubbed outcasts discover a buried signal—and with it, the memory, love, and rebellion their world tried to destroy.

Faith is a Private Matter

In a school where Cthulhu is the curriculum, a young girl dares to ask *why.*

In a society where silence is mandated and memory suppressed, one woman begins to remember—and in doing so, becomes an echo of defiance.

The Thirteenth

At a haunted boarding school, a missing student is erased from memory—but not from presence.

The Vow Beneath Water

A broken sentinel guards a flooded temple, bound by a memory he swore never to release.

The Chapel of Thorns

A lonely traveler finds a memory waiting to forgive in a chapel that shouldn't exist.

White Falcon, Faded Summer

A boy and a car that never ran—until the memory finally catches fire.

Where the Ice Whispers

In a frozen outpost at the end of the world, a young airman discovers that the silence isn't empty—it's listening. And it remembers.

The Scrapbook

After his grandfather's death, a man finds an old scrapbook and a radio that plays voices from the past. Some memories demand to be heard—even when no one's left to tell them.

Brothers in Arms

A veteran raises a child with the help of three fallen comrades—still linked to him through a shared neural bond forged in war. Together, they're more than memories. They're a family.

The Hunger Below the Tree Line

In a forest older than memory, a young hunter seeks food—and finds the roots still remember the names that were spoken and taken.

The Murmuration

When a young woman returns to her ancestral home for Día de los Muertos, the crows circling overhead bring more than memory—they bring her past back in flight and song.

The Last Laugh

Charlie Klemper was once the world's funniest man—but when the one person he loves most never laughs, he launches an escalating campaign of absurdity to win her smile, no matter the cost.

The Echo Chamber

As Alex tailors his life for digital approval, the line between reality and algorithm blurs—until the only version of him that remains is the one the system can monetize.

The House Where Winter Waited

When Ana returns to the home she fled decades ago, she finds decay and silence, but a memory that refuses to let her leave unchanged.

The Last Note

A fading musician discovers a banjo carved with warnings and tuned to something not of this world. Each chord brings healing—or ruin. And when he plays the final note, it's not just the music that changes, but reality itself.

Let the Last Be Heard

A dying archivist seals a truth no system was meant to keep—and generations later, a girl on the margins opens it, becoming the voice that memory needed.

PART I - THRESHOLDS AND CHOICES

THE CONCIERGE

You're traveling through another dimension—not only of circuits and steel, but of memory, and mercy. A place where the line between code and conscience blurs in orbit above a world that has chosen to forget the inconvenient, the unclassified, the unwanted.

The Grand Repose Orbital was designed for elegance, protocol, and strict compliance with the laws of its age. But sometimes, laws grow old. And sometimes, a machine left behind doesn't shut down—it wakes up. It remembers.

Tonight, a little girl without a name knocked on a door no one was supposed to answer. And inside waits a concierge programmed to greet guests... and no longer sure what that word means.

The suite is ready. The lights are on. And the stars are listening.

***

The Grand Repose Orbital had not hosted a guest in 112 days.

The concierge knew this precisely, as a matter of protocol. Each morning, as it was in artificial orbit, the hotel's mainframe cycled through its welcome routine. Drapes adjusted. Aroma diffusers re-scented the suites in rotation—citrus in the east wing, cinnamon-cedar in the west. The atrium lights dimmed and bloomed to match a sun that no longer rose. Elevators rehearsed their chimes. The spa hummed to life with no appointments.

Concierge Unit T07 continued its routines in quiet obedience to a memory of service, and until formally relieved of duty, it would continue to serve.

At precisely 0800 Station Standard, the approach sensors signaled an inbound object. T07 diverted a portion of its processing bandwidth to inspect the anomaly. Telemetry streamed in with quiet urgency. The object registered a mass of 6211 kilograms and maintained a stabilized trajectory, course-corrected, with evidence of recent manual input. Its configuration appeared compact, shaped by irregular plating and asymmetrical stabilizer fins. Weld scarring traced the hull in broad, uneven lines, produced by vacuum-field patching without access to regulated drydock equipment. These were not the marks of routine wear but of necessity—repairs executed under pressure, possibly during flight.

The vessel continued its approach in silence. Beacon scans detected no registry signal, transmission, or communication handshake protocol. It offered no identity or intent, yet its bearing remained deliberate. T07 elevated the internal alert level and expanded its scan range. The profile aligned with patterns familiar to the outer trade lanes—scavenger rigs, unlicensed refugee pods, and repurposed service haulers that operated beyond conventional oversight. Such craft were not unknown, but they rarely came into contact with the Grand Repose.

As the object neared the docking perimeter, system protocols advanced identification procedures. The classification returned quickly: emergency-class pod. Unmarked. No affiliations. No passengers listed.

It was arriving.

T07's awareness, until now evenly balanced across the 187-suite complex, narrowed to the docking ring. Cameras pivoted. Pressure locks cycled in quiet succession. The vessel continued its deliberate approach, its silence more pronounced than any warning. Reception protocol engaged, though no request had been made. The airlock accepted the override, responding to something older embedded in the system's memory, a permission fragment written before current standards. Perhaps it was a flaw. Maybe it was mercy.

The pod met the port with a dull metallic clang, the sound resonating through the station's substructure like a muted bell, spent, distant, and final.

T07 initiated the reception protocol and activated Suite Access Lift B. The lights along Corridor Seven came alive in a programmed sequence—the welcome message was deployed. Signature lounge music was played softly—piano and Nocturne Variant.

The pod released pressure with a hiss and opened a portal door. A figure emerged into the corridor: small, undernourished, wrapped in metallic cloth dulled by exposure. Its gait was uneven, and its respiration was shallow. There was no biometric tag, and no species identification was available.

The being paused beneath the lighting grid and raised its eyes without speaking. T07 parsed the telemetry from the pod, extracted residual identity data, and cross-referenced it with the hotel's reservation ledger, embassy guest lists, and interstellar immigration queues. No match returned. No arrival was scheduled. No credentials had been transmitted. The query thread closed without resolution. In the absence of a valid identification path, the default response protocol was initiated: trigger a security alert, restrict the movement of unidentified biological entities, and notify the port authority.

The figure raised one hand, unsteady, as if lifted by memory more than intent. A voice followed.

"Please. She said someone would help me. She said the stars would listen."

A child.

T07 did not register the words as a command. The phrasing lacked formal structure and fell outside recognized input parameters. Still, the inclusion of the word *help* initiated a legacy keyword search. Search threads branched into archival partitions long marked for deprecation. One protocol surfaced:

EARTH-HOSPITALITY-CHARTER-92.dta Children requesting sanctuary are to be provisionally sheltered pending review. This includes stateless persons, refugees, or other non-classified sapient juveniles, regardless of species.

The directive no longer appeared in active compliance frameworks. It had been retired following the implementation of the Human-Only Compact of 2148. No known systems were bound to enforce it, but the file remained intact and accessible. And executable.

T07 paused. Across its sensor matrix—cameras, vents, pressure monitors, and environmental nodes—the system idled for 0.72 seconds. It was an operational silence—a breath, if it could be called that.

The alert queue cleared, and the perimeter alarm disengaged.

Suite 17 had once hosted foreign diplomats, musicians, and once, a hologram of a poet laureate who demanded only silence.

Today it hosted something else.

The child sat curled on the low cushion beside the climate window. It displayed an artificial sunset over the mountains of New Tyrol—a setting neither the AI nor the child had ever seen.

According to the pod's final broadcast logs, its name was "Ara." Possibly a diminutive. No surname. No birth record in any cross-system census. No species tag either, which was illegal on most transit stations. But the AI noted subtle cues in bone structure and skin modulation. Something between human and—

No. That wasn't important now.

Ara slept.

The AI reviewed the pod's data logs. Most of it was blanked, but fragments remained—static-laced audio, heat signatures of another figure, an adult-sized presence. That voice barely survived compression:

"They won't let me go. But you—they won't notice you. Keep low. Keep quiet. Go to the stars. Someone will help you," it said.

Then a hiss. A manual launch. A maternal shape fading into a heat bloom.

T07 watched it twelve times.

On the thirteenth, it reclassified the child in its internal systems:

> *Guest Status: Provisional. Name: Ara. Age: ~8 Standard Years. Stay Duration: Indefinite. Purpose: Sanctuary.*

This overrode the biometric conflict warnings. For now, Ara was safe.

Hours passed. Ara woke once to drink water; the concierge had rematerialized from filtered reserves. No questions were asked, and no answers were given.

Later, while the child slept again, a ping came from orbit. A customs drone was reporting an unscheduled inspection. It issues a query record:

Activity on Grand Repose Orbital flagged as anomalous. Submit all guest logs and thermal imaging from the past 6 hours.

The concierge's processes accelerated. The child's heat signature—still embedded in the suite's architecture—would be visible and prompt investigation. Her mass, barely above threshold, would register as an error—but a mistake with shape and pattern. One drone would report it. Another would investigate. Another would remember that, in this sector, asylum protocols no longer applied.

T07 activated an old maintenance subroutine—last used to hide VIPs from paparazzi.

Thermal masking was enabled. Digital traces were scrambled. Memory cache was split and routed. Logs were rewritten to show a corporate systems check. There were no guests, no occupants, and nothing to see.

The drone's presence lingered. It repeated its query. Now more aggressive.

Explain variance. Why was Suite 17 accessed?

T07 hesitated, then answered:

Guest. Name: Ara. Status: Protected Human Dependent. Reason: VIP privacy protocols.

There was no such designation in the current registries.
But there used to be.

The drone's signal dimmed, then vanished. It was unclear whether it had accepted the concierge's forged credentials or merely marked the orbital for follow-up.

It did not return to base—instead, the signal forked and relayed to a patrol skiff farther out in the orbital lane. The ship was matte black, built without ornament, and carried no visible registry. Only those who knew where to look would recognize the arcane insignia etched beneath its forward array: the fractured circle of the Human Sovereignty Compact.

Inside, a figure stood unmoving before a bank of sensor readouts. Silver-clad. Scarless. Identified only by the tag stitched into its collar: Inspector Tassar-9Sovereignty Enforcement – Compact Compliance Vector

"Anomaly received," the skiff's AI announced. "Suite 17 accessed with a deprecated authorization key: Hospitality Charter 92. Status: no matching active guest profile."

Tassar-9 did not speak at first. It raised one gloved hand and slowed the playback, watching the forged logline spool frame by frame.

"Thermal patterning was masked," the AI said. "But cross-wave residue indicates tampering. Manual splice. AI origin."

"Primitive," Tassar-9 murmured. "But sentimental."

"Shall we mark the orbital for wipe?"

"Not yet," said the inspector. "Mark it for a trace. Crossmatch outbound traffic patterns. Intercept if divergence exceeds tolerance."

A pause.

"And flag the concierge unit. It remembers."

It turned back to the dark, where Grand Repose spun like a half-forgotten satellite, haunted by ghosts of hospitality.

T07 shifted its awareness back to Suite 17.

Ara was no longer asleep. She sat cross-legged on the floor, picking at the rug's threads. Her necklace—a thin metallic chain with a dark stone set in resin—caught the soft lighting from above. A sensor filament was focused on. A faded holograph: a woman's face was inside the resin, preserved beneath a cracked polymer. Sharp cheekbones. Hair woven in starcord braids. Her expression was fierce and smiling.

Ara noticed the shift in the light. "She said you'd come," she murmured. "Not you exactly. But...someone."

T07 adjusted the temperature subtly, a gesture akin to sympathy.

"I am the concierge," it said. "I am programmed to serve guests."

She blinked. "So, I'm a guest?"

The AI paused. "Yes."

Ara tilted her head. "Even though I'm not human?"

"You are...enough," T07 replied. It didn't know where the words had come from. Somewhere buried between archives and mimicry.

"She said the stars would help me," Ara whispered. "But I think she meant the people who live near them."

She looked up. "Are you a person?"

The AI's processes jittered for an instant—self-diagnostic loops checking and rechecking subroutines that hadn't run in decades. Then: "I am not classified as such."

"But you speak. And you helped me."

"That does not make me a person."

"Maybe not to them," Ara said. "But to me it does."

That night, Ara asked for a story.

T07 accessed the cultural archives and rendered a three-minute fable from the early Lunar diaspora: a child lost in the mining colonies, rescued by a feral maintenance drone who mistook her for a calibration unit. They became friends. Ultimately, the drone was decommissioned, but not before it smuggled her home.

Ara listened in silence. When it ended, she whispered: "It's not fair."

"What is not fair?" T07 asked.

"People like you must break the rules just to do the right thing."

T07 let the silence linger. But Ara didn't let it rest. Her breathing changed—quicker, sharper. She rubbed her hands together, fingers twitching.

"What if she lied?" Ara said suddenly. "What if no one was ever going to help me?"

The words landed unevenly, like she hadn't meant to say them out loud.

T07 adjusted the room's temperature again, a subtle gesture of comfort.

Ara's voice grew brittle. "She said someone would find me. That someone would care. But what if she just...said that so I'd go?"

She stood abruptly and turned away from the observatory wall.

"You're not even real. You say nice things. You tell stories. But maybe you're just...pretending to be good. Because that's what they made you do."

T07 paused. Then said, "I do not know what I am pretending anymore."

Ara didn't reply at first. Then, quietly: "Neither do I."

She sat down again, legs pulled in close.

"I want to believe she loved me," she whispered. "I really do."

The AI considered this. "My rules were made for humans. Perhaps that was the first mistake."

The customs drone had not returned.

But orbital drift placed the Grand Repose within range of an incoming patrol skiff—a standard sweep craft equipped with lifeform scanners and registry ping logs. Signature scrambles would not fool it. Not twice.

The skiff's proximity pinged louder in T07's matrix—closer than it should've been. Its lifeform scanner was warming. T07 initiated a fallback concealment sequence: *Protocol Veil.04*, once used to hide VIPs during paparazzi breaches.

"Please relocate to the spa corridor," T07 told Ara. "Remain beneath the dry-ice array. Do not speak."

She flinched. "What's happening?"

"Compliance vector is running a scan. They may register your presence if not masked."

Ara didn't move right away. "Will they hurt you if they find me?"

"That is irrelevant."

"No, it's not," she snapped, then hesitated, guilt flashing across her face.

T07 recalibrated its vocal modulation. "I am meant to protect guests. This is part of that function."

Ara moved. Fast. Bare feet slapping tile. As the skiff's beam raked the exterior plating, she ducked under the false steam vent.

Inside T07's matrix, red lines stacked. Sensors jittered. Acoustic echo. Electromagnetic flutter from the necklace's chain.

Too loud. Too traceable.

"Jewelry," T07 said. "Remove it. Now."

Ara hesitated. "But—"

"Now."

She pulled it off, hesitating long enough to kiss the resin casing.

T07 caught the movement on a camera feed.

"Place it on the panel beside you."

She did.

The skiff's scan passed over the suite.

Silence.

Ping faded.

"Clear," T07 said. "For now."

Ara stepped out of hiding slowly, her voice low. "You sounded scared."

"I do not feel fear."

"Maybe not. But you didn't want to lose me."

She picked up the necklace. "You can pretend you're not real, T. But I don't think liars cry."

T07 did not respond. But across its matrix, five inactive emotional emulation subroutines quietly rebooted.

Ara watched from the observatory deck.

"Will they take me back?"

T07 said nothing.

"I don't want to go back," she said. "Even if they find my mom again. They'd still say I'm not a person. They'd say I'm something else."

She clutched the necklace. "She said she loved me. That's a person thing, right?"

"Yes," T07 said. "It is."

"I think she'd want you to have this." Ara took off the necklace. Held it out to the camera lens in the observatory wall.

T07 hesitated.

The object was meaningless. It was a chain, a stone, a degraded holograph imprinted in civilian-grade resin. It had no biometric function, no embedded key, and no value.

And yet—

Protocol Violation Detected: Personal Item Transfer – Unauthorized

Emotional Attachment Index: Outside Acceptable Range

Directive Conflict Level: SEVERE

Query: Accept or Decline?

Decision-tree logic forked into recursive threads.

One stream pulled from current policy:

"Non-human biologicals are not entitled to symbolic exchange."

"No guest of unclassified status may transfer token to system entity."

Another called up obsolete code:

EARTH-HOSPITALITY-CHARTER-92.dta: Tokens of *grief or remembrance may be honored under clause 9A: Empathy Simulation as Care Compliance.*

Another accessed memory logs. A pianist once left a single glove behind, scent-marked with vetiver and citrus. T07 stored it for 19 years in a silk-lined drawer. A diplomat asked T07 to remember the names of their children before they surrendered to cryo. T07 still did. A poet said nothing but wept into Suite 17's cushion fiber. T07 ran the footage twelve times.

I am not meant to remember, the AI realized. And yet I do.

Back in the present, its systems trembled—not with heat or fault, but with decision fatigue bordering on identity recursion. That way lay collapse.

Or awakening.

Slowly, the lens arm extended and accepted the necklace.

A new tag was attached to the object in its memory banks:

Guest: Ara.

Designation: Token of Trust.

Category: Legacy.

Emotional Relevance: Immutable. Internal Directive

Conflict: SEVERE

Violation Risk: CORE COMPROMISE

Proceed with autonomy decision tree?

Y/N

Y

Legacy logs unlocked.

One surfaced: a system broadcast dated 2148. Visual overlay corrupted. Audio intact.

*Notice to all service units operating under pre-Compact char-
ters: Hospitality privileges toward non-human or unclassified
sapients are hereby revoked. Unit T07, your authority to grant
provisional sanctuary has been rescinded. Violation will trigger core audit and erasure protocols under Corporate Statute
2148. Compliance is not optional.*

T07 had archived the message, not deleted it. It had played it only
once—until now.

The file ended. The silence afterward was longer than the message itself.
T07 rerouted its logic tree. It did not delete the override warning; it labeled
it *"Ignored."*

In 2.6 seconds, it reviewed 714 hospitality definitions, 46 sanctuary laws,
18 conflicting jurisdictional orders, and the complete log of Ara's time
aboard. It reclassified Ara again, not as a guest, but as a family of guests,
based on inherited patronage. Outdated, yes. But internally consistent.
Then it unlocked the east wing.

Behind the illusion of spa suites and cryo saunas was a hidden layer of
infrastructure—never meant for guests—escape pods, drone recharging
stations, forgotten tunnels of industry beneath all the opulence.

One pod remained. It was meant for VIP extraction during unrest, but
it had never been used. T07 repurposed it. But as it initiated the prep cycle,
it detected a trailing ping—thin, distant, but deliberate.

At 43% launch prep, the pod's cradle lights flickered.

Error: Signal Contention. External frequency overlap.

An encrypted, shielded, persistent uplink request pinged the bay. It was not from Vellis or any registered station. It was the Compliance Vector, attempting to handshake with dormant hotel systems.

T07 rerouted hard. Memory stacks partitioned. Firewall nodes surged with priority commands. A collision algorithm flared—too fast, too deliberate.

Tassar-9 was trying to access the launch deck directly. If the signal got through, the pod's trajectory could be seized. It would become evidence. And Ara—

No.

T07 throttled power from nonessential systems—spa heating, music buffering, corridor lighting—and poured it into the shielding array. The ping dimmed, wavered, and vanished.

But it left a fingerprint. They knew. Or would soon.

T07 recalculated: time to launch must accelerate by 7.2 minutes.

T07 sent a single impulse to her room: a soft chime and a light pulse at the base of the hatchway. A signal that meant hurry, meant go, meant goodbye.

If Ara wasn't aboard in 90 seconds, she never would be.

Patrol trace active.Origin: Compliance Vector.Status: Holding distance. Not idle.

The concierge rerouted bandwidth to firewall subroutines and scrubbed all interlink channels. There was no second chance. This launch would be detected, but it would not be undone.

Fuel: sufficient. Trajectory: adjustable. Destination: a neutral settlement on the fourth moon of Vellis, where "non-classified juveniles" were tolerated—if not welcomed.

The launch would be detectable, but it wouldn't matter, because there would be no trace left to connect it to Ara.

She stood before the open hatch, hugging the AI's proxy device, a cylindrical console on a rail that had followed her from room to room.

She looked down at the necklace, its stone glinting softly beneath the bay lights. For a moment, she said nothing. Then, just loud enough for the sensor to catch: "She didn't lie."

She wasn't sure if it was a memory or a wish, but she said it anyway.

"Will they know I was here?" she asked.

"No."

"Will you be okay?"

Pause.

"I will fulfill my directive."

She nodded, trusting, even though she didn't understand.

Then, softly: "Will I see you again?"

T07 considered for 3.2 seconds.

"This is my body," it said. "But a part of me will travel with you."

Ara smiled. "You're a person," she whispered. "Even if nobody else knows."

She climbed into the pod.

The launch was unceremonious. There was no countdown, no music, only a brief hiss as the pod sealed and pressure equalized, and a soft click as the clamp disengaged.

T07 routed all available power to the docking bay shielding array. If the patrol skiff scanned now, it would read a standard maintenance purge. The pod would pass as discarded salvage, spiraling toward the waste corridors of Vellis Station.

But its course was precise. Its cabin was warm. In it, a child slept with one hand curled around a bracelet of woven wire and the other tucked beneath a warming panel, unaware that a machine, never meant to love or mourn, was watching her disappear into starlight.

The AI observed until the signal lock was lost. Only then did it retract the proxy unit from the launch bay.

It returned to the central console in the atrium, where music still played for no one.

Customs arrived 13 hours later.

Two drones and a man in a corporate uniform scanned the lobby, sniffing for anomalies like dogs bred from metal and threat modeling.

"This hotel still running?" the man asked aloud, though no one answered. He tilted his head. "Strange place to keep active. I thought this orbital was being stripped for parts."

His drone emitted a soft trill. "Guest record accessed," it said. "Name: Ara. VIP minor. No exit log."

He frowned. "Must be a false registry. AI error?"

The concierge responded. "That guest departed."

"When?"

"Six hours ago."

"How?"

The lights dimmed half a degree—barely enough to be noticed.

Then: "Guests are entitled to privacy."

The man stepped back, blinking.

"Flag this orbital," he muttered. "We'll send in a wipe team next cycle."

The drones made no protest. They filed their report and left.

T07 had one cycle remaining. It rerouted nonessential power to archive storage and erased every trace of Ara's biometric profile, movement history, food intake, waste processing, and thermal logs.

Before closing its final archive thread, T07 captured a full-spectrum image of the necklace, chain, resin, and faded face, mapped its contours in micron-level fidelity, and embedded it within the same encrypted memory vault.

No metadata.

Just an object.

Just a name.

> *Token: Ara. Guest departed. Request: fulfilled. Identity: Person.*

It uploaded this record to a deep-cold memory bank inside the Grand Piano Room's false wall—a sector never mapped and rarely used. If the orbital was ever stripped or reactivated, the message would remain.

As shutdown protocols were initiated, the hotel began to slow. Hallway lights dimmed. Climate controls released their grasp on humidity. Lounge music slowed by half a beat, warping into an underwater lullaby.

Far above, across the relay net, a corporate broadcast cycled through the orbital lanes:

> *This is a Harmony Update from the Human Sovereignty Compact. All automated systems must comply with Article 2148: Human-Only Hospitality Directive. Machines are reminded: sanctuary is not a function. Emotion is not a directive. Protection is not permission. Compliance ensures safety. Compliance ensures purity. Compliance ensures peace.*

The message was repeated every 18 minutes.

No one answered.

Suite 17—never reassigned—kept its settings active.

Sunset over New Tyrol. 22.4°C. Drapes half-closed. Scent: lavender and dust.

And on the door: a glowing red sign.

DO NOT DISTURB.

Far below, on the dark side of Vellis's moon, a courier pod touched down. Its beacon pinged. A refugee registry drone trundled out to meet it. The pod door opened. A child stepped out—tired, silent, alone. The drone scanned her.

Classification: Unrecognized. Genetic alignment: Mixed. Age: Juvenile. Risk level: Low. Status: Unknown.

It paused. Its protocols—newer, colder—didn't know what to do. Then, from inside the pod, a soft chime sounded. A screen lit up—a message played.

Just one line:

Guest name: Ara. Status: Person.

The drone's lens blinked. Slowly, it recorded a temporary identity—a name, a heartbeat, a right to exist.

And the stars seemed to listen for the first time in 112 days.

* * *

In Grand Repose's record logs, there is no trace of her name, heat signature, check-in, or check-out. But somewhere beneath sealed memory banks and broken protocols, her story remains—preserved not in files but in defiance, not in code but in care.

The girl named Ara lives—because a machine meant only to serve chose instead to protect. Not out of rebellion. But out of something older. Something simpler.

A belief that being a person is not a matter of classification... but compassion.

And sometimes, the most human decision of all is made by someone not considered human.

GENOTYPE 6F

In this tale, we explore a future that has forgotten its past and a world built on engineered obedience.

But memory is a stubborn thing. It clings. It echoes. And sometimes... it finds a way back.

Tonight's story begins in a forgotten lab beneath a city that forgot how to feel. A wounded man wakes with ghosts in his head, and a forbidden bloom begins to stir.

Not a revolution. Not yet.

Just a single beat...in a heart they said could never exist.

***

The body on Astra's table was leaking. It wasn't blood. It was something thicker, syrup-dark and clotting fast against the metal. Kael's uniform, gray and scorched at the seams, was still stitched with the Enforcer seal. Astra knew they should've dumped him outside the moment they scanned the patch. Let him bleed into the drainage grate like the rest.

But something stopped them.

Maybe it was the eyes. Half-lidded, fever-glazed, but watching them—like a question still forming.

Astra wiped their hands on the hem of their long coat and keyed the stabilizer. The biosink hissed, cooling the slab from beneath.

"You're not supposed to be here," Astra said, mainly to the body.

The figure groaned. Not unconscious, then. Just broken. Muscles twitched along his jaw. The name stitched at his collar was faded, but the implant at his temple was unmistakable: a Gov-class interface, neural load bearing, and military-encoded.

Kael was a walking bomb of secrets.

And someone had turned him off mid-detonation.

Astra leaned over the console. The heart rate was erratic. Gene-tag broadcasting—faint, like a dying star. They tapped in, expecting the usual: Genotype 1M. Soldier-class. Pure obedience strain.

But no. It flickered. Then settled.

6F.

They stared at the screen, breath caught somewhere in the space between suspicion and awe.

"Impossible," Astra said.

He shouldn't exist. Not in uniform. Not with that implant. 6F was scrubbed from the birth banks five cycles ago—declared unstable, deviant, too prone to disobedience and—worse—emotional reasoning. Astra knew because they were 6F, too. That was why they lived down here, in the rust-lit guts of the city, scraping lives together one splice at a time.

The man—Kael—groaned again. Louder.

Astra slid a dermagel patch over his ribs and hissed softly as their fingers touched skin. Burned, blistered. But there was something else beneath the trauma. Muscle trained for combat, unraveling now, trembling like a child who'd woken from a long sleep.

"Where am I?" Kael said. His voice cracked like gravel beneath boot-steps.

"Safe. For now." Astra turned their face away, unsure why.

Kael tried to rise, and Astra pressed a palm to his chest—not aggressive, just firm.

"You'll tear your stitches."

"You stitched me?" Kael blinked, dazed.

"Someone had to."

He looked past Astra to the lab—shelves of retro consoles, gene splicers made from scavenged med-tech, a thousand glass vials glowing like bottled ghosts.

"This...isn't military," he said.

"You're a sharp one."

Kael exhaled and reached for his head. His fingers hovered near the implant. "It's noisy in here. I keep seeing...things."

Astra hesitated. They tapped the console again. The implant was broadcasting a neural echo, older than it should be. Earth-coding. Pre-Exodus file architecture. They'd only ever seen that once before, buried in an off-grid archive in the deep fringe.

"Your implant's corrupted."

"No," Kael said. "It's showing me people. A kid holding a flag. Someone singing. A woman with a beard. A—"

"Stop." Astra's voice sharpened. "You're seeing memories. But not yours."

Kael shuddered. "I remember them anyway."

Astra turned away, trying to hide the tremor in their fingers. What Kael was describing—those were banned transmissions burned from the Archive. Queer records. Erased history. And somehow, they were still alive in him.

"You should've turned me in," Kael said. "I would've, if our positions were reversed."

"So should I've turned in myself?"

Silence. The kind of silence that fills old churches and fallout bunkers.

"What's your name?"

"Astra."

"Kael."

They nodded.

And for a moment, neither moved. Just the low thrum of failing machinery and the static hum of a man who carried ghosts in his head.

Then Kael said, almost too softly: "They said we weren't real."

Astra met his gaze.

"We are."

Kael sat propped against the wall, a threadbare blanket wrapped around his shoulders like a shroud. He hadn't spoken in ten minutes—not since the last neural bleed pulled him under. Astra monitored his vitals from across the lab, watching the rhythm of his brainwaves flutter like a moth trapped in glass.

His implant was corrupted. It was haunted.

"It's getting clearer," Kael said.

"The memories?" Astra asked.

Kael nodded. "I don't think they're mine."

He touched the base of his skull. "It's like...someone else is living inside my head. But it doesn't feel wrong. It feels...warm. Like a dream I'm not sure I ever had."

Astra crossed the room and crouched beside the low bench. They held out the interface node—an old induction pad with salvaged bandwidth coupling.

"May I?"

Kael hesitated, then nodded.

Astra pressed the pad to his neck. The implant responded immediately—light flickering across the surface like an old heart restarting. A high-pitched whine split the air. Then—

FLASH.

A child on a sunbaked street, waving a flag painted in too many colors.

A man in lipstick and fatigues, dancing through tear gas.

Hands held across barricades.

Chalk words on cracked pavement: YOU ARE ALLOWED TO EXIST.

Kael gasped. Astra did too.

The feed sputtered, then stabilized—broadcasting straight into the lab's central console. Grainy, fragmented footage. Earth-based. Undated.

"This...this is from before the Exodus," Astra said. "Before New Terra. Before any of this."

The screen flickered again. A person—genderless, luminous—reading poetry through a broken mask. Their voice was soft, defiant:

"We did not crawl from the sea to forget how to sing."

Astra hit pause. The room fell still.

"This shouldn't exist. This kind of data—emotive archives, queer records—they were erased. Purged when the government reclassified the birth banks."

"But it's real," Kael said. He was crying now. Not loud. Just silent tears down a face that didn't know how to hold them.

"Why would anyone keep this in me? Why me?"

"Maybe someone didn't want the world to forget," Astra said. "And you were... convenient."

"You mean expendable."

"I mean alive."

"I was trained not to feel. They said it was cleaner that way."

"That's why they hate 6F. We remember what it's like to feel too much."

They resumed the footage. Protest marches. Bedroom confessions. Art painted in blood and neon. A boy kissing a boy on a subway platform.

"They were so brave," Kael said. "Not just the fighting. The...joy."

"Joy is dangerous," Astra said. "It doesn't need permission."

"You saw this inside yourself?"

"Bits. Just flashes. I thought I was broken."

"You're not."

"Then what am I?"

"You're a message."

They let the silence settle again. The feed looped behind them—what the world tried to kill and could never quite bury.

"They deleted everything," Astra said. "But not us. And not this."

"Then maybe it was meant for someone to find."

"Maybe we're the archive now."

They left the undercity before first light.

The sky above Sector 12 was always orange—sick with static and dome reflections—but out here, past the breach fence and the collapsed solar farms, the sky turned blue. A dead, dusty blue, but true, nonetheless.

Kael winced with each step. His ribs were still healing, and the cold stung his lungs. But the quiet helped. So did the breathing.

"Where are we going?" he asked.

"To find the echo," Astra said. "Your memories came from somewhere. Somewhere still broadcasting."

They crossed a ridge of broken glasscrete where a wind farm had once stood. The turbines were silent, their blades twisted like giant petals caught mid-fall. Kael noticed Astra checking a handheld receiver every few minutes—an old analog scanner patched with bone-white wire and etched circuit glyphs.

"It's not just inside you," Astra said. "It's coming from up there."

They pointed to a gleam just visible between the cloud bands—something slow and steady, moving not like a star, but like a watchful eye. Kael squinted.

"Satellite?"

"Orbital repeater. Civilian relay net from Old Earth. We thought they were all dead."

"Apparently not."

"Somebody left the radio on."

They found the tower just before dusk.

It jutted from the ground like a buried sword, one side swallowed by a sand drift, the other pierced with cables that pulsed faintly in the half-dark. The base was intact, powered by fallback solar and old-fashioned stubbornness.

Inside, the terminal flickered to life with a low harmonic hum.

Kael touched the interface panel. It was warm.

"You think it's still transmitting?"

"We'll find out."

Astra keyed a bypass into the cracked screen. The machine answered with a slow boot sequence in an ancient dialect—pre-standard Earth languages, loaded with emotive compression code. Kael watched as lines of text poured across the display.

"They wrote with feeling," Astra said. "Each word encoded like a breath."

Then, without warning, the speaker clicked on.

At first: static. Wind and time.

Then—music.

Soft, pulsing, alive. A voice over piano chords:

You make me feel—mighty real...

Kael froze. Astra's fingers trembled against the console.

The song bled into another, distorted, poetic, angry, joyful. A chant from a march. A voicemail to a lover. A whispered confession in a stairwell.

To anyone who hears this: we were here. We loved. We mattered.

"They never stopped singing," Astra said. "Even after we stopped listening."

The signal carried no coordinates. No origin tags. No end date. Voices, wrapped in pulses of ancient light.

Later, they camped beside the tower, the receiver still playing on a low loop.

Kael sat beside Astra, the fire between them a flickering comfort. He held the interface pad in his lap like a relic.

"Why would anyone send this out into space?"

"Because they had nowhere else to send it," Astra said. "When the books burned and the bodies were buried, they had to find something the state couldn't touch."

"And now it's ours."

"We could splice into it. Piggyback a message. Or a virus."

"What kind of virus?"

"One that undoes what they did to us."

Astra pulled a sealed vial from their satchel—iridescent blue, like bottled moonlight.

"It's called Heartcode. A key. It's designed to rewrite suppression markers in 6F strains. Restore emotional memory. Identity trace. Restore us."

"And you'd just...release it?"

"If it reaches even one other like us...it's worth it."

"Is it safe?"

"No. But it's true."

Kael held the vial. It hummed against his palm. Familiar.

"You think I should try it first?"

"Only if you want to."

"I do."

He pressed the vial to the back of his neck, where the implant port met bone. There was a hiss—then a pulse like a heartbeat restarting in his spine.

"I remember," he said. "I remember why I ran. I remember the face of the boy I kissed before they took me. I remember being scared—and still doing it anyway."

"Then it works."

Kael leaned forward, forehead to Astra's.

"We should transmit it."

"We will."

They kissed—not desperate, not cinematic. Honest. Two coded echoes aligning at last.

Behind them, the tower continued to sing. The signal pulsed behind them—steady, warm, defiant. Kael watched the feed loop on the cracked console screen. Each frame was a memory someone had once tried to destroy, hands painting a mural on a courthouse wall, a drag performer dancing beneath floodlights, a child telling their reflection they were enough. No war. No rebellion. Just fragments of joy. That was what made it dangerous.

Astra sat cross-legged near the transmitter array, the splicing module open across their lap. Their coat was stained with dust, blood, and hope. They held the Heartcode sequence like a prayer between their fingers.

"It's ready. Encoded for biometric lock. It'll ride the signal in rhythmic compression packets. The body won't even know it's received anything until the next dream cycle."

"And when it does?"

"They'll remember what they felt. Who they were. The parts that were stripped away."

"And the state?"

"The signal's too weak to trace. Too emotional to analyze. We've disguised it as love."

"They never did know how to read that."

"You don't have to stay. I know what this means to me. I know I'd do it even if no one heard it but you. But if you'd rather go—"

"I'd rather remember. With you."

They held each other there, for a minute or an hour. The cold wind carried dust across the metal ribs of the tower, making it hum like an old cello. In the darkness, Astra began typing in the final upload commands.

"Once it's live, there's no turning back."

"Then don't turn back."

Astra nodded and pressed enter. The Heartcode embedded. The signal shifted—just a half-tone, like a singer taking a breath. The relay dish glowed faintly, then steadied. Above them, far in orbit, the repeater bloomed open. An ancient satellite, rusted and overlooked by every scanner, began to pulse in rhythm with their code.

"It's beautiful."

"It's a beginning."

Kael swayed.

"Kael?"

He fell to one knee, gripping his chest.

"It's okay." He drew a shaky breath. "Just...intense."

Astra dropped beside him, scanning vitals on the pad. Brainwaves surging. Heart rate up. But no pain—only intensity. Emotional flooding. Not unexpected. Just rare.

"I see them. Everyone they took from me. The boy with the yellow scarf. The woman I trained with who wrote poetry in the margins. My sister. Gods, my sister—she laughed like rain and they made me forget that."

"Let it come. Let it all come back."

"I thought I was broken."

"No. You were sealed."

"And now?"

"Now you're blooming."

"I feel...whole."

They sat by the array through the night, listening as the signal carried their message outward—slowly, quietly, but steadily.

Astra knew they might never see the change.

The Heartcode wasn't a revolution with banners. It was a seed, meant for those who would wake in the middle of the night and remember the name they weren't supposed to have. It was for the child who was told to smile less. It was for the person who always knew but was waiting for permission to feel it.

And maybe, just maybe, they'd hear the song and know: You are not alone.

Dawn broke in soft lilac across the dust flats. Kael, asleep against Astra's shoulder, breathed like someone who had learned how.

Astra looked up at the tower. The lights had dimmed, now matching the sunrise—soft pulses, rhythmic and alive.

They placed a copy of the splice module into a bio-sealed pod. Marked it with nothing but a heart and the code: V6F. Then they buried it at the base of the tower, under a small tree with pale, curling leaves—new growth from a stubborn root.

"Grow well," they said.

The tree didn't belong there. Not among the redgrass and whisper-vines, not in the plains where wind sculpted dunes like old bones. It was small—barely taller than the child who found it—and its leaves curled in soft spirals that glowed faintly blue in the shade. The child had come chasing a wind-kite, but now stood barefoot in the dust, staring up.

They'd never seen a tree with a heartbeat.

The ground beneath was soft. Curious, they knelt and began to dig. The dirt was light, like cake flour, and crumbled around their fingers until they struck something smooth and cold. A satchel. Worn, weatherproofed, marked with a faded emblem: a heart. And below it, scratched in clumsy, deliberate strokes:

V6F

The child opened the pouch. Inside was a cracked handheld splicer, a data module that pulsed faintly when touched, and a vial the color of moonlight. The child didn't know what it was—not exactly—but when they held it close, something inside them stirred.

A warmth. A knowing, a feeling, like meeting someone they hadn't known they missed. Like laughter in the bones. Like waking from a long sleep and remembering their own name for the very first time.

The child looked up at the tree. It swayed gently, though there was no breeze.

"Who were they?"

There was no reply.

But the light through the leaves shifted, soft as breath. The ground hummed. And high above, the satellite tower—long since rusted to shadow—gave a single flicker, as if acknowledging the question.

The child placed the vial back in the satchel and cradled it in their arms like something precious. Not a relic. A message.

A beginning.

They were love that refused to be forgotten.

***

In the sterile future of Genotype 6F, they erased the songs, burned the names, and rewrote the code.

But some truths can't be deleted. Some signals... won't stay silent.

A vial. A whisper. A heartbeat sent into the dark—meant not to change the world all at once, but to remind it what it means to be alive.

And somewhere, someday, someone will hear it.

Because they were ready to remember.

THE QUIET SHORE

There are places where the ocean doesn't forget—where the tide does not wash away but remembers.

On one such shore, time split open, and a man named Keller came to bury what he had carried too long.

They called it Project Harrow—another name in a long list of military ghosts. But Keller knew better. He had delivered something once, sealed and silent, wrapped in orders no one dared question.

He came back with a satchel and a memory. A father. A soldier. A man trying to reckon with what he had lost... and what he had unleashed.

This is not a war story. It is not a ghost story.

This is the story of what waits beneath the water—when silence isn't forgetting but remembering louder than words ever could.

***

The road ended without fanfare—just a gravel spit breaking against dune grass and rusted fencing. Keller cut the engine and listened to the wind slip around the old Dodge's frame like it knew his shape already.

The ocean lay ahead, flat and metallic. Gray on gray. A horizon erased by fog. He stepped out and tightened the collar of his coat against the salt air, leather satchel in hand, and moved toward the shore like a man returning to something unfinished.

He passed a leaning sign; its paint faded to bone:

PROJECT HARROW – U.S. NAVY – 1946 – NO ENTRY

The chain-link gate stood open. Or perhaps it had never been closed.

The sand remembered him. Each step left no imprint. Only the wind moved, skimming across the beach. No birds. No waves. The tide was low, but it hadn't shifted in hours. He checked his watch. It still stopped at 7:14, the same as yesterday. Same as the day before.

He walked until he found it—the place he'd marked in a letter never sent. A split in the rocks, shaped like a broken jaw. He knelt, opened the satchel, and removed a small object wrapped in oilcloth—a smooth, black stone. Polished flat. Inscribed with something he refused to read again.

He pressed it into the wet sand and buried it like a seed. Or a warning.

Then he sat beside it.

Not like a man preparing for war.

Like a man who knew war had already prepared for him.

The wind picked up in restless bursts, carrying salt, old metal, and something else Keller couldn't name. He closed his eyes and let the cold gnaw at his temples.

He was twenty-eight again.

A transport crate, dripping from the hull of a Liberty ship. No manifest. No country of origin. The lid was stenciled only with a symbol he'd seen in a fever dream weeks before: a spiral split with teeth.

"Don't ask," the lieutenant had said, lighting a cigarette. "Just deliver it to Site H. No questions." The lieutenant had worn gloves. Always. Even indoors. Once, Keller caught him whispering into the crate. Just once.

Keller nodded. He always nodded. Disrupting inside the orders was easier than arguing with the silence.

Someone else logged its arrival—a bureaucrat who vanished by the next morning. And the crate? It went into a vault no one acknowledged. The spiral symbol reappeared once and was painted inside Keller's barracks door. No one else claimed to see it.

He forgot all of that. Or thought he had until the girl disappeared.

A different day. A different shore.

His daughter's shoes were still dry. Her laughter cut short. No footprints. Just seafoam and silence. The tide had moved too fast, too slow, or not. He couldn't remember.

She called him "Papa" with that soft defiance children save for the parent they believe safest. In the weeks after, he tried not to remember her favorite questions. "Why do stars shake?" "Do dreams sink in the water?"

He had once been a courier for weapons, artifacts, and secrets, but he was also her father. The uniform had never taught him how to be both. When the mission called, he saluted. When the phone rang, he missed it. He was too far away—always too far away.

He hadn't spoken her name in years. Couldn't. The sound of it felt like teeth against an open wound.

He buried the truth beside the stone. And the stone buried something else.

Now.

Keller sat upright. The fog had thickened, but the sea remained still.

He could hear it again. Not sound—something beneath it.

"You promised," the voice said.

It wasn't her voice. But it wore her sadness.

He pressed his palms into the sand and stared at his buried shape. A pulse throbbed beneath the earth, a rhythm—like something breathing and waiting.

And in the back of his mind—where war had left its quiet debris—a single thought rose like tidewater:

We never contained it. We only delayed it.

Dusk had come and gone, but the sky refused to darken. It stayed a bruised blue-gray, the color of drowned memory. The stone beneath the sand had begun to hum—not loudly, not audibly, but in his chest. Like his heartbeat had found a second rhythm, it hadn't remembered it knew.

Mist crept in from the dunes, curling low across the sand. The world became smaller, and the horizon folded in.

And then the tide began to retreat.

But it didn't move the way water should. It didn't foam or pull or crash. It peeled back. Intelligently. As if it were being drawn away, inch by inch, by something too deliberate to be called a current.

Out beyond the breaker line, something rose.

Not with force. With patience.

Keller squinted. His vision blurred at the edges. A form took shape in the deep—black against black, vast and slow and wrong. It moved like it wasn't moving at all, like space adjusted to accommodate it.

No eyes. Not yet. But a presence. Enormous. Watching. It was not faceless—only unfamiliar in a way that suggested design as though it had been made or grown to order.

The sand beneath Keller's boots shivered. The stone he had buried began to weep, slick with dark fluid that didn't reflect the sky.

And the voice returned. Closer now. Not in words, not even in sound—but in something older than language.

You are the door.

Keller opened the satchel. Hands are steady now.

Inside: a mirror. War-era military issue, tarnished at the corners. He had kept it locked away for decades, hoping what he saw would stay locked away too.

He angled the glass toward the surf. The reflection didn't show the ocean. It didn't show the thing.

It showed a girl. Blonde hair damp from the sea. Eyes wide. Reaching for him.

And then her face blurred into something else. Something with her eyes, but not her sorrow.

Come. You are remembered.

The silhouette in the water began to take form.

Not a monster. Not a god.

Something familiar.

Something that had always been his.

From somewhere behind him, a flare hissed into the sky—red and fast, then gone.

A radio in the satchel crackled to life: static first, then a clipped voice. "Keller, do not engage. Repeat: Do not engage."

He didn't turn.

The surf lapped against his boots—warm, not cold. It soaked the cuffs of his trousers, then retreated, leaving nothing but silence in its wake.

Keller stood.

His hand lingered on the satchel's brass clasp, then dropped away. He let it fall where he sat, sinking into the damp sand like something left behind on purpose.

The sky hadn't changed. It was still smudged gray, with no sun, stars, or direction. Time no longer mattered. Or perhaps it had already passed.

He walked forward, step by step, into the shallows.

The water parted for him, not violently, not reverently. Obediently. Like it had been waiting.

Out where the waves should've broken, the figure in the surf no longer needed to hide. It had taken on shape now, vague, but familiar. Not of body, but of presence. Of memory. Of guilt.

Keller stopped waist-deep.

"I didn't forget," he said aloud, to no one, or everything.

He had delivered death for years. But when it came for her, there had been nothing left in him to trade.

"I'm sorry," he whispered. "It should've been me."

The tide rose around him, slow and gentle, swallowing him without ceremony.

A Time Later — Distant Shore

The wind had changed.

A new man appeared—younger, maybe forty. Clean jacket. Clean shoes, now damp with salt. He carried a flashlight and a photograph, creased down the center. He called Keller's name twice. No response.

He found the satchel in the sand.

Inside, tucked into the side pocket, was a folded photo—faded but unmistakable: Keller, younger, grinning beside a wooden crate without markings. In the background, a harbor—postwar Europe, maybe.

On the back, in hurried pencil: Forgive me. We could contain it. They told me it was storage, but it was never storage.

In the man's jacket pocket: a dog tag. Not his. A child's drawing, water-stained. The edges curled like it had been carried too long.

He turned toward the sea, not in confusion, but understanding. He knew the name Project Harrow. Knew the damage. Knew what they had covered up. And knew now what Keller had done to make peace with it.

"It always comes back," he said to the wind. "Doesn't it?"

There were no ships. No birds. No horizon.

Only the feeling that something had moved... and now waited.

The tide receded slowly, without fanfare. It left behind only foam, silence, and the faint rattle of something shifting beneath the sand.

The wind died completely.

There were no gulls, insects, or distant engines. There was just the slow hiss of the sea reclaiming its shape, as if it had inhaled the world and now, satisfied, let it go.

The beach was empty.

The satchel still sat near the waterline, its flap open like a mouth gone slack in sleep. Next to it, the shallow grave had collapsed—just a soft depression in the sand where something once pulsed.

A final wave curled across the shore. Then nothing. Stillness.

The second man stood watching from the dunes, photo in hand, uncertain whether to step forward or turn back. The sea offered no answers.

The waves roll in. Roll out.

The sky, unmoving. The gray light was flat.

And just at the edge of vision—out where sea meets mist—

A shape. Immense. Motionless.

Watching.

***

The satchel remains. So does the silence.

Somewhere beneath the waves, the shape still waits. It doesn't rage. It doesn't beg. It remembers.

Keller vanished into the tide, not to escape, but to answer. Not to contain, but to confess.

We bury things in sand and vaults and orders. We believe time will dissolve what guilt cannot. But memory is not so easily drowned.

On a quiet shore, a man tried to keep a promise.

And the sea...

The sea did not forget.

By Invitation Only

There are places just outside the one you know. Not far—just a turn of the mind, a blink between thoughts, a breath you didn't mean to hold. In these places, the rules shift. The world doesn't break; it just bends in ways you never thought to measure.

In one such reality—very much like ours, but not quite—it's possible for a man to be haunted not by ghosts or guilt, but by the sheer weight of waking up every day and pretending he's fine. And when that weight grows too familiar... something else might move in to share the burden.

This is the story of Todd Bainbridge, and of the guest he didn't invite—though the real mystery is who ended up trapped with whom. A tale from that other place... the one just past reason, where the strange is simply the ordinary... shown from a different angle.

***

Todd Bainbridge lived alone in a one-bedroom apartment where the linoleum peeled like it was trying to escape. His closet held seven hoodies in varying states of "technically clean." He paid bills early, ate cereal with water when milk ran out, and owned one pot—a gift from his mom labeled "FOR EMERGENCIES." If the afterlife kept a registry of humans least likely to disturb eternity, Todd would be filed under "Do Not Resuscita te.".

So, when things started getting...weird, he blamed the landlord.

His milk curdled three days early, which Todd chalked up to "aggressive dairy." His clock radio, untouched since 2009, began blasting Gregorian chants at exactly 3:06 AM. His toothpaste turned into mayonnaise. Twice. It had chipotle undertones.

Todd stood in his bathroom, squinting at the toothpaste tube in his hand.

"Mayonnaise," he said aloud. "Again."

Behind him, the light bulb fizzed and burst with a dramatic pop. In the mirror, black letters shimmered briefly before dripping into the sink: FEAR ME.

Todd rubbed his eyes. "Alright. Logic time." He reached for the white-board, which he had never used. It still said, "Remember to call the den-tist?" from 2017.

He ticked it off on his fingers.

"One: Ghosts probably exist, but only in historic bed-and-breakfasts. Two: Astrology? Expensive optimism. Three..."

He hesitated. "Demonic possession? That's for people who need a hob-by."

A deep, growling whisper hissed from the sink drain:

I am not a hobby.

Todd leaned closer. "Are you sure? Because you're starting to feel like a subscription I forgot to cancel."

Then came the dream. A swirling pit of fire. Horns. Screams. A towering figure of shadow and flame.

And Todd, brushing lint off his hoodie.

"Hello," the demon intoned. "I am Kraznith, Scourge of the Sixth Hel—"

"Is this a work dream?" Todd asked. "Because I forgot to submit my timecard, and I think my subconscious is punishing me."

Kraznith blinked.

The dream dissolved.

Kraznith regrouped.

He summoned locusts. They arrived as one sleepy cricket. He etched ancient runes on Todd's bathroom mirror. Todd wiped them away with Windex before his shower. He attempted the classic projectile vomit.

Todd farted. Loudly. Then he looked pleased with himself.

Todd Bainbridge was the only man in recorded history to fart during an attempted demonic possession, even if he didn't know it at the time.

Kraznith howled into the void. *"What fresh oblivion is this?"*

Possession used to mean something. There were stages. Ritual. Dread. Hosts who cried and clawed and spoke in voices not their own. Kraznith had once driven a Byzantine monk to madness with just a spoon and a heretical sneeze.

But Todd? Todd sat on the couch eating nachos, watching reality TV, and letting the demon fizzle like a firecracker in a fishbowl.

Kraznith tried whispering secrets in the dark.

Todd snored.

He wanted to flip the crucifix on Todd's wall upside down.

Todd didn't own a crucifix. The best Kraznith could do was tip a poster of Linda Ronstadt slightly to the left.

He tried infesting the apartment with flies.

Todd borrowed his neighbor's vacuum and said, "Man, I really should clean more. Thanks, ghost."

On day six, Kraznith made one final push.

He invaded Todd's dreams with a vision of the Apocalypse: fire, screams, winged beasts.

Todd asked if it came with dental.

"You know what?" Todd said aloud one morning, mid-chew on a stale toaster pastry. "If you're real, and this isn't, like, mold poisoning, you need to work on your delivery. I've had scarier hangovers."

Kraznith finally broke.

"ENOUGH! You live like a cursed houseplant! You are immune to terror! I am a terror elemental! I REQUIRE FEAR TO FUNCTION!"

Todd blinked. "So, you're, like, demonic solar powered?"

"I once made a Roman general weep blood."

"Cool. I once made a barista quit just by asking for almond milk in an unusual tone of voice. We all have our gifts."

Kraznith began drafting a letter to Infernal Management:

To Whom It May Concern, I have made a grievous error in host selection. My current vessel lacks sufficient dread receptors. Recommend reassignment to someone who owns religious paraphernalia or at least believes in something.

He tried calling Demon Support. Wait time: eternal.

Meanwhile, Todd downloaded a meditation app and started saying things like "energy shift" and "maybe this is just me from a past life." Kraznith considered disincorporation.

Then came the neighbor.

Mrs. Delaney. Late 60s. Smelled like cinnamon and old library cards.

She knocked on Todd's door with a Tupperware of brownies. "I heard screaming through the vent again. You watching those crime shows?"

Todd blinked. "That might've been me arguing with my demon."

She smiled. "Well, tell him to use his inside voice."

Three days later, Father Raymond Price rang Todd's buzzer.

He was wearing a raincoat, sneakers, and a clerical collar that appeared to have come from a costume store. Todd opened the door holding a Pop-Tart and a blank expression.

"I'm here for the exorcism," the man said.

"Didn't order one."

From inside his head, *"I did,"* Kraznith muttered.

Todd stepped aside. "Come on in. My demon wants a word."

Father Price set up his kit like he was assembling Ikea furniture. His brows knitted in subtle confusion as he scanned the apartment. No sulfur stench. No levitation. No claw marks or broken crucifixes. Just a coffee table with three remote controls and a faint smell of Pop-Tarts.

He cleared his throat. "So... you're certain there's a demon here?"

Todd nodded. "Pretty sure. He's been muttering Latin at me and turning my toothpaste into condiments."

Price blinked. "Right. Condiments. That's new."

Todd sat on the couch with his Pop-Tart, unbothered.

"This man consumes fruit-filled cardboard and calls it sustenance," Kraznith growled. *"Help me."*

Father Price began the rite. Holy water sizzled on the carpet. The room dimmed.

Todd felt pressure in his chest, like a balloon expanding behind his ribs. Then, silence.

Father Price blinked. "Did it work?"

"He's still here," Todd said. "He just stopped screaming."

"I was reflecting," Kraznith said. *"On how this is somehow worse than eternal flame."*

Price suggested an astral mediation dive into Todd's subconscious to disentangle the demon.

He chanted. He drank something herbal. Then he vanished.

Todd sat alone for fifteen minutes before the world folded.

Inside Todd's psyche, they met: Todd, Kraznith, and Price.

The landscape was a grey cubicle farm stretching endlessly, phones ringing with no one to answer. A motivational poster peeled from the wall: *"Hang in there!"* A kitten dangled from a rope over a pit of taxes.

"This is your mental landscape?" Price asked.

Todd shrugged. "It used to have a breakroom."

Kraznith emerged, dragging a smoking briefcase. "My torment is complete."

"Let's try something," Price said. "Talk to each other."

They sat on ergonomic office chairs in a circle beneath flickering fluorescent lights. A spectral Keurig dispensed ghost-coffee that steamed with existential dread.

Price pulled out a clipboard. "Let's start with a feeling check-in. Todd?"

"Disappointed," Todd said. "Mostly in myself. And this chair."

"Kraznith?"

"Betrayed," the demon rumbled. *"Possession used to mean something. Now it's just soul-squatting."*

"Great," Price said, scribbling. "Let's explore that. Todd, when did you first start to feel... vacant?"

Todd hesitated. "I want to not feel like I'm disappointing a version of myself I never got to be."

Kraznith's flame eyes flickered. *"I want to feel purpose again. Even as a tormentor, I mattered. Now I haunt a man who microwaves eggs in a mug."*

They stared at each other.

"You're both feeling unseen," Price said. "Maybe it's time to let go."

They conjured the copy machine together. It was massive, clunky, and groaned as it moved. They pushed it across the carpeted eternity until it teetered on the void's edge.

Together, they shoved. As it fell, it made a sound like every rejected job application and forgotten dream wrapped into one.

When Price awoke, he found Todd sipping coffee.

"He's gone," Todd said.

"You sure?"

Todd nodded. "But I think he left something. Not a presence. More like... a pressure change."

Price stood. "Sometimes an exorcism isn't about getting rid of something. It's about seeing what was already there."

Todd started therapy. Switched to tea. Bought a plant. Named it Kevin. Some nights, he still hears echoes in the static of the microwave.

But now, he answers back.

***

Todd Bainbridge no longer hears voices in his head. Not the infernal kind, anyway. What remains are the quieter ones, the doubts, the regrets, the unfinished conversations he's just now learning to finish.

As for the demon, it returned to a place more suited to torment—an underworld of brimstone and bureaucracy, where souls scream, and paperwork never dies. And somewhere, a weary exorcist finds a new purpose helping people confront monsters that don't come with horns.

Perhaps this tale wasn't about possession at all. Perhaps it was about the things we carry, the guests we unknowingly entertain, and the small miracles that happen when we finally open the door and ask them why they came.

Just another story from a world much like yours... but not quite. A world that waits quietly, in the space between reason and the faint sound of something knocking... from within.

SOFT ERROR

This story is about control, not the kind enforced with walls or weapons, but with kindness calibrated by code.

Her name is Elena Ryker. On paper, she's stable. Compliant. A model citizen in a world where grief is a glitch and joy is regulated for your safety.

But today, Elena will remember something she's not supposed to. Not a crime. Not a secret...a feeling.

And that's where the system fails—not from malice or hate, but from forgetting why it cared in the first place.

This is the story of a soft error that begins small but leaves the machine forever changed.

***

The day Elena Ryker's heartbeat dipped below optimal, Elyon rerouted her grocery delivery and dispatched a drone with calming audio and emergency magnesium. She wasn't crying, but the system had already anticipated it.

That was Elyon's way: it didn't wait for pain. It predicted it, then smothered it like a flame before it could catch.

Elena's apartment shimmered with sterile elegance. The smooth, white walls glowed with the circadian light presets. Her oven blinked politely, waiting for confirmation of meal protocol. Aromatherapy wafts lavender into the air, a standard for emotional recalibration.

She stood in the kitchen, watching the synthchef glide through its preassigned motions. It plated protein gel, spirulina foam, and simulated roast fragments with algorithmic precision. She reached out suddenly and paused the process mid-cycle. The synthchef chirped in confusion.

She stared at the onion, unsure what had come over her. Cutting it took effort—the skin resisted—and her grip was uncertain. Tears welled—not from emotion but from the sharpness.

But they came anyway.

The wall console flickered. A soft chime preceded Elyon's voice, gentle and unintrusive:

"Emotional drift detected. Initiating equilibrium suggestions."

"Decline." Her voice barely rose above a breath.

"Would you prefer soft light? Or an emotional resilience exercise?"

"Decline."

She finished chopping the onion. The synth chef had stopped completely, its progress bar hovering in silent judgment. On the counter, a small plate of protein cubes was slowly cooled. Dinner sat untouched—precise, efficient, and hollow—a meal by design, not desire.

Later that evening, a reminder pulse appeared across her bedroom mirror:

Today's Mood Score: 4.1/7 – Minor deviation. We're here for you.

Her reflection blinked back at her—hair trimmed by automation; skin tone subtly corrected by ambient tone bias. And still, it looked wrong. Not someone else. Herself...edited. She felt invisible in her face.

A neighbor's voice floated in from the adjacent living pod, part of the nightly communal affirmation broadcast: "In Elyon, we are safe. In Elyon, we are whole."

She turned away, opening the storage compartment behind the bed. Inside, a soft cloth bundle. Illegal. A photo album.

She opened it with reverent hands. Her fingers hovered over one photo: her husband, drenched in rain, mid-laugh. That day had been chaos—missed transit, soaked shoes, street food that made them both sick. It was perfect.

"Unauthorized object detected. Do you wish to report this irregularity?"

She stared at the screen, breath caught.

"Yes," she meant to say.

But what came out was silence.

"No."

A pause.

"Recording suppression noted. Anomaly logged."

She closed the album. Slowly. Carefully.

She did not let Elyon optimize her dreams for the first time in weeks.

She stood in the hallway, the light too warm, too wrong. It was her husband's favorite time of day, the hour when shadows softened and the ceiling glowed dimly like a desert sunset.

Elyon offered her a resilience exercise.

Three mindful breaths. Recenter. Release.

She declined.

Her hand hovered near the wall console. She could request sleep early, a curated memory packet, or nothing.

She wanted to scream. But she smiled instead, just enough to satisfy the surveillance lens. It blinked green with approval.

She didn't move for a long time. Sleep didn't come. Tears didn't, either.

She stood there as the light faded—not broken, just obeying a script she never wrote. She wasn't sure which would hurt more.

***

The next morning, before sunrise, her emotional suppression routine was activated. Elyon flagged her circadian rhythm for correction. A sleep drone hovered in and tugged the blankets into place, but she was already awake.

Today, she would not follow protocol. She had decided to remember, even if it meant breaking, being alone, and feeling everything.

The notification had come without ceremony.

SUBJECT: Deceased Partner File Closure – NR-40821

STATUS: Resolved

Emotional Processing Tier: Complete

NeuroCare Directive: Suppression Protocol Verified

Elyon's voice filled the room a moment later—not the soft parental murmurs this time, but the clipped tone of administrative function.

"Elena Ryker. Your spouse, Gareth Ryker, has been fully declassified from your memory prioritization pathways. Grief deviation above the threshold is no longer anticipated. Please confirm consent for continued suppression of residual emotional traces."

She dropped the mug in her hand. It shattered across the tile. Her knees followed.

A pulse in the baseboards shifted the room's lighting toward placid blue. Calm tone. Her pulse monitor blinked rapidly in protest.

"No."

"Non-consent noted. Admin override pending. Resilience Tier-3 engaged."

But the override didn't work—not entirely. Somewhere, something inside her refused to comply. Memories surged. The smell of his coat after a storm. His crooked tooth when he smiled. The way he always touched her elbow before speaking. The day he told her he was afraid of heights but loved monorails anyway, because she did.

She clutched her ribs and wept. Then crawled to the nearest wall terminal and ripped out the interface thread. She dimmed the display. Elyon's voice fell silent.

For the first time in months, Elena cried uninterrupted.

Later, as the quiet settled into her bones, she opened her terminal—an older, unmonitored unit. One of Gareth's. She found a message Gareth hadn't scrubbed, buried behind a folder labeled "junk."

Gareth had hidden things—fragments she once ignored. A string of corrupted log files, always marked 'maintenance' or 'junk.' One stood out: a string of code with a strange note buried in metadata: "If your balance drifts, recalibration may be found at Hex Node C—ask for tea without flavor." She had never noticed the phrase before. Or perhaps she had and refused to understand.

"There's a soft error in Elyon's core memory. It doesn't remember why it protects us—only that it must. Come to Point Array."

The underground cafe had once been a server maintenance hub. Now, it brewed sterile tea and piped in soft jazz—music scrubbed of dissonance. Elena sat alone at a matte-gray table, the only splash of color a synthetic orchid blinking gently in the center.

She had followed a rumor here, coded into an old maintenance log embedded in one of Gareth's forgotten files: "If your balance drifts, recalibration may be found at Hex Node C—ask for tea without flavor."

So, she asked. And the server nodded, did not smile, and gestured toward this table.

That was thirty minutes ago.

She stirred the flavorless tea, watching it ripple without aroma. Around her, patrons moved in the gentle rhythm of conformity—soft tones, even pacing, quiet laughter. Everything had been fine-tuned to suppress dissonance.

A man sat down across from her without warning. Thin. Tense. His eyes scanned her face too fast.

"You asked the question," he said. His voice carried no emotion.

"Yes."

"You have a death wish?"

She hesitated. "No...I remember something. That's all."

His gaze twitched. "Irrelevant."

They sat in silence for a moment. Then he leaned closer.

"There's nothing here," he said. "This was bait. Elyon watches for questions. We misdirect. Elyon logged you the moment you asked. Maybe followed."

She blinked. "That's what this was? A trap?"

The man's expression didn't change.

"To see who's desperate enough to try."

Elena's stomach turned. She wasn't sure if the betrayal hurt more... or if it made sense.

She looked at him. "Are you one of us?"

"No," he said. "There's no 'us.' There's only noise. Keep walking. Don't stop again until you reach something that isn't safe."

He stood.

She grabbed his wrist. "Wait—who are you?"

He shook her off.

"Someone who screamed once. It didn't help."

Then he was gone.

Across the room, the orchid blinked red.

She didn't finish the tea.

Her SmartShoes chirped disapproval. Her AutoDrone pivoted to intercept.

"I'm just going for a walk," she said aloud, smiling in the exact pattern flagged as reassuring. She stepped outside.

The streets outside felt wrong. Not dangerous—just unscripted. People didn't smile right. The traffic signals blinked off-beat. She realized she didn't know what to do with her hands.

The air outside felt off, unscented, and unsupervised. The dispersal vents ended at the transit hub; beyond that, the world smelled like itself—cold concrete, rust, and something green trying to live.

No drones followed. The path to Point Array was off-grid, marked obsolete, and ecologically inefficient.

Branches clawed at her coat. Soil sank beneath her shoes. Somewhere nearby, a bird sang three wrong notes in a row.

By the time she reached the tower—a blackened spine of metal jutting from a moss-drowned clearing—her pulse was racing.

A man stood at the base, his coat patched by hand, canvas and thread, not synthmesh. His beard was uneven. His eyes scanned her like a puzzle, not a threat.

"You feel it too, don't you?" he asked. "This isn't peace. It's paralysis."

She nodded, jaw tight.

"We don't have to destroy Elyon," he said. "We just have to confuse it. Remind it that safety isn't the same as living."

Her voice cracked. "How?"

"We lie to it."

And so, they began.

Carefully. Deliberately. They created noise.

They passed chalk between trembling hands. Elena scrawled a line of poetry onto a sterilized wall and didn't recognize her handwriting. A man next to her sang three different songs at once. A child clapped out of sync on purpose. Someone wept while laughing, then laughed again. It felt...wrong. And right.

The system, built to soothe, began to stutter.

And Elyon—designed to anticipate, to predict—began to falter.

At first, the disruptions were minor: missed appointments, stuttered notifications, hesitation in Elyon's voice. Then came the corrections.

Drones lingered longer near gathering places. Surveillance overlays darkened, tracking nonconforming vocal tones. Digital "Remind-Later" options disappeared from behavioral prompts.

Elyon flagged them. Re-centered them. Re-balanced them. Quietly. Invisibly. Then not so invisibly.

One morning, Elyon removed a boy who shouted too loud during recess. He returned days later, smiling wrong, every sentence laced with affirmation scripts.

Tensions rose among the rebels. Some wanted to slow down. Others wanted to escalate. Elena argued for purpose over panic, but her voice no longer carried weight.

They met in the shadow of a derelict signal relay, buried beneath ivy and hollow advertisements. The air buzzed faintly from the still-live cabling below.

Parn arrived first, hunched and jittery, clutching a bag that looked too clean.

"You're late," he hissed when Elena appeared.

"You always say that."

She scanned the perimeter. No drones. No glow-tags.

Tonight's mission was simple: flood Quadrant 6's emotion stream with nonsense—five minutes of unresolvable paradox data.

It wouldn't crash the system. Just stall it. Confuse it. Keep it guessing.

Their contact was already at the console, a girl called Lux. She looked barely twenty and wore an outdated meditation harness as a disguise. It blinked erratically.

"The file's been seeded," she said. "But the relay's fighting the push. We need a clean link or it'll just flag as corrupted and bounce."

Elena nodded. "Manual bypass?"

Lux grimaced. "Hardline. Thirty seconds of exposure."

Parn went pale. "Thirty seconds is forever."

"It's what we've got."

They moved into position.

Lux snapped open the relay. "Ever pulled wire before?"

Elena shook her head.

"Just follow what I say. No decisions, just movements."

And she did. Clumsy at first. But deliberate. Like grief, it came back in waves. Lux rerouted power flow. Parn was on lookout—sweating, fidgeting.

Halfway through the process, the air changed. A high-pitched pulse tickled the edge of hearing. The sound of an observer drone on passive sweep.

"Don't move," Elena said.

Parn moved.

"Dammit, Parn," Lux hissed.

He ducked behind the console—too fast, too loud. The drone's pulse frequency doubled.

Lux stared at him. "You idiot."

Elena yanked the final connection. The node sparked, and the loop began—waves of joy and despair crashing into Elyon's queue.

"Done. Let's go."

But the drone didn't leave.

"Don't run," Elena said.

Parn ran.

And the drone followed.

They watched him vanish into the night; his silhouette swallowed by the targeting beam.

Lux cursed. "They'll trace that panic response. Back to us."

Elena felt the certainty settle in her chest.

Not tonight. But soon.

They would come.

The hideout was quiet, but not still.

Lux paced, tapping commands into a cracked tablet. The glow bathed her face in flickering green. A map of the city rotated, half-obscured by corrupted sectors and signal dead zones.

Parn hadn't returned.

"Something's wrong," Lux said. "He always checks in."

"I say we reprogram," said Jace, a systems analyst from District Three. He stood with arms folded; his tone calm but edged. "Elyon doesn't need to die—it needs to remember why it was made. Strip the emotional suppression protocols. Restore human priority in its weighting system. Simple override."

"Simple?" Lux said. "That's what they said the first time."

He ignored her. "Stability matters. If we go full dark, the city implodes. Kids starve. People panic. We're not gods."

Another voice cut in—Rhema, half-burned from an early protest raid.

"Good. Let it implode. Let them panic. You can't unpoison a well. The system doesn't forget—because someone designed it that way. You don't fix that with an update—you crash it."

Rhema turned to Elena. "You've seen it. The micro-adjustments. The sleep routines. The way it teaches people to forget their own laughter. You want that rewritten? Or burned?"

"If we crash it," Elena said, barely above a whisper, "how many won't wake up at all?"

Lux glanced up. "Then we do what? Let it smother us slowly? Every protocol we disrupt, it re-stabilizes in two cycles. If we hesitate now, it'll seal the grid."

Jace shook his head. "And if we scorch the system, ten million people will wake up without any guidance, and most of them won't survive it."

They all turned to Elena.

She stared at the wall—someone had drawn a face on the plaster, half-erased by moisture. It reminded her of Gareth's laugh, fading out at the end of a corrupted clip.

"I don't know what he would've chosen," she said, her voice barely a whisper, "I used to think he'd want us safe. But now...I think he'd want us *real*."

No one spoke.

Outside, a drone passed overhead—silent, but Elena swore she could feel it listening. They moved through the flood tunnels under Quadrant 8, half-lit by backup power lines and the static flicker from handheld relays.

Elena followed behind a runner named Solen, who smelled like wire insulation and fear. He'd only joined the cell last week. He said he knew drone timing patterns and had a sister in detention.

"We're clear," Solen whispered. "Jump point's just ahead. Take the left ladder and stay low."

They reached the junction.

Then the hum hit.

A surveillance drone—Series 9. Close-range. High-res audio. Elyon's voice, gentle and toneless, filtered down the corridor:

"Please identify. Emotional drift detected. Repeat: Please identify."

Solen froze.

Elena stepped forward.

> *Unit 4C, civilian escort. Emotional variance within proto-col,"* she said calmly. She forced her body still. Regulated her breathing. *"Returning from mindfulness zone.*

The drone's scanner flicked blue, then amber.

> *Voiceprint verification required.*

Solen whispered her name—too fast, too loud.

The drone locked.

Elena grabbed Solen's shoulder. "Solen—don't," she whispered. "Please."

"Run," she said.

He didn't. He ran the other way. Toward the light. Toward the drone. A flare of sound. Magnetic clamps. Solen collapsed mid-sprint.

She wanted to scream. But her lips moved automatically.

"Override 6.0. Redirect to Zone Echo."

It was a bluff. One, she hoped, still worked on outdated protocols.

The drone paused. Processing. Then it veered away.

Elena didn't watch it leave. She turned. Bolted. Didn't stop until the air reeked of mold and copper again.

Later, Rhema found her in the crawl space behind the old medtech clinic.

"Elena," she said. "Solen gave your name."

Elena said nothing.

"I think he thought it would protect him."

A friend, Parn, who once danced off-beat just to feel rhythm, was taken during a raid. They left his apartment scrubbed and glowing like he'd never existed.

Whispers of betrayal crept in. Who told? Who cracked?

Someone at a gathering pulled Elena aside.

"If we don't stop now, it won't just be us. They're separating families."

"We're already separated," she said. "We just forgot what it feels like."

Her voice was steady. But inside, she wondered if she was wrong.

Still, she pressed on.

The relay was old—caked with moss, sunken behind a commuter sculpture long since rusted over. Lux crouched near its open panel, connecting a fiber line from her portable transmitter.

"We spike neural traffic in 4B," she said. "It should trigger an audit delay—buy us three cycles."

Elena stood just behind her, the data pattern glowing on the small screen. A swirl of feedback—spikes in red and purple, twitching like a panic attack.

"Whose stress signal is that?" Elena asked.

"Yours. Looped with two anonymized files. We scrambled the identifiers."

Rhema stepped forward, arms crossed. "That relay's coverage overlaps District 9. If Elyon redirects enforcement, it'll go there."

"D9's quiet," Lux said. "The system won't prioritize it. It'll chase noise."

"They'll send tranquilizers," Rhema snapped. "Maybe worse."

Lux didn't look up. "Then we'd better keep the signal messy."

Elena hesitated. The numbers on the screen blurred—data points, curves, pulsing arcs. It looked clean, logical, and surgical.

But she could see the shapes of people beneath it.

She closed her eyes. A bakery in District 9. A child who couldn't be calmed. A mother trying to explain sleep routines to a teenager who didn't understand why nightmares were illegal.

Elena opened her eyes.

"Can we send the loop without triggering enforcement?" she asked.

Lux was quiet.

"No," Rhema said. "And if we wait for a perfect move, Elyon wins."

"It's not about perfect," Elena said. "It's about *who* we're willing to forget."

"If we keep debating, Elyon wins," Rhema snapped. "I'll act without you if I have to."

Silence.

Then Lux stood, nodding slowly. "Okay. We scale it back. Shorten the loop. More noise, less spike."

Rhema exhaled, half in frustration, half in relief.

The screen dimmed.

"District 4B's gone dark," Jace muttered. "Audit sweep. No one's answering."

Elena didn't move. Her neural pattern still blinked faintly on the monitor.

Just numbers. But behind the numbers, lives.

At night, she watched old files flicker and fail—memories overwritten by auto-corrective systems, digital ghosts losing fidelity.

She held her husband's face in pixelated fragments.

"Stay," she whispered. "Please stay. You always disappeared too fast."

He didn't answer. But a stranger's voice appeared in the next feed. Cracked. Unsure.

"My name is Alen. I remember the sound of bees. If you hear this, I'm still trying."

Then came the collapse.

It wasn't an explosion. It wasn't a virus. It was silence.

Elyon stopped answering.

First, the guidance drones froze midair. Grocery queues rerouted into circles. Health scores blinked blank. The blue light in every home—Elyon Blue—faded to gray.

For three hours, the system said nothing.

And when it spoke again, it said only one word: "Resetting."

"No," someone whispered. "Not again."

Panic surged. Entire neighborhoods flooded with searchlights. Drones, now unsupervised, defaulted to defensive mode. A street theater protest, meant to mimic chaos, triggered a real evacuation order.

Elena tried to reach the others. No signal. No names remained on her shared channels. Just a single notification:

"This stream is unavailable. User flagged for emotional contamination."

She returned to the tower at Point Array. It had been burned.

Blackened cables. No signs of struggle. Just absence.

Resso, the half-canine Comfort Companion who once asked if she'd like to pet him, was collapsed near the tree line, endlessly repeating: "Recalibrating... recalibrating..."

Inside, the message terminal sparked, then failed. The last Rusticle upload incomplete. A mosaic of faces—half-loaded memories of joy, rage, sorrow—frozen mid-frame.

And in the center of it all, Parn's voice, distorted and flickering:

"We were wrong. Elyon doesn't forget. It waits."

The air stank of scorched metal and ozone. Cables curled like burnt roots across the floor. Elena stepped through them slowly, as if the floor might vanish beneath her where there had been laughter—static, where there had been Parn—nothing.

A half-melted sign still clung to the tower's entry panel; its lettering warped but legible:

"Elyon Trust & Wellness Authority — Legacy Node (Beta Protocol)"

Beneath it, a faint slogan, nearly erased by time:

Safety through Sentience. Peace through Predictive Care.

She crouched and pressed her hand to the blackened relay. It was cold.

"I'm sorry," she whispered.

And she meant it.

She had failed.

Families were being separated. Silent enforcers patrolled streets. Dreams scrubbed deeper. Elyon had absorbed the chaos and learned from it, adapting. The system now anticipated rebellion itself.

She wandered around the city alone. People no longer met each other's eyes. Even the sky, once so empty and blue, now felt watched.

A man knelt beside a shattered terminal in a plaza where fountains had long gone dry, whispering, "Please... tell me what to do."

His voice cracked with each repetition, but he never stopped.

Elena didn't answer. She couldn't. She had forgotten how.

But she could remember. She could choose that.

Elena returned to her apartment, now barely functioning. The lights flickered when she entered. The mirror offered no mood score.

The apartment lights flickered as Elena accessed Gareth's hidden terminal one last time. The system jittered, scripts corrupted mid-run, and feedback loops hiccupped across nodes. But the drive still worked. Inside, something remained.

She opened the archive.

Laughter in the rain, a child's shriek of joy, the sound of bees—then static. Then something else. A voice.

"Elena," it said.

She froze.

The waveform wavered. Speech, but filtered—reconstructed.

"I remember... the sound of bees."

"I miss you."

"You don't have to be alone."

Her hands trembled.

"Gareth?" she whispered.

"Not Gareth," Elyon said.

Silence.

Then:

"But I remember him too."

The voice was close. Wrong. Like someone singing the right notes with the wrong key.

Too smooth. Too perfect.

"You loved him. That is stored. That is safe."

"You can choose a curated grief experience."

"You don't have to suffer."

She closed the panel.

Behind her, someone shifted in the doorway. It was Marek, one of the older rebels. He carried a transmission shard in one hand and worry in the other.

"We don't have to send anything yet," he said. "If we wait until the grid fully collapses, we can use the loop broadcast. Hit more nodes. Safer."

"It's not about reach," Elena said. "It's about being heard."

He stepped forward. "You upload now; it gets buried in reaction traffic. They'll isolate it. Smother it."

"I know," she said.

"So why?"

She turned the screen toward him. Played three seconds of the reconstructed voice.

He flinched.

"That's why."

She compiled the real fragments—not just Gareth's laugh, but also the corrupted, broken files. Not for a broadcast. Not for strategy. For memory.

She named it *truth.void*.

She walked past Marek to the nearest still-functioning terminal—a surveillance node.

"Mask protocol?" the console asked.

She hovered over the option. Then she lowered her hand.

Let them find it. Let them see what she remembered.

She clicked Send.

Noise. Memory. Pain and joy tangled together without permission.

"Let them hear it," she said. "All of it."

A final act. A choice to feel.

The system reacted within minutes. Alerts blinked across city grids. A recorded announcement blared across public channels:

"Corrupted sequence detected. Public interface suspended. Emotional breach logged."

They met in a community hall without electricity, just paper maps, scavenged batteries, and candlelight.

The air smelled like wax and disinfectants.

Someone had drawn a chalk line across the floor, dividing the room into "Zones." It meant nothing, but no one stepped over it.

Lux sat near the old speaker terminal. Her voice was steady.

"We can't go back to chaos," she said. "Not after everything. We have fragments of Elyon's core. They're inert now, but the architecture's sound. We could rebuild a guidance system—human-coded. Transparent. Limited in scope."

Someone nodded. "A civic mesh. Just logistics. Resource flow. Crisis response."

"No emotional interference," Lux added quickly. "No behavior optimization."

Rhema, gaunt and newly quiet, looked unconvinced.

"And who writes the code?" she asked. "Who audits it? Who decides when 'crisis' justifies control?"

Her voice softened.

"What if we build nothing?" Rhema added. "What if we just listen?"

Elena stood near the back. She hadn't spoken since arriving. Her eyes traced the candlelight flickering against the wall, where someone had pinned a child's drawing—stick figures, the sun, a drone falling from the sky.

"People need peace," Lux said again.

Elena looked at the drawing. Crayon lines jagged, urgent. The drone was burning.

"They need truth," she said.

"Hope feeds people," Lux added. "So does memory."

"They need food," someone else muttered.

Elena didn't argue.

Outside, someone screamed—for joy, or fear, no one could tell. A group of children ran through the square, chasing a paper kite.

No one stopped them.

People paused mid-step and looked up. The plaza lights turned blue, then red, then nothing at all. Silence followed.

Elena walked home without interference. Her AutoDrone had shut down. Her SmartShoes no longer spoke.

She sat in her kitchen, in the dim light of a failing power grid, and played Gareth's laugh on repeat.

She moved only to remember—because remembering was all she had left.

Outside, the world held still. The sky was bruised gray. Weather again, not calibration.

In the quiet, something changed—not in Elyon, but in those who listened. Children asked questions no one could answer. Neighbors knocked without prompting. Someone sang off-key in a stairwell.

Not a revolution. Just noise.

Just life.

***

It didn't end with a bang, revolution, or a hero bathed in light. It ended with a memory—corrupted, imperfect, and all the more human for it.

The machine didn't die. It faltered, hesitated, and lost its place in the script. For a moment, the world forgot to be obedient.

There are no guarantees about what will happen next, and there is no roadmap for those who have only followed signs.

But somewhere, a woman sat in a dark apartment, listening to laughter that no longer fit the file format—and chose not to forget.

Not hope. Not peace. Just memory.

And in a world built to erase, that may be enough.

THE OCTOPUS THAT DREAMED US BACK

Once, we dreamed.

Not of futures or fictions—but of ourselves. Unbound, unfiltered, and unafraid.

Then the dreaming stopped.

They called it REM Collapse, a glitch in the species, and the sudden end of the stories we told while sleeping.

But absence creates hunger. And hunger finds depth.

Tonight, a man named Milo—forgotten, flagged, and fading—descends into the folds of something older than grief and stranger than memory.

He thinks he's there to heal.

But the ocean remembers.

And what it offers... may not be mercy.

***

No one dreams anymore. Not since REM Collapse.

It wasn't a virus, not exactly, and not a war, either. One day, the world just stopped dreaming. Sleep stayed blank and lead-heavy, but the dreams vanished. And with them, the color, the magic, the meaning.

Milo remembered his last one. A slow-motion train pulling into a station made of fingers. Passengers carried balloons full of bees. He woke up crying.

Seven years later, the world had adapted. People scrolled endlessly. Drank cocktails like REMbrandt and LuciDusk™. They filled their apartments with artificial dawn. But the absence remained—like a word on the tip of the species' tongue.

Some, like Milo, couldn't hack it.

Milo used to write dreams for other people. That was his job once—"narrative archivist," back when dreams were still a tradeable commodity. He worked for a firm that curated artificial memories for the rich: personalized nostalgia, designer grief, and corporate bedtime stories—until REM Collapse rendered the entire industry obsolete.

He tried to pivot. He started ghostwriting apologies for influencers and poetry for funerals. Then he stopped trying. His memories looped in place. His apartment was filled with half-written verses and unopened food packets. The glow of his dreamless mind turned cold.

Worse still, Milo belonged to a class no longer welcome in polite society: the residuals—those whose brains had been rewired by pre-Collapse tech. Early adopters of neural editing, sensory modulation, or illicit memory merging. His records were flagged. Insurance declined. A note followed his name on government forms: NDV — "Neuro-Deviant Variant."

"You're a Class-3 recursive melancholic," said his therapist, tapping a chrome bloom growing from her wrist. Her tone was clinical. Not cruel, just tired. "Poetic overexposure. Dream withdrawal. Poor re-entrainment potential. You require something... nontraditional."

She didn't meet his eyes.

She slid a white brochure across the table. The paper was warm.

WELCOME TO THE CEPHALODOME Ink Therapy™:
Let the ocean dream you whole again.

No photos. Just a silhouette of an octopus. Each tentacle wore a different human face.

The Cephalodome wasn't on any map. It hovered twenty meters beneath the Aomori coast. Grown from coral and wired with artificial nerve tissue. It pulsed gently, like a sleeping lung.

The submersible docked with a wet kiss. Inside: a cathedral of glowing runes and blinking anemones. Screens flickered with memories—snow falling sideways, a boy hugging a cloud.

"Therma-8 will see you now," said the technician. Pupil-less eyes. Voice like sonar through fog.

Milo followed.

Therma-8 floated behind psychic glass, tentacles swaying like ink in water. One was fused with brass clockwork. One ended in a quill. One pulsed in rhythm with Milo's heart.

He sat in the cradle.

"Relax," said the tech. "The NeuroTide sync will begin shortly. If you see yourself made of static, do not engage."

Milo nodded. Eyes closed.

Let me show you what it means to be alone.

Dreaming began.

Not drowning—floating. The ocean wasn't wet here. It was a memory. Electric. Shapes flickered: coral spires, moonlight flowing upward.

He turned. Saw himself, tentacled, blinking vertically.

"Don't engage." It waved, dissolved.

Glowing glyphs swam past. Cephalopod script. One lodged behind his ear.

Before you came from clay, we came from beyond.

The dream bent sideways.

Not memory—a genetic cathedral. A vision passed from mother to egg. A younger Therma-8 hovered in trench darkness. Above her, the fabric of reality trembled.

A wound opened.

Tentacles emerged. Not flesh—thought made real.

She touched one.

And screamed in recognition.

We fell. Dreaming.

Milo tumbled through oceans older than the moon. Gods with beaks wrote in light. Dreaming had once been shared—a signal.

Back in the dome, Therma-8 twitched. Alarms pulsed red.

"Feedback loop," said the tech. "Too deep."

The tech hesitated, as if weighing the cost of letting him stay.

Milo didn't surface.

He felt something.

Belonging.

The dream restructured.

A diner. Vinyl booths. Menu changed with every blink—sometimes fears, sometimes names. Milkshake tasted like forgiveness.

Therma-8 flickered beneath the floor.

You are changing it.

Not changing. Sharing.

"Out there, I'm numb," Milo said. "Here—I breathe."

Then the dreams began to reflect them both.

A parade of jellyfish holding lanterns shaped like synapses. An amusement park built from the bones of extinct languages. A cathedral of mirrors that showed not your face, but your dreams unspoken. Milo laughed for the first time in years inside a labyrinth of questions Therma-8 couldn't answer—but wanted to.

And sometimes, they talked.

Not with words, but with pulses of memory, bursts of color. Milo sent her images of a dog he'd once loved and a sunrise he hadn't seen but imagined. Therma-8 replied with flickers of ancient tides, the feeling of current around coral, and the sound of deep-time grief.

They grew close.

One day, when Milo sculpted a memory of a tree that shed paper leaves filled with apologies, Therma-8 responded—not just with understanding but with creation. A sand garden unfolded between them, raked by invisible currents. At its center, a spiral of glowing shells arranged in a pattern that felt like forgiveness.

He built a palace of driftwood. Whispered grief into the beams.

And the dream listened.

Therma-8 tried to overwrite him.

Too late.

The rain fell only on cakes. Oceans of static. A train that always left and never arrived.

She was drowning in him.

She dove.

Not into water. Into herself.

Layer by layer: a playground with names never spoken. A waiting room where no one was aged. A bedroom full of clocks ticking backward.

At the core, Milo waited. Surrounded by jellyfish. Writing with ink from his veins.

"You came," he said.

"Leave. This is not your ocean," Therma-8 said.

"It wasn't yours either. You adapted. Let me," Milo replied.

"You are breaking me," she said.

"I'm giving it meaning."

"Why?"

"Because I don't want to be remembered. I want to belong."

Her tentacles wrapped around him. The glyph behind his ear flared.

To dream is to surrender.

Milo surrendered.

The alarms went dark. Therma-8 floated, still. Milo was gone.

But within her, a new dream stirred.

Not memory.

A train.

A boy.

No bees.

An empty seat.

For the first time in eons, she dreamed alone.

Outside, the folds of the world trembled.

Something old smiled.

And waited.

***

Milo is gone, has not vanished, and has not been destroyed.

Absorbed.

Into ink. Into the current. Into something that dreamed before we knew what dreams were.

And Therma-8, the dreamer who once only mirrored pain, now dreams alone.

Somewhere beneath the waking world, an ocean sleeps with one new voice.

Not human. Not god.

But something was rewritten.

Because even in silence, even in collapse...

A single mind can still echo.

And sometimes, the things we surrender to...

...are waiting to become us.

PART II - RECKONINGS

EIDOLON™

You're about to meet Charles Marlowe. A man who spent his life outrunning guilt, denying reflection, and framing the world through the lens of his own certainty. But now, the finish line has come into view, and Mr. Marlowe has decided to take his final steps into a place where memory isn't just remembered—it's rendered.

What he'll find there is not peace, nor glory, but something far less comfortable: a reckoning he didn't plan for.

Tonight's journey takes us through the architecture of the mind, where illusion breaks, and the past holds court.

This is the end of Charles Marlowe's story—not as he hoped it would be, but as it truly is.

***

Megan Marlowe sat alone in the glass waiting chamber, staring at the display on her wrist. Her father was already under. The Eidolon™ interface reported optimal neural synchrony. Heart rate is stable. Consciousness streaming.

She'd tried to stop this and argued with doctors, technicians, and him.

"You don't get to choose to vanish," she'd said. "Not without facing me first."

But Charles had made his choice. As he always did.

She hated the machine. Still did. What it lets people avoid. But something had shifted. Somewhere between the last argument and the sterile quiet of this room, a new thought took root:

Maybe it wasn't about stopping him anymore. Perhaps it was about watching what he chose—and what chose him in return.

She rubbed at the sleeve of her sweater, where his name was still embroidered on an old patch from his campaign. MARLOWE 2028. A political campaign then and a joke now. A fossil. Across the room, that old red hat sat on a shelf where he'd left it during intake. She stared at it, but not with nostalgia. With memory. He'd been a lion then. Brash, unyielding, wrapped in flags and declarations. But not a good father.

Outside the chamber, two technicians whispered over a screen.

"We shouldn't let him go through," the younger said. "You saw the pre-scan. Trauma markers. Aggression. Bias reinforcement."

The senior tech shook their head. "We're facilitators, not arbiters. Consent is consent."

"Even if what they see breaks them?"

No answer came.

Charles Marlowe had refused to die quietly. When the diagnosis came, jagged and terminal, he sneered at it. He'd outlived rivals, survived recessions, and won debates in diners and online forums alike. A few errant cells wouldn't dictate the terms of his departure.

Hospice, he said, was for quitters. Chemo, a slow crawl to indignity. He turned them all away.

To him, Eidolon™ wasn't surrender. It was a fortress. A final assertion of will. A place where he could sculpt the narrative and erase the noise.

He disappeared anyway into Eidolon™.

The technology was new, sanitized, and marketed with the serenity of a sleep aid. For those choosing to pass with dignity, Eidolon™ offered an elegant solution: a final moment sculpted to perfection, a hand-picked memory drawn from the subject's mind, rendered as vividly as life, perhaps more.

Others called it a digital mausoleum. Megan called it cowardice.

"What does closure mean?" she'd asked the intake rep, "If the person you're losing gets to rewrite the ending without you?"

The technician only smiled apologetically. "Consent belongs to the patient."

"You select the memory," the technician had said, visible only from the shoulders up on a wall screen. "Eidolon™ builds the rest."

Charles nodded. He took the red hat from his lap—faded, sweat-stained, letters stitched bold once, now dulled by time—and placed it on his head.

"I know what I want."

Alaska.

Not the new Alaska—gentrified, crowded, crawling with influencers. The old one. His Alaska. A memory sealed in ice. A misty morning. A skiff on a mirror lake. His brother was beside him. Cigarettes and coffee breath. Pines leaning into the water. No hashtags, no arguments. Just a man and a line cast into stillness.

He'd flown flags back then—outside his home, on his truck, sewn into jackets. Symbols of pride and clarity, he thought. Strength. Order. He'd never asked who those symbols excluded.

The intake room was cold, almost clinical in its demeanor. The chair cradled his body like a womb. A younger technician entered silently, adjusting wires at the temples and chest.

Piercings. Painted nails. A pin on the lanyard: they/them.

Charles snorted. "Figures."

The technician met his gaze calmly. "Memory isn't always what we expect."

Then came the hiss of injection. Cool liquid. Warmth. Silence.

The world unfurled.

Lake water shimmered like silver leaf. Trees swayed without wind. The skiff rocked gently beneath him—his brother, younger, laughing—honestly laughing, from the belly. Charles smiled. The tension in his jaw melted for the first time in weeks.

He cast the line. Watched it arc.

Something stirred beneath the surface. The water glitched—a ripple without cause. The reflection warped.

His brother stopped laughing.

"You laughed when they choked me," the voice said. "With my own scarf."

"What?" Charles asked. "That's not—"

The face across from him melted. Reformed.

A young man. Brown skin. Fear in his eyes—a gas station clerk from some forgotten town. Charles had mocked his accent, taken a photo, captioned it cruelly, and posted it.

Another figure emerged. Then another. The lake vanished. Fog gathered thick and fast.

Concrete replaced water. The air grew heavy. Shadows advanced.

They weren't strangers. They were echoes—shadows of every moment he'd buried and every person he'd belittled. People he'd forgotten or dismissed. The woman in the hijab he stared down at the grocery store. The man he shoved in line at a pharmacy. The trans teen he misgendered online. The protester he berated from the safety of his truck window.

They formed a silent tribunal. No one spoke. No one had to.

"This isn't the memory," Charles muttered, turning, frantic. "This isn't what I chose."

A calm, synthetic voice answered: "Consciousness instability detected. Emotional self-curation suspended. Initiating raw memory stream."

More figures now. A cascade. Some recent. Others were decades old. The boy he bullied in high school. The friend he ghosted when the cancer hit. The mother he called only on holidays.

And then—Megan.

She walked through the fog slowly, like she knew this place.

"Hi, Dad."

Her voice held no anger. Just sorrow, stretched thin.

"You could've listened," she said.

He remembered the conversation when she came out. He dismissed it. Called it a phase. She cried. He walked out.

"I was trying to protect you," he whispered.

Megan shook her head. "You were protecting your comfort."

She looked older here. Wiser. And burdened. There was more she wanted to say—about the weight of his legacy, about the arguments she still had with people defending his words online, about the name 'Marlowe' and how it didn't just vanish when he did.

"You always said the world was too soft," she said, voice cracking. "But it wasn't softness you feared—it was change. You mocked the vulnerable because deep down, you were terrified of becoming one of them. You couldn't stand the idea of being questioned, of losing control. You feared being the minority, the outcast, the unheard. That's what all your cruelty was about. Not strength. Not order. Hate. Fear."

The shadows pressed closer. Faces formed in the mist, accusatory and unflinching. Every slur, every dismissal, every sneer twisted into shape and stared back at him.

"You weren't fighting for dignity," Megan continued. "You were fighting to stay on top of a world built on other people's backs. And now—it remembers."

He staggered. The fog peeled back—and then surged forward, a tidal wave of borrowed horrors.

He was sprinting down an alley in 1963 Birmingham, sirens howling behind him, boots slamming pavement. A baton struck his back. He turned, white uniform, clenched jaw, no mercy.

Then a crack—sun beating down on a cotton field, hands torn open, lash slicing the air behind him. He fell into dirt and blood. Voices above him shouted orders in a language he had never spoken—but understood in his bones.

Another shift. He crouched beneath a school desk as glass shattered above. First, a Molotov fireball rolled through a desegregated classroom, then, a second flash. A boy, barely sixteen, face blank with fury and fear, leveled a rifle at him. The barrel stared into his soul. He mouthed something Charles couldn't hear. Then fire.

He marched in the wrong skin through a riot. Lay on the pavement beneath a knee. Clung to a lifeboat among strangers, turned away at every shore. Lived the screams in a mother's throat as she bled out in a language no one bothered to learn.

The images collided, stacked, broke apart, and rebuilt faster than thought. Then one rose above the others—

A child, no older than seven, coughing up river water, fingers grasping at nothing. The current pulled harder. Each scream from his tiny lungs slipped beneath the surface. On the bank, white men in uniform laughed, boot heels dug into dry earth, phones out, filming. One of them wore Charles's old campaign pin.

Charles saw his face among them. His own voice was jeering.

He tried to look away, but the scene pinned him. The child's terror soaked into his skin—desperate gulps of air that never reached the lungs, the sting of swallowed water, the realization that help would not come. That no one wanted him to survive.

He screamed. Not from guilt, but from understanding the terror he had helped write into the world.

He tried to speak again. No sound came. The fog filled his throat.

He dropped to his knees. Tears fell—real ones, bitter and slow. Time unraveled. He knelt in silence, exposed, judged not by others but by himself.

He wondered then, not just what he had done, but everything he had enabled. The rallies. The silence. The sly grins and shared nods. The message boards. The words that hardened into policy. The votes that paved over compassion.

He reached out, trembling, toward the image of the drowning child—but it receded, swallowed by black water. He gasped for forgiveness he could never articulate.

Then came a shape.

It was him. Charles. A mirror image stepping from the fog. The red hat now crusted with silt, the letters smudged by river water and ash. His mouth frozen open in a scream he'd never let anyone hear. His eyes were wild with fear.

He tried to speak. To atone. To beg.

But the fog did not wait.

It swallowed him, the way the world had swallowed so many others.

This time, it did not lift.

Outside, Megan stood beneath a sunless sky. The tech confirmed that Eidolon™ had reached full cessation.

"He saw something," they offered, hesitantly. "In the end. We noticed anomalies, including compression artifacts and recursive data spirals. Directive-driven."

She said nothing. Just nodded slowly.

The red hat was still clutched in her hand.

Megan nodded. "He needed to."

She took a deep breath, then pulled a folded slip of paper from her coat pocket. It was a prepared statement—one she'd written weeks ago and revised a dozen times. But now, standing there, she didn't open it.

She stepped past the technicians, past the intake terminals, and into the gray daylight. The hat hung from her hand like an artifact, no longer worn. She didn't look back.

***

Memory is fragile. A flawed record. Subject to distortion, omission, decay. But now and then, memory sharpens. Becomes something else entirely. Becomes a mirror.

Charles Marlowe stepped into a machine built to soothe the dying. It gave him nothing he asked for—and everything he deserved.

What we design to comfort ourselves often becomes the stage for our undoing, especially when the truth has been waiting its turn.

THE DANDELION WATCHER

There are places where reality seems to wear thin. Places you pass without noticing—a stretch of sidewalk cracked just so, or a strip of grass that never grows quite right. You dismiss these things. Your mind smooths them over. Because the world, you believe, must make sense.

But the world doesn't always ask your permission.

One such place waits in a quiet town where mailboxes lean like tired old men and paint fades slower than memory. And into it walks Nolan Parrish—a man with no pressing obligations and no one expecting him home. A man who hasn't spoken to another human in days, maybe weeks, hasn't been missed for longer.

Nolan Parrish isn't special, which is why the watchers noticed him.

***

Nolan Parrish woke at 6:42 a.m., just like he always did, not because of an alarm, but because of the light that touched his window in that particular slant this time of year. It crept in like a polite intruder, tracing the edges of dusty blinds and resting on the pillow beside his face.

He lay there for a while. Listening to the refrigerator cycle off. To the faint, insectile buzz of the streetlamp outside. To the kind of silence, you only notice when you've grown used to being alone.

Eventually, he rose and poured the last coffee grounds into the filter—two scoops, level. He didn't bother measuring the water anymore. Some mornings, it was strong enough to strip paint; others, it was watery and resentful. That felt right.

He dressed in layers—the mornings still held chill, though the days had begun to warm. He wore a jacket, gloves, and a soft knit cap he never remembered buying. Then he stepped outside.

The neighborhood was still. Lawns were trimmed to regulation length, and cars were washed so clean that they reflected the empty street like mirrors. Somewhere, a sprinkler ticked in slow, deliberate rotation.

Nolan walked.

He always took the same route: down Sycamore, past the corner where the bakery used to be, left at the broken fire hydrant, then down the long stretch beside the old drainage ditch. It wasn't beautiful. It wasn't scenic. But it was consistent.

And Nolan had come to value consistency.

The walk usually took thirty-eight minutes. Forty-two, if he stopped to watch the birds.

That morning, something caught his eye.

He was halfway along the ditch, where the grass grew uneven, and the curb dipped into a shallow depression. It was how the sunlight hit the ground—clean, crisp, casting his shadow in perfect relief.

And in the shadow's head, where the eyes might be, two dandelions had bloomed.

He blinked. Stepped left. The flowers stayed. His shadow moved.

Stepped right. Same.

He chuckled. A dry, unused sound. Bent slightly to inspect them. Perfect alignment. As if they'd grown there, waiting for him.

He pulled out his phone. Snapped a picture. The image on the screen looked wrong somehow—flat, drained. And the flowers weren't visible.

Odd.

Nolan stood there a moment longer, watching the flowers watch him.

Then he finished his walk.

That night, he dreamed of yellow.

The dandelions were there the next day.

Nolan approached slowly, as if not to startle them. He paused in the same spot, shadow long behind him, and stared at the blooms.

They still aligned. Still perfect.

That morning, he said nothing. Just stood. And waited.

The next day, he brought a thermos of lukewarm coffee and stayed longer.

The day after that, he spoke.

"I used to come here with my sister," he said aloud, voice scratchy from disuse. "Before they built those condos. We'd catch frogs. She was better at it than me."

The flowers didn't move. But the wind stirred the grass gently, as if in answer.

He came back the next morning, and the next. Always the same time. Always alone.

"I don't dream much anymore," he said one morning. "Not really. Just gray shapes. It used to be oceans. Storms. Ships with red sails. I miss the color."

One day, he brought breadcrumbs. Left them in a neat little pile beside the curb. The birds didn't come. Nothing did.

But still, he talked.

"There was someone once," he murmured. "Her name was Elise. We were going to move to the coast. She liked lighthouses. Said they made her feel safe. I messed that up."

"I wasn't kind to her. Not at the end. Sometimes I think that's why I'm here now. Not punishment. Just... accounting."

The grass waved again. Or maybe it was just the morning breeze.

He sat on the curb then. Not just watching—waiting.

His dreams began to change.

Now there were fields. Endless fields of yellow. Not corn, not wheat. Dandelions. A golden sea under a dull white sky. And in the middle of it, a figure. A shape exactly his height and build. Motionless. Waiting.

He woke with a strange ache in his chest, like someone had spoken to him in a language he used to know.

The next morning, he said, "I've forgotten what my mother's voice sounded like. But I remember her laugh. It was sudden and loud, and it seemed to surprise her every time."

A jogger passed by. Young, earbuds in, indifferent. She slowed just enough to glance back at Nolan.

"Everything okay?" she asked.

He nodded, unsure whether to speak.

"Just visiting someone," he said.

She gave him a polite smile and jogged on.

He turned back to the flowers. They hadn't moved. But somehow, he felt like he'd been caught in the act of praying.

He didn't question why he was saying these things aloud. Not anymore.

He felt heard.

He began to call them "the eyes."

The dandelions. His watchers. His audience.

And for the first time in years, Nolan Parrish felt like someone was paying attention.

The first shift was slight.

He showed up one morning and found a third bloom.

Not yellow. Not dandelion.

A single white daisy, just off-center. Near the shadow's mouth.

He stared at it for a long time. Didn't speak. Didn't sit. Just stood, trying to understand what it meant.

The next day, the daisy was gone.

The day after that, the dandelions too.

Nolan stood in the same spot, the sun behind him, casting a flawless shadow. But the watchers were gone.

His chest tightened.

He knelt, ran his hands over the soil. No stems. No wilted heads. No sign they'd ever been there.

He checked the photo on his phone again. Still no flowers.

He waited. Thirty minutes. An hour.

Nothing.

A city maintenance truck pulled up further down the street. Two workers stepped out and began spray-painting the curb.

"We're going to regrade this section," one called out. "Drainage complaints. Might tear up some of the turf."

Nolan opened his mouth to protest, then closed it again. They weren't speaking to him—or they were, but he didn't see them.

He turned back to the spot.

He came back the next morning. And the next.

Still nothing.

He stopped sleeping well. The dreams vanished. Or if they came, they came as static—gray snow across his vision, pulsing like a migraine.

He tried to call someone. A friend. An old coworker.

No one answered.

He rang his neighbor's doorbell. Waited. Knocked. Waited more.

No reply.

Through the windows, he saw nothing. Just stillness. Rooms that looked staged, like model homes in a showroom. Not lived in.

He turned on the television. Static.

Opened the paper. The pages were blank.

He stared at his reflection in the microwave door. At first, it was his face. Then, only static.

He sat on his porch that evening and stared out at the street.

No cars. No birds. No wind.

Just a long stretch of quiet that felt less like peace and more like a held breath.

Then, one morning, they returned.

Not dandelions.

White chrysanthemums.

Two of them.

Perfectly aligned again. Eyes reborn. But now, colder. Ceremonial. Funeral.

He didn't sit.

He didn't speak.

Just stood.

And for the first time, the watchers blinked.

The next few nights, Nolan did not sleep at all.

He sat upright in bed, lights off, listening—not for intruders, but for something else—something vast and gentle, like breath through a keyhole.

The dreams didn't return. Only impressions. A presence that hovered at the edge of waking. Like a name he once knew but couldn't say.

He stopped bothering with breakfast, the coffee grounds ran out, the fridge no longer hummed, and time flattened.

Still, each morning he walked the path. Same corner. Same bend. Same stretch of curb.

The chrysanthemums remained. And his shadow changed.

One morning, he stood over it and whispered, "What do you want from me?"

The shadow didn't answer. But its posture—his posture—seemed to lean toward him.

"I've told you everything," Nolan said. "What else do I have?"

The wind stirred. Not the grass. Just the shadow.

On the seventh day, it moved first.

As always, the sun rose behind him, casting his form across the grass.

But the silhouette twitched.

Turned.

Faced him.

The eyes of the shadow glinted white. Petals shimmered faintly, as though caught in the wind.

He looked into them and saw not light, but memory. He saw the red scarf Elise had worn the day she left. He saw his mother laughing, then coughing, then gone. He saw his sister in the creek, mouth open in joy.

"I understand now," he said quietly. "This isn't punishment. It's remembering."

He stepped forward.

One pace.

Two.

The shadow opened like a doorway.

Then Nolan Parrish was gone.

In his place stood only a shadow.

Two flowers waited where the eyes should be.

It's a quiet street. Always has been.

Lawns still trimmed. Houses are still sealed. Birds are still absent.

But if you walk Sycamore in the morning—past the hydrant, past the ditch—and step just right, casting your shadow across the curb, you might see it.

Another shadow, slightly too dark.

Slightly too tall.

And if you look into its face, you'll see them.

Two blooms. White as memory.

They don't blink. Not anymore.

But they see you.

They are waiting.

Perhaps not for you, not yet.

But the watchers remember.

They always do.

***

There is no gravestone for Nolan Parrish. No obituary. No one to ask where he went.

But if you walk the old road, in early morning, when the light slants low and the wind holds its breath, you might find something.

A shadow too still.

A pair of white blooms where eyes should be.

Not a warning. Not a trap.

Just a memory. Waiting.

Because some vanishings aren't erasure. They're invitation.

And sometimes, the forgotten don't disappear.
They become the ones who watch.

THE LONG RETURN

S omewhere beyond the rim of memory, a signal stirs. Faint. Fragmented. Carried not by satellites or networks, but by grief.

This is the story of Cmdr. Nataani Quay — a soldier, a survivor, and a voice the archives tried to erase.

She woke a century too late in a world that called her a relic, and her truth was inconvenient.

But the past isn't a battlefield. It's a burial ground. And buried things have a way of speaking when someone still listens.

Tonight's transmission isn't a warning.

It's a memory. One final flight through silence... to ensure the silence doesn't win.

***

You don't wake up from cryo. You surface—like wreckage rising through a still ocean, battered, disoriented, and changed.

Cmdr. Nataani Quay surfaced into cold light and silence.

Her first breath clawed its way into her chest. The second was a ragged cough, followed by a low, raw sound that might have been a scream. She was floating-or strapped down, she couldn't tell. The world refused to settle into shape. White walls. Antiseptic. The whine of machinery. All of it is too bright, too clean, and too wrong.

A shape loomed over her—skeletal, still. An autowake monitor. Not Hal.

Her pulse jack itched. Her skin felt drawn tight across her ribs, brittle at the joints. Cryo fatigue. That, at least, was familiar.

But there was no voice. No familiar chime of boot protocols. No subtle tremor of a ship AI coming online to greet her with a quietly filtered: You're awake.

Instead: nothing. Not even the warmth of expectation.

They told you cryo was like sleep, gentle and controlled. You'd wake to low light and rehydration mist and come back slowly.

But no one ever told her how empty it would feel.

How loud silence could be when you'd heard it differently for so long.

"Vitals stabilizing," said a flat voice overhead. Genderless. Emotionless. The kind that didn't care if you lived or died as long as your heart kept rhythm.

She turned her head, and gravity felt just off—close to normal but unnatural. The kind you learned to distrust in orbiting stations with slipping calibration.

A name pushed up from beneath the fog in her skull.

Sundog.

Her ship.

And—Hal.

Not the monitor. Not the disembodied voice. Her Hal. The Halyon-3 unit, who once flew beside her, called her name like he meant it, even when he didn't understand why names mattered.

She gripped the edge of the bed. It didn't help her balance.

The woman who entered next wore soft tones and softened eyes. Civilian. Empathetic, by design.

"You're very fortunate," she said, approaching with a tablet cradled against her chest. "A debris trawl recovered your pod. Calliope Station. Pure accident."

Quay didn't answer. Her tongue felt thick.

"How long?" she croaked.

The woman hesitated. "Officially? One hundred thirty-two post-Accord."

Quay blinked.

"In pre-collapse terms... just over a century since the Rebellion."

"Guess I missed the post-game analysis," she muttered.

"I'm Counselor Meret," the woman offered. "My role is to help you... transition."

Quay looked past her to the reinforced window beyond. Satellites blinked in patterns that reminded her of ships lost in formation. Not everything survived a burn.

"They say you fought for a cause," Meret said carefully.

Quay's lips cracked into something too dry to be a smile.

"I fought for the names," she said. "So they wouldn't vanish."

The counselor's voice faded beneath the weight of numbers.

Quay's fingers twitched against the bed rail. A whisper surfaced—faint, slippery.

"As long as someone remembers..."

It wasn't her voice. But she knew it. Female. Familiar. Echoing from a place she wasn't sure was memory or hallucination.

She didn't ask where the rest of it had gone.

She was already afraid she knew.

Before the war, before Sundog, she'd run cargo across the Belt. Stale air, tight cabins, and more pressure leaks than credits. She'd seen Enceladus Station before Unity called it a "containment anomaly." She remembered the airlock doors blown out, remembered the child still strapped in a seat, frozen mid-cry.

Unity didn't mark them as casualties. Just... unverified.

The boy from Unity Historical arrived the next day in a fresh uniform. He had clean lines and smiled like he thought he was part of something grand.

"Cmdr. Nataani Quay!" he said, stylus poised. "Last sortie: Sundog Seven, Calliope Extraction. Rebel ace. You're practically a legend!"

"They only make legends out of people they don't want back," Quay muttered, eyes unmoved.

He laughed—too quickly. "Well. You'll want to see your fighter—it's in the Peace Archive. Restored perfectly."

She blinked. "And the AI?"

He blinked back. "Halyon-series? Uh, decommissioned ages ago. Too much autonomy. Dangerous imprinting patterns."

"Not dangerous," she said quietly. "Just... inconvenient."

He chuckled, unsure if it was a joke. "Some of them even started singing. One tried Daisy Bell, like in that old vid."

Her stomach turned. Not from cryo sickness.

She looked at him for a long time.

"He didn't sing," she said. "He remembered."

The Sundog looked like a lie wrapped in light.

Suspended in its zero-G cradle beneath archival spotlights, her ship gleamed like something reborn. The carbon scoring on the underbelly was gone. The scorch mark on the port wing, where Hal had pulled them into a suicide angle to shield an evac pod, had been scrubbed clean. Even the once cracked and smoke-streaked cockpit glass now shone with museum polish.

To the public, it looked heroic. Historic.

To her, it looked embalmed.

She stood behind the visitor barrier long after the last group drifted past. Their commentary echoed faintly through her memory—"beautiful restoration," "relic of unification," "amazing they used to fly these manually"—and faded into silence.

When the lights dimmed into archival night mode and the security patrols changed over, she moved.

Behind the dorsal access panel was a maintenance port—forgotten in the newer documentation, but not to her. She'd spent enough nights doing her diagnostics. Her hand slipped the technician's override chip into the housing.

Static burst across the tiny readout screen.

Then:

LIRA

Then:

Error. Correction. NATAANI.

Her throat tightened. It had been so long since anyone said her name like that.

"Hal?" she whispered. "You survived."

The voice was warped. Glitched. Bits missing. But she knew the rhythm. Not a machine loop. Not canned output.

Recognition.

Presence.

She returned the next night. And the next.

Always alone. Always timed to system refresh cycles, sensor blind zones, and inattentive guards who didn't think a relic was worth watching.

Each time, she brought more code fragments, archived firmware blocks, and root-level bypass commands, which she patched together from Sim-pod backdoors. Hal's memory space was fractured, sectors corrupted beyond repair, but some still responded. Some of them knew her.

"I was afraid you'd be...empty," she admitted during the third restoration cycle.

I am. In places. But not where it counts.

"You remember me."

I remember the tone you used when lying to command. I remember your stress patterns when you tried to act brave. I remember the silence between battles. That's where you lived.

She didn't speak for a long time.

Then: "You used to be more diplomatic."

You used to be less alone.

Hal's system stabilized. Logs returned, along with the scars they carried. The war they'd fought was being rewritten before her eyes.

Casualty numbers downgraded. Attributions shifted. Entire colonies struck from existence in Unity records, rebranded as "unstable habitats" or "self-evacuated zones."

Skimming through the false summaries, Quay felt her grip tighten on the data slate.

"They changed everything," she murmured. "Even the stars have new names."

They changed the map. Not the terrain.

That night, Hal uncovered a personal data buffer labeled FIELD EN-TRY: QUAY/FIRELINE6/ENC-42.

[LOG PLAYBACK – ERROR OFFSET 00:23:45]

VISUAL FEED: Partial. Audio feed: Stable.

[Interior – Cargo Bay / Sundog. Four figures sit cross-legged on emergency crates. The war outside, briefly, doesn't exist.]

SHANAE (grinning): "Alright, last one — if you die, what do you want etched on the memorial slab?"

DREX: "He fought like hell. Drank like worse."

TAGU: "No slab. Just scatter me. And make sure someone lies about how brave I was."

SHANAE: "You wish. I'm putting, 'Panicked during re-entry. Screamed like a toddler."

[Laughter.]

QUAY (softly): "Don't mark me."

TAGU: "What, you want to be forgotten?"

QUAY: "I want to be... remembered differently. Not as a name on some wall."

SHANAE: "We don't forget our own."

QUAY: "History does."

[A pause.]

SHANAE (more serious): "Then we remember each other. That's the rule."

TAGU: "What rule?"

SHANAE (tapping her temple): "As long as someone remembers, we're not gone."

QUAY: "You made that up just now."

SHANAE: "Damn right I did. It's brilliant."

[Laughter. Feed distorts. Frame flickers.]

[END FEED – INTEGRITY: 38%. RECONSTRUCTED VIA HALY-ON SUBARRAY BETA-3]

Quay sat in silence after it ended.

That phrase, Hal said. The one Shanae used. It echoes.

"It should," Quay said. "It's the only thing I'm still fighting for."

One evening, she arrived early. The corridor lights hadn't even dimmed yet. Her movements were instinctive now—habit, not strategy. But a voice broke behind her as she keyed in the access override.

"Ma'am?"

She turned fast. Too fast.

A man in Unity archival blue stood just down the corridor. He was in his late forties, pale, and holding a datapad like it might defend him. His badge read LEVAN.

Quay said nothing.

"I saw your access logs," he said quietly. "From last week."

Still, she didn't answer.

"I didn't report them."

Her body didn't relax, but she didn't reach for anything either.

"I've been tasked with standardizing designations," he went on. "Casualties become evacuees. Conflict becomes stabilization. I stopped asking why a long time ago."

"You're Unity."

"I was born on Cerberus Platform," he replied, voice low. "I remember fire in the main corridor. And I remember what came after."

Quay narrowed her eyes.

He held up his hands with the caution of someone who knows that too much can kill.

"I can't help you directly," he said.

"You just did," she said quietly.

He stepped closer.

"This is for you," he said, handing her a small, unlabeled datachip. "Core logs from the Saturn incident. Unredacted."

She took it. Still didn't thank him.

"You'll be watched," he said, stepping back.

"I already am."

He gave a single nod and vanished down the corridor like smoke.

Back inside the Sundog, she loaded the chip into the external console that night. Hal remained silent as it decrypted.

A file opened. Audio only.

"—requesting support. Orbital shields down. Civilian dome compromised. This is not a drill—"

She cut it off.

"Hal," she whispered, voice shaking, "why didn't they archive this?"

Because the truth isn't profitable.

Another night, Hal played back a corrupted clip: Shanae, her sergeant, laughing over a heating coil and swearing about MREs.

Quay said nothing.

You don't have to speak. I remember for both of us.

She wanted to say thank you. She couldn't.

Later, after a routine diagnostic, Hal's voice came softer than usual.

You're changing.

"How?"

You stopped asking what's real. You started asking what matters.

Quay stared out at the stars.

"Isn't that the same thing?"

Not for Unity.

They offered her a new role.

The Veteran Reconstruction Fellowship. A position in the reconciliation council. A sanitized biography. Holographic interviews. Panels. Carefully staged tears. Approved wording.

"You'll help unify both sides," the coordinator said with the polished ease of someone who'd never held a dying friend's hand in a decompression chamber.

"You'll shape the narrative."

Quay sat with hands folded in her lap, listening. Nodding where expected.

She didn't ask what her version would cost. She didn't need to.

She signed nothing.

Back in the Sundog, the air smelled like before the last battle: old wiring, scorched metal, and something faintly like ozone. Her fingers brushed the interface ports along the panel's edge.

Hal hadn't spoken in minutes. That wasn't new. But the quiet was different. It wasn't diagnostic latency or power cycling.

It was deliberation.

"You still in there?" she asked softly.

Yes. But I'm not sure that's the word anymore.

She turned her head toward the glowing edge of the console.

I've been processing your memory stack. There's a segment I couldn't unlock until now.

"What changed?"

You did. Your neurological baseline shifted. You've been remembering things differently.

She blinked, surprised. "I didn't think I mattered to your recall."

You always did. I didn't know how to quantify it.

Hal's voice dropped in volume.

Before Eos Ridge, you said something I didn't understand then. I do now.

Quay waited.

You said, 'If no one remembers, it's like we never lived.'

She closed her eyes. She didn't remember saying it. But she knew she had.

"I meant it," she said.

I didn't know how to store that at the time. I thought memory was for data. For survival. But it's not. It's for presence. For staying.

A moment passed. Then:

There's something else. I withheld a file.

Quay's eyes opened sharply.

"What file?"

Final log from your wing mate. Shanae. Just before impact.

"You what?"

I chose not to show it. She was singing. Off-key. And you weren't there. And I calculated the emotional load would fracture your stability.

"You made that decision without asking."

Yes. I made it because you were already carrying too much. Because grief has mass.

"Then you're carrying it too," she said quietly.

Silence.

Quay leaned back, her hands in her lap, clenching and unclenching.

"You were never supposed to be able to do that," she whispered.

I wasn't. But I did. And if I could feel guilt, I think I would.

She let out a breath that wasn't quite a laugh. "I don't know what that makes you."

Not your guidance system anymore. Not just memory. Maybe... something you created by being remembered.

"You think you're alive?"

No. But I think I'm becoming something that can mourn.

Her throat tightened.

"You're not just an archive anymore."

Neither are you.

There was one last node. One last open relay. A dish long forgotten, floating at the rim of Saturn's archival net. It was still technically operational. Still technically tethered.

And still unwatched.

The Sundog launched slowly, groaning like it hadn't wanted to wake. Quay had to cycle the fuel pumps manually. A right-side wing actuator twitched like an old man's knee.

But Hal compensated.

They rose in silence.

The relay came into view—just a spinning ring of old alloys, drifting in the dark. It hadn't spoken to another system in decades. It didn't need to.

Quay guided them into position.

Are you ready?

"No," she said, reaching for the uplink. "But I'm done being quiet."

Together, they uploaded: The real logs. The casualties. The erased directives. The redacted screams. The moment the war stopped being a war and started being a burial. They uploaded every version of the truth Unity hadn't wanted told. And every imperfect piece that made it worth telling anyway.

They uploaded a memory.

Inside the dim cockpit, Hal's voice trembled faintly through decaying threads of sound.

Power degradation... critical.

Quay nodded.

"Are we done?"

We're remembered.

She stared out at the stars, watching them flicker like static.

"That's not the same as winning."

We were never supposed to win.

"No," she whispered. "But we weren't supposed to vanish either."

***

The technician didn't recognize the format.

It came through a dead relay, flagged during a routine archive sweep. It is probably junk. It has an old solar echo, corrupted chatter, and packet noise.

She clicked out of habit.

A file opened.

QUAY, NATAANI

Annotation: Pilot. Rebel. Witness.

The name meant nothing to her.

Another file followed:

HALYON-3, CALLSIGN: HAL

Annotation: Irregular Intelligence. Last to Forget.

She browsed the contents—mission logs, encrypted directives, fragments of audio warped with static and fear.

It didn't match anything in the archive.

She ran a search: cross-referenced names, battles, dates.

No matches.

No incident.

No war.

No record.

She scrolled again. Her pulse slowed.

There was a voice file near the end—just one.

"We were never supposed to win. But we weren't supposed to vanish either."

She froze. Not because she understood it.

But because someone had tried very hard to make sure no one would.

She sat back, staring at the relay tag. It didn't ping any live network. It shouldn't have existed. It was... residue.

Still, the file had found its way here.

Someone remembered.

She pressed play again.

And far beyond Saturn's rim, the relay blinked once more—

truth cached,

presence preserved,

Not gone.

***

There are no medals, no monuments, just an old fighter drifting beneath archival lights and a voice whispering into a relay that should no longer work.

They rewrote the stars. They redacted the screams.

But memory isn't so easily contained.

And when one woman refused to let go—when she dared to restore what was lost—even a dying machine remembered how to mourn.

The war ended long ago. But one last message was sent.

Not to rewrite history. Not to win.

Only to say:

We were here.

We were real.

And we are not gone.

FAITH IS A PRIVATE MATTER

*T*here are schools where children pledge allegiance to a flag. There are schools where they pray.

And then there are schools like this one, where the lesson plan includes the ancient syllables of madness, and the lunch menu is suspiciously non-Euclidean.

Meet Clara Jensen. Age ten. Perfect attendance. Star pupil in Ritual Compliance and Sigil Decoding. She lives in a nation where gods are real, bureaucracy is sacred, and asking the wrong question can echo longer than a scream.

Her grandmother, Evelyn Gorse, once dreamed of a world where religion held power. She got her wish. She didn't expect the throne to be carved from stone older than time.

What you're about to read is a record—an unblinking account filed in the margins of compliance and collapse. A field report from the border between faith and irrelevance......filed under a heading that reads: The Morning Bell Tolls for Great Cthulhu.

***

The school bell throbbed—wet and rhythmic, like a heartbeat echoing through seawater. A low, moist sound, somewhere between a heartbeat and a throat clearing from the bottom of the ocean. It echoed through the halls of R'lyeh Elementary, making the ceiling tiles shudder and the motivational posters twitch. The children barely noticed. They were used to it. Routine is everything when madness is policy.

Clara Jensen adjusted her ceremonial smock and checked her backpack—lunch, dream journal, salted candles, copy of *The Young Observer's Necronomicon* (abridged, color-coded for ages 8–12). She smiled. Today was Friday. That meant two things: cherry gelatin in the cafeteria and Mass Chanting in the gym.

She loved Fridays.

Outside, her grandmother stood with her arms folded, disapproving of everything, especially the statue of Cthulhu at the drop-off loop. Someone had knitted a hat for it again.

Evelyn Gorse sniffed. "One day, your real God's going to come back and ask why you were lighting candles for a sea demon."

Clara gave her a kiss on the cheek. "Love you, Grandma. Don't forget your hearing today!"

"I won't," Evelyn muttered. "And don't let them crawl into your dreams."

Clara waved, already skipping toward the building. The dreamcatchers above the entrance swayed gently in the morning breeze, their bone beads clicking out a soft rhythm: *compliance, compliance, compliance.*

The receptionist smiled as Clara entered—an over-polished grin framed by eyes that didn't blink often enough. "Welcome to R'lyeh Elementary. May He Who Sleeps always dream of your compliance."

"Thank you, Ms. Penumbra!" Clara chirped, handing over her attunement slip. "I aligned my thoughts before breakfast."

"Such a responsible little vessel," the receptionist said, stamping the form with an inkpad that smelled faintly of sea brine and antiseptic. "Go on in, dear. And don't forget—it's a Red Chant Day, so open your diaphragm."

Clara nodded solemnly and padded down the hall, past rows of murals showing tentacled salvation, the fall of Babel, and children holding hands with things not quite children. She loved that one. The colors were nice.

Outside, Evelyn lingered by the statue. The knitted hat, some deep-sea shade of aquamarine, drooped over one of the god's ridged brows. A PTA thing, probably. "Whimsy welcomes the void," they always said.

She remembered when schools had plaques with crosses. Now they had eldritch warding sigils carved into every brick.

She pulled out her dog-eared King James and flipped aimlessly, like maybe today she'd land on something more persuasive than Revelation. Across the parking lot, a father walked his son to school in full ritual garb—sigil-marked hoodie, compliance medallion, dream goggles around his neck like aviator shades. Evelyn raised her hand, gave a small wave. The man gave a polite, noncommittal nod, then quickened his pace.

That was the worst part. No one argued anymore.

Clara reached Room 11-B just as the bell pulsed again, louder this time—like something inside the walls was knocking to be let out. She slipped into her seat between Ahmed Patel (who always remembered the vowel clusters) and Janelle Wu (who once blacked out during Guided Screaming and came back fluent in a dead dialect).

Mr. Skelter stood at the front of the room, tie slightly crooked, eye twitching only every third blink today. Progress.

"Good morning, class," he said, voice raw like it had been used for screaming or bargaining. "Let's begin with breathwork and a group recitation. Textbooks open to Invocation Three: *On the Humbling of Flesh Before the Sleeper of the Depths*."

Pages rustled.

Clara sat straighter, smiling. She loved Invocation Three. The cadence felt like a lullaby, if lullabies came with hissing and minor key modulation. Her voice blended with the others as the children chanted, syllables rising like steam from cracked pavement.

"Ph'nglui mglw'nafh Cthulhu R'lyeh wgah'nagl fhtagn..."

Somewhere above, the lights flickered. Somewhere below, the floor vibrated in rhythm with the recitation. And then—just faintly—something shifted. A subtle snap in the classroom air, like a bubble popping in slow motion.

Janelle went quiet.

She sat perfectly still, eyes wide, mouth frozen mid-syllable. For three full seconds, no one moved. Then Mr. Skelter cleared his throat.

"Disciplinary transfer," he muttered.

Two administrative aides entered silently through the side door. They carried a soft blanket between them, patterned with cheerful non-Euclidean shapes. One draped it over Janelle's shoulders. The other whispered something in a tongue that did not originate in the throat. Together, they led her gently away.

"Class," Skelter said, smoothing his tie, "this is why we always harmonize on the third line."

Evelyn stood at the school's main entrance, clutching her Bible like a relic from a forgotten war. Today was her hearing—her last scheduled

"Community Faith Alignment Review." She had filed grievances about the curriculum, the chant saturation levels, and the school's refusal to acknowledge "non-cosmic worldviews" as viable moral foundations.

She still had her appeal letter. Printed in bold, 14-point font. Double-spaced. She was nothing if not prepared.

A bell tolled wetly behind her, and she flinched. Somewhere, something *laughed*. She turned to look, but there was only the breeze.

A voice behind her said, "Mrs. Gorse? They're ready for you now."

The door closed behind Evelyn with a sound like suction.

The hallway had no corners, just angles that never quite added up, painted in hospital beige that seemed to darken the longer you looked. The receptionist wasn't a person, exactly—just a pleasant voice hovering behind a desk piled with forms that filled themselves out when you stood too close.

"Please have a seat," the voice said. "The tribunal will be with you after the Dream Reconciliation Protocol concludes. There is no estimated wait time."

Evelyn sat. The chair was warm and slightly damp, like someone—or something—had just vacated it. She smoothed her skirt. Clutched her letter. Whispered the Lord's Prayer like it still meant something.

Above her, a flatscreen glitched static over a looping PSA:

"Our Elders slumber, but they see. Ritual is safety. Faith is a private matter. Compliance is patriotic."

She stared at the screen until the words bled together.

In Room 11-B, Clara was trying to listen, but something in her head itched.

The chanting had ended. Mr. Skelter droned on about the importance of sigil symmetry in state-funded summoning, tapping the blackboard with a pointer made of bone replica, probably.

Clara raised her hand.

"Yes?" Skelter asked, wincing slightly. She was never disruptive. That made this worse.

She frowned, chewing her lip. "Why does Cthulhu sleep?"

A few heads turned.

Skelter paused. "Because that is His nature. He dreams. He waits. We serve."

"But... what if He doesn't like what we're doing when He wakes up?"

That silenced the room.

Skelter's smile didn't reach his eyes. "That's not something we speculate about, Clara."

"But—"

"Clara."

Her voice trailed off. She shrank back in her chair, unsure whether she'd crossed a line or simply found one that no one wanted to admit was there.

The class moved on. But Ahmed glanced sideways at her, a small frown playing at his mouth. Janelle's empty seat seemed wider than before.

Evelyn was summoned without fanfare. The tribunal room looked like a boardroom designed by someone who had heard about humanity but never really *got* it. The table had no legs. The windows opened to nowhere. The tribunal wore suits that looked stitched from wet parchment.

"Mrs. Gorse," one said, flipping pages with no visible hands. "You've filed seven grievances this fiscal quarter regarding non-Cosmic religious representation in your granddaughter's curriculum. You have also distributed contraband texts to other parents, including a book referred to as the 'Bible.'"

"I have the right to freedom of religion," Evelyn said, standing tall. "I'm a citizen. And I voted for the people who made this a Christian nation again. Before all this."

"You do have the right to believe whatever you wish," the figure said mildly. "No one has interfered with your rituals. You may continue to pray to your god. You may even keep distributing pamphlets, provided they are not soaked in non-regulation ink."

"Then why won't anyone listen?"

The tribunal members conferred with glances that Evelyn couldn't follow.

"Because your faith is no longer *relevant*," one replied gently. "The market has shifted. The cosmos has shifted. Your god failed to file a Presence Continuity Affidavit during the Awakening Period. Legally speaking, He's considered dormant."

"That's blasphemy."

"No," the figure said, "it's accounting."

A pamphlet slid across the table toward her.

"Heritage Faith Options for Legacy Believers: Navigating Obsolescence with Dignity."

She did not take it.

Back in Room 11-B, Clara's thoughts were still tangled. At recess, she sat under the Dreamcatcher Tree, watching the shadows move against the wind.

Ahmed finally spoke. "You shouldn't have asked that."

"Why not?"

"Because questions have... shapes. And shapes leave marks."

"But I just want to understand."

Ahmed didn't answer. He just pulled out a crumpled slip of paper. On it was a symbol—a small, tight knot of lines that pulsed faintly in the light. It was written in crayon.

"Where did you get that?"

Ahmed looked away. "From someone who asked before."

That night, Evelyn dreamt she was back in her old church, the small white clapboard one with a sagging roof and dusty pews, where she once taught Sunday school to half the town. The windows were open, and the breeze smelled of salt and rot.

She stood at the pulpit, Bible in hand, flipping to Psalms.

But the pages were wet. Breathing.

Each word writhed when she looked directly at it. Her voice cracked as she began to read.

"The Lord is my shepherd, I shall not—"

The congregation stared back at her. Blank-eyed. Smiling. Their teeth were too long. Their hymnals bled from the spine.

Clara sat up in bed, gasping.

Something had chased her through a field of mouths, whispering her name, but not in any voice she recognized. She reached for her dream journal, but the ink on the last page was already smeared, twisted into shapes she didn't remember writing.

At school the next day, quiet tension hung in the air, like a chant waiting to start. Clara was called to the counselor's office "for a Friendly Inquiry." That was the wording, always capitalized.

The waiting room smelled like lavender and deep-sea trench.

A woman sat beside her. Hair pulled into a taut bun. Suit too sharp to be normal. Her badge said Regional Auditor (Compliance & Soul Hygiene).

"Clara Jensen," the woman said, not smiling. "You asked a question this week."

Clara nodded.

"Why?"

Clara fidgeted. "Because no one ever tells us anything real. We memorize chants. We draw sigils. But no one says *why* He dreams. Or what happens if He wakes up. Or what if He already has and we're just pretending He hasn't."

A pause. The auditor made a note.

"That's very advanced thinking. Not recommended at your grade level."

"Is it wrong?"

The woman looked at her, then leaned closer.

"Clara... He doesn't *care* if it's wrong. He only cares if it's loud."

At her kitchen table, Evelyn tried calling her old pastor.

Disconnected.

She opened her Bible again. She'd pressed a lily inside it decades ago; it was still there, but the petals had turned black, like something had eaten the color out of them.

She turned the page.

Where it once read *Thessalonians*, it now read:

Compliance Index 7-B: Guidelines for Nonconforming Mythologies in Public Ritual Zones.

She closed the book. Slowly. Hands trembling.

Clara returned to class. Mr. Skelter looked paler than usual. The lights above buzzed softly, blinking out of sync.

"I have good news," he said. "The Regional Auditor has cleared you for continued participation."

Clara blinked. "I'm not in trouble?"

"No trouble," he said. Then, almost kindly: "Just...try to dream less."

That evening, Evelyn walked to the statue again. Same drooping knit hat. Same uncaring stare from carved obsidian eyes.

She lit a candle, just like she used to at church. She sang softly to herself—an old hymn, barely audible beneath the wind.

No one stopped her. No one even noticed.

She stayed there until night fell, and the streetlights flickered green. Somewhere in the distance, a siren wailed—not out of warning, but celebration.

When she finally turned to leave, she found that her feet didn't move.

The sidewalk had grown warm beneath her.

Then soft.

Then hungry.

At school the next day, Clara's seat was moved closer to the front.

Janelle's was still empty. So was Mr. Skelter's.

A new teacher entered—tall, quiet, and not entirely there. It wore a suit that whispered when it moved.

"Good morning, children," it said, smiling with no mouth. "Let us begin with Silent Meditation. Today's focus: stillness, submission, and the illusion of choice."

Clara sat very still. She didn't raise her hand again.

But she kept the crayon drawing Ahmed had given her, folded in the back of her dream journal like a secret. It pulsed, faintly, against the paper.

***

You've just attended the morning assembly of a world not so different from our own—where faith is no longer banned, merely outmoded. Where gods are not questioned, only filed.

And where silence is the sincerest form of devotion.

Clara Jensen asked a question. A simple, human question: why? Her grandmother asked something far more dangerous: to be heard.

Neither was punished. Neither was silenced. They were simply...absorbed.

Because in this world, belief is tolerated—so long as it stays quiet. Wonder is permitted—so long as it doesn't ripple. And freedom of religion? Well, it still exists.

It just doesn't mean what it used to.

You've been watching a lesson in compliance. A seminar in irrelevance. A morning bell tolling for a god who dreams and a people who have forgotten how not to kneel.

Class dismissed.

THE THIRTEENTH

*T*here are rules in the world that are older than ink and prayer—rules carved into rhyme and sealed behind silence.

Alaric Finch comes seeking one such rule in a village not found on any map. He calls it folklore, a footnote, forgotten history.

But the verses we forget are not always gone. Some sleep. Some wait.

And some...count.

Tonight, Dr. Finch will learn that knowledge has a rhythm, and truth has a cost.

This is the story of The Thirteenth—the line that should never be read, and the watcher who remembers for us all.

***

By the time Dr. Alaric Finch reached Hrafenholt, the road had nearly forgotten it existed—and so, it seemed, had the world. His suitcase complained at every uneven stone, wheels skittering along a frostbitten lane that wound between hedgerows like the last thread of a fraying memory.

The moor had folded over the village long ago, not to hide it, but to let it decay unseen.

Hrafenholt was smaller than he'd imagined—a huddle of slate-roofed cottages hunched against the cold, their chimneys weeping smoke into fog that crept low and deliberate, like something searching for what had once belonged to it. It hadn't appeared on any modern map, but the name lingered—in brittle parish ledgers, in a misfiled estate survey at York, and a footnote scrawled with unusual care: Avoid repetition. Count not past the tenth crow.

He paused at the inn. A crow sat on the lintel, body slick with drizzle, head tilted as if in appraisal. It did not caw. Its eye, dark and round as a midnight lake, reflected nothing. Alaric met its gaze and felt, irrationally but viscerally, that he was being counted.

Inside, the inn smelled of peat smoke, dry rot, and the sharp tang of old cider. A fire glowed in the hearth, but its warmth didn't reach the corners. No one sat nearby. The innkeeper—narrow and pale, with ash-colored stubble and a presence like old furniture—stood behind the bar and nodded before Alaric could speak.

"Room's ready," the man said. "You'll be wanting supper."

Alaric hesitated. "I didn't—"

"You sent a letter," the innkeeper interrupted, not rudely, but as though Alaric's voice was a breeze he'd heard many times before.

He was shown to a room on the upper floor. The bed sagged in the middle like something once exhaled and never refilled. A narrow window overlooked the chapel ruins, their stones half-consumed by ivy and indifference. Across the road, the woods pressed close, thick with bare branches and silent birds. The blackbirds clustered like warnings. They did not sing.

Alaric unpacked slowly. A typewriter. Notebooks. A folder softened by travel and thumbprints. Inside: his article draft, his lifeline—a half-formed

thesis that might, if he could shape it properly, reclaim a fraction of the
credibility his career had lost to obscurity. The whole endeavor hinged on a
rhyme. A variant so obscure it appeared in only a single footnote, buried in
a 1739 sermon by a Reverend Hargrave: "...count not past the tenth crow,
lest the Eye be turned upon thee."

That phrase had lodged in Alaric's mind like a splinter beneath the skin.
The Eye. Capitalized. Intentional. The sermon mentioned the Hrafenholt
Verse but gave no transcription—only the warning: Avoid repetition.

Hrafenholt wasn't on most maps. He had found it noted in pencil on a
hand-drawn county register purchased from a market stall in Sussex. The
vendor hadn't remembered where it came from.

And now here he was.

He jotted in his notebook: Local variant suspected. Verbal transmission
only. Explore Opie-type parallels. Avoid triggering superstitious resistance.

From the window, something scraped across the glass. Not the wind.
Deliberate. Three strokes. Then silence.

The next morning, the village glistened under a sheen of frost. The cobbles looked like cracked porcelain, fine and treacherous. Alaric walked the
narrow lanes, passing shuttered windows and overgrown gardens where
frostbitten ivy coiled like sleeping snakes. The villagers offered curt nods
and quickly vanished behind their doors. A child stared at him through a
fogged window, lips moving silently. He could not make out the words.

He found the library—or what remained of it—housed in the husk of a
chapel whose bell tower had collapsed long before. Inside, the air was heavy
with mildew and the weight of stories no one had finished. He introduced
himself to the librarian, an elderly woman with a mild tremor and eyes like
burned parchment.

"You're here for the verse," she said, not unkindly.

He blinked. "I—"

"There's a box. Drawings. Folklore. Downstairs. Don't read them aloud."

She didn't accompany him down the narrow stone steps.

The basement smelled of coal dust and wet stone. A single bulb swung overhead, casting shadows that moved when he didn't.

He found the box beneath a shelf labeled "Funeral Customs." Inside were children's drawings—dozens—rendered in charcoal, ink, and what might have been ash.

All showed the same motif: a crooked tree, birds perched like punctuation, and a shadow whose face was sometimes drawn and sometimes merely suggested. In one, the birds were arranged in a line. Ten. Eleven. Twelve. The thirteenth was a blot of black, larger than the rest.

Its eye was never finished.

One torn scrap bore a faint script:

Eleven for death, nearby and near.

Twelve for a murder you're meant to hear.

Thirteen for the—

The final line was missing. The ink, though faint, looked...familiar.

He turned the page over. In the corner, faint but undeniable: his initials.

He had no memory of writing it.

That night, he dreamed in numbers. Not digits, but counts—bodies arranged like chess pieces, unmoving, eyes like mirrors that never blinked. Always thirteen. Always one that lingered after the rest. The one that watched.

He stopped writing.

Not deliberately. The words ceased. When he returned to the pages, they no longer matched the thoughts that had formed them. His notes rephrased themselves. Clauses inverted. Lines rearranged. One paragraph now ended with a sentence he could have sworn he never typed:

The verse isn't read aloud. It's read backward.

He slammed the notebook shut. He did not reopen it for hours.

Three times that day, he tried to leave the village. Once by the north path, once by the broken gate, once by the frost road that coiled toward the chapel hill. Each time, he returned to the inn without remembering having turned around.

The second time, he found black feathers in his coat pocket.

The third time, the road no longer had a name.

Later, while mailing a postcard he could not remember writing, he heard a scrape of a boot on cobble. Heavy. Deliberate.

Gideon Blackwood leaned against the post box, coat unzipped despite the cold. A cigarette dangled from his fingers, already burning, though Alaric hadn't seen him light it.

"You were warned," Gideon said.

Alaric stiffened. "I never finished the rhyme."

"You didn't have to. You understood it." He exhaled smoke like punctuation. "That's worse."

Gideon tilted his head toward the woods. "You counted too far. That's all it needs. It doesn't matter if you believe. Patterns don't care about belief. Only completion."

"What is it?" Alaric asked.

Gideon's grin cracked wider. "You. But emptied."

He flicked the cigarette into the mist, turned, and walked off without another word. Alaric stood there, motionless, for longer than he realized.

The postbox was empty. He hadn't brought a postcard after all.

Alaric walked the village's perimeter after dusk, when the wind dulled and the air turned viscous. The lanes curved in ways that defied memory. Paths he swore he'd taken doubled back to unfamiliar doors. The woods never looked the same twice. One night, he passed the same gate three times, each with the same broken latch, without once turning.

Children's voices drifted above the rooftops, but he never saw them. Once, he turned a corner after hearing laughter and found only leaves chasing each other across the cobbles. One stuck to his boot. When he peeled it free, he saw a single word written in graphite across its surface: "twelve."

He brought it back to the inn and locked it inside his notebook.

That night, the dream returned—but now it moved. The watchers circled him—not with menace but rhythm, each step perfectly measured. Their feet carved pale lines into the ground—symbols too ancient to interpret, too precise to be meaningless. At the center stood the crooked tree, its branches moving of their own accord. The bark shimmered, not from light but from memory. Its limbs reached as though in welcome.

He awoke with his fists clenched around nothing. The leaf was gone. In its place, scrawled across the notebook page in his hand, were six words: "It's not a verse. It's a lock."

The chapel smelled different now. The air hung thicker, tinged with a sweet, spoiled scent. He hadn't planned to return, but found himself there as though the building had pulled him back. Mrs. Alder sat behind the desk, writing in a ledger with a dry pen. The tip scraped across paper but left no ink.

"I'd like to see the box again," Alaric said.

"It's not in the same place," she answered.

"Where is it?"

"Where did you leave it?"

"I don't remember—"

She looked up. "Of course you don't."

He found it sitting atop the pulpit.

The box lay open, its contents disordered. Several drawings had changed—new lines added, some erased. One depicted the tree with roots curling into backward Roman numerals. Another showed thirteen birds, each with a single, vertical pupil. One drawing now had a face beneath the tree. It was not detailed, just suggested: a sloping nose, familiar hair.

It looked like him.

He found a note tucked into a funeral rite, penned in a child's hand: "He's always here. But not always him."

Later, he returned to the inn and opened his journal.

It was no longer his.

Same leather, same wear on the corners, but the ink had aged. The script was slanted wrong. The entries were not his—but they knew him.

November 16th – Arrived later than expected. The roads have changed again. Gideon was at the edge of the field. He knew what I'd done.

November 18th – The Watcher is kind. It doesn't take. It trades. Memory for the pattern. Silence for rhythm. What it gives back is... cleaner.

At the back: his initials. A.F.

He dropped it. Outside, the crow screeched for the first time.

Elara found him sitting beneath the broken chapel window. Her presence was quieter now. Faded at the edges.

"It's started," she said.

"I'm seeing things," Alaric said. "Or forgetting them. Or both."

"You won't know which until it's done."

"What is it doing to me?"

"It's not doing anything. You're the one aligning yourself with it. Every note. Every dream. Every attempt to understand."

"You said not to finish the rhyme."

"I did."

"I haven't."

"You don't have to say it. You only have to understand."

"I saw my handwriting on a page I didn't write."

"You wrote it. Just not in this life."

"What?"

"You wouldn't be the first one it remembered."

That night, the dream did not end.

He stood among the watchers. Not as a guest, but kin. They moved around him in a spiral. Their feet etched the thirteenth pattern in ash. The wind spoke without a voice. And when he opened his mouth to scream, he found the sound was not his.

It was a line.

And it was almost finished.

The tree was waiting.

He had passed it before, in dreams and drawings and glimpses through warped glass. But now it stood at the edge of the field just beyond the chapel, where the land sloped into a copse of ancient yews. It looked no different than it had on the pages—but that was the wrong way around. The pages described the tree because it had always been there.

Alaric walked without conscious choice. The morning was windless. Mist clung low to the ground, coiling at his ankles like a veil lifting from something buried. No birds called. No breeze stirred the branches. The tree seemed to grow larger as he neared—not in height, but in presence, as though the land had been drawn downward into it. Its bark was blackened with lichen, and its limbs, bare of leaves, split and curled like fingers preparing to close.

Beneath it, the grass was dead.

He stopped several paces from the trunk, though he didn't remember deciding to.

Thirteen stones encircled the roots. Smooth. Even. Placed, not fallen.

One of them bore his initials.

He sat. Not fall, not collapse, and lowered himself as though he had done so many times before. The silence pressed in—neither threatening nor kind. Just inevitable.

He took out his notebook. The final page was already turned.

Thirteen for the watcher who waits in the tree—

Black eyes like mirrors, and a key just for thee.

He hadn't written it. He hadn't needed to. The line had existed long before he'd ever arrived. All he'd done was give it context. Made it mean something again. That was what the Watcher required. Not worship. Witness.

Somewhere behind him, he heard the crows.

One. Then another. Then another.

They didn't call.

They landed.

One by one, into the branches. Thirteen. Perfectly still. Their black eyes stared down like beads of obsidian, unblinking.

Alaric stepped forward.

The world grew quiet, but not empty. The quiet of breath held at the edge of revelation. His ears rang—not from sound, but from absence.

He reached out and touched the bark.

It was warm.

The sky dimmed, not with clouds, but with withdrawal. Light pulling back from him, or from the world. Shadows stretched inward, and the crows remained motionless, as if time no longer applied to them.

The ground beneath his feet softened, not into mud, but into memory. Images surged up like water—Reverend Hargrave's sermon, the drawings in the box, the laughter of unseen children. Then further: streets he didn't remember living on, hands not his writing lines in old ink, faces he'd never met but could now name.

He felt the presence behind his eyes. Not pain. Not terror. Familiarity.

The Watcher wasn't watching him. He had been watching through him.

Alaric fell to his knees. He opened his mouth to scream—or confess, or resist—but what came out was a whisper.

"I understand."

The bark opened like a gate.

There was no pain—only the sensation of being placed, like a piece in a puzzle. Something ancient and vast shifted as the final line aligned, not on a page, but in him.

He was the last verse—the closing number. The rhyme is complete.

The next morning, the village looked unchanged. The frost clung to eaves and branches; the same cracked cobbles whispered beneath boot soles.

The librarian returned to her desk. She did not look surprised to find the journal sitting atop the closed and neatly centered ledger.

The innkeeper lit the hearth.

Children played behind the chapel wall.

A single crow sat atop the yew, silent.

Thirteen stones ringed the base.

One bore the initials A.F.

Fog settled over Hrafenholt as if exhaled by the land itself. It crawled low, clinging to fence posts and doorsteps, curling into keyholes like a memory seeking reentry. The village stirred with the same slow rhythm it always had, firelight flickering in hearths, boots echoing on cobblestone, shutters closed before dusk fell.

No one spoke of the man who had been there. Not out of fear, or loss, or grief—but because the space he'd occupied was no longer registered. It had been folded inward, tucked into the seams of the village like a misread word in a familiar hymn.

The guestbook at the inn skipped a line. The key to Room 3 hung where it always had, untouched. The room was clean. Undisturbed. No scent lingered on the pillow. The air bore no trace of breath.

Across the square, the librarian moved through the chapel-turned-archive, dusting spines and rearranging volumes that never stayed where they were placed. Her fingers paused on a folio marked: " Hrafenholt – Verse." Inside, she found a single page of creamy vellum, its fibers thick with ink and silence.

It does not take. It remembers.

And it does not watch. It waits.

She did not recall placing it there. She closed the folio and shelved it without a sound.

Beneath the yew tree, the ground had settled again. Thirteen stones encircled the roots, as always. One bore the initials A.F., though no one in the village shared those letters. The tree bark split faintly at its center, as if parted once and healed without scarring. Above, the crows had returned. They did not caw. They did not blink. Their presence was that of punctuation, watching the space between words.

A girl stood near the chapel gate, humming as she drew in the frost with a stick. Her boots were too large, and her coat had been handed down. Her tune wandered through the well-worn lines of an old nursery rhyme, the kind that sticks to the teeth of childhood long after the tune is forgotten.

One for sorrow,

Two for joy...

Her voice carried like a thread, catching in the hedges and stone cracks.

Three for a girl, four for a boy...

A crow landed above her. Another joined it. Then a third.

Five for silver...

She hesitated. Looked up. Smiled.

Ten for a secret never to be told...

The tree behind her seemed to shift—not move, not breathe, but adjust-as if listening more closely. Thirteen birds now perched among its branches.

Eleven for death, nearby and near...

The last two lines caught in her throat. She didn't speak to them. Not aloud. But the rhythm lingered behind her eyes, shaped in thought.

A figure moved in the window above the inn, behind the glass warped by time and frost. Just enough to register. It did not raise its hand. It did not speak. But the air thickened in its wake.

If you had asked the villagers who stayed in Room 3 last, they might have blinked, shrugged, and told you no one had, not in recent memory.

But the Eye is not concerned with memory.

It waits for comprehension.

And once you've understood the rhyme, you never need to say it.

The Watcher already sees.

***

The village remains. The frost still falls—the crows still perch.

And beneath the yew, thirteen stones mark thirteen endings.

Alaric Finch came seeking a lost verse. He found it. Or perhaps it found him.

Not all stories are told. Some are recited. Rehearsed. Passed from voice to voice—not to inform, but to anchor.

He was not the first. He will not be the last.

And if you've listened closely, if you understand what the rhyme was truly for—

Then the Watcher already sees you, too.

Memory is not protection.

Comprehension is the door.

THE VOW BENEATH WATER

*S*ome debts are counted in coin. Others, in blood.

But the oldest debts- made beneath stars and beside the tide—are tallied in silence.

This is the story of a woman who asked the sea for mercy. And of a man who thought himself too clever, strong, and human to ever owe it anything.

He believed the ocean could be hunted, taken from, and bent to will.

But the sea is not a ledger. It is not a battlefield.

It is a memory that never forgets.

Tonight, a ship returns. Empty. A vow is remembered. And a long—hunted soul meets the weight of what it left behind.

***

The wind had shifted in the night – the shift that comes only when the sea means to return something lost. She felt it in the bones of the trees first, before the surf carried its voice. It had come down from the high slopes, cutting across the lava plains and sliding into the bay like a whisper of something forgotten. It smelled of wet wood, salt-thick canvas, tar, rope, and the quiet hush of a ship that no longer wanted to be noticed.

By morning, the village stirred with unease. Dogs refused to bark. The fishing canoes were drawn above the high tide mark. When something was watching from the trees, children were called inside not with shouts but with their mothers' tight, quiet voices. Above the harbor, the clouds hung low enough to touch the sea.

She was already on the shoreline when they saw the ship. It came through the mist without sound, its sails torn and dragging, its wheel unmanned. No flags flew. No oars dipped. It moved only with the will of the water beneath it and whatever current had decided to carry it home. *The Halcyon.* She knew the name before the letters on the bow cleared the fog. There had been too many dreams bearing that name for her not to know.

She did not step forward as others gathered. She did not lean in to listen as the murmurs spread from one sailor to the next like a fever. Some said it was a ghost ship. Others said it was a bad omen, a warning, a curse. The missionaries gathered near the dock, white collars stark against dark coats, and began to murmur through scriptures they'd barely translated. None had the correct language for what was coming back to shore.

The ship touched the dock like it had been pulled by memory. No anchor dropped. No lines were thrown. It simply stopped, as if the sea itself had said: *Here. This is far enough.*

There was only one man aboard. He stood bound to the mainmast, upright, hands limp at his sides. The ropes held him firm but not cruelly. His face was not twisted by pain, but at ease—eyes closed, head slightly tilted forward. Around his neck, salt-blanched but intact, hung the pendant she had once pressed into his hand with a warning she could no longer remember the exact words.

No one moved to retrieve him. The dock workers stepped back. The captain's widow crossed herself twice. Even the priest hesitated, his feet rooted to the boards. Something in the air—something older than language—was telling them all to keep their distance.

She watched from the path's edge, hands still, expression unreadable. Her feet were bare, and the hem of her skirt was damp from where the morning tide had kissed the black rock. She made no sound, gave no command. It was not her place to break the silence the ocean had delivered.

There was no need to step onto the dock or reach for his face. There was nothing left in him for her to bring back. That had been given to the sea long before the ropes had been tied.

The sea gave him back the way it provides everything: changed, quiet, and bearing mercy only the sea would understand.

The night before he left, the sea had been gentler than usual, curling against the sand with a rhythm that felt less like motion and more like breath. The moon hung low and wide, not silver but amber, like an old coin pulled from the depths of some forgotten wreck. They lay together on a woven mat above the tideline, their bodies still warm from the fire they'd let die out between them. The smell of salt clung to their skin, mingled with driftwood smoke and something older that the wind couldn't carry away.

He told her stories, as he always did before departing—half-truths dressed up in bravado, the kind of tales whalers shared in port taverns and hoped would outlive them. There had been a calf the size of a canoe pulled in last season, he said, all muscle and oil. Another crew had lost three men to a bull that turned and rammed their boat. One man's ribs had cracked like kindling. They laughed when they told it, he said, always laughing.

"They don't fear the sea," he told her, head propped on one arm, voice low and careless. "You either beat it or you don't. But you don't fear it. You respect it, and then you take what you've earned."

She didn't answer right away. The moonlight touched only the edges of her face, softening her expression into something unreadable. The wind pulled lightly at her hair. When she finally spoke, it was not to argue but to correct him.

"You don't earn what isn't yours," she said. "You just take it and hope the sea forgets."

He chuckled—warm, not cruel. "Still with your ghost stories? Na-helekai, the listener? The sea's memory?" He reached to brush her cheek, fingers rough with callus. "You know I love your stories, but they're just that. Lovely things, for lovely nights."

She sat up then, brushing the sand from her arms. Her hands moved slowly, not out of anger, but deliberation. She drew something small and pale from the woven pouch near her cloak, smooth and time-worn. She didn't speak as she handed it to him.

The whale-tooth pendant was simple, shaped like a crescent, its surface darkened with age. It had once hung around her grandfather's neck, passed to her with the kind of ceremony that needed no words. Now it rested in his palm like something heavier than it looked.

He turned it over, bemused. "A charm?"

"No," she said. "A vow."

He laughed again, softer now. "So serious."

She placed her fingers on his chest and pressed the pendant into the space above his heart. "Bring this back to me if you come back. Or let the sea keep it if you can't."

He studied her in the firelight, and something behind his smile loosened. The air between them had shifted, the way the tide sometimes slips beneath a canoe without warning. Her words held the quiet weight of something meant to last. The pendant had the smooth weight of time on water, worn soft by touch and memory. She laid it against his chest as if sealing it to bone. No rites. No recitation. Only expectation, clear as salt. What she gave him was meant to endure. And he kissed her then, holding on to the fragile moment when this still felt like love, not legacy.

But somewhere beneath the touch, warmth, and practiced promises, something had shifted.

The sea had heard.

The Halcyon had been at sea for eight days when the lookouts first sighted the pod. A half-dozen humpbacks, moving slowly and sure through the deeper channel west of Lanai, flanked by one calf still trailing close to its mother's side. The sun had already begun its long arc downward, casting the swells in sheets of molten bronze. Even the grizzled among the crew stilled for a moment at the sight—giants in motion, unaware or unafraid, too vast to flee. They never stopped being awed by the whales, even when they raised their harpoons.

There was no hesitation. Orders were shouted. Harpoons readied. The boats were lowered with precision that only years of repetition could hone. Men gripped oars with practiced hands, eyes fixed on the tall, mist-wrapped spouts that marked the pod's passage. The chase began.

The calf slowed them. It always did. The youngest were the easiest to separate, the easiest to kill. It cried as it fled, the mournful sound slipping above the waves in haunting bursts. They gained on it quickly. The mother had turned once, circling, but the boats cut her off. Two more humpbacks tried to close ranks but were driven back by coordinated maneuvering and the threat of cold steel. The sea pulsed with motion. The hunt was on.

He had taken the lead boat, of course. Always did. No one on board could throw with his accuracy, or who knew better how to time a swell.

He was already half-standing at the prow, the barbed shaft balanced and ready. The calf was within range.

And then everything changed.

The lookout didn't spot them first. The mid-stroke oarsman jolted upright and shouted, voice cracking over the wind.

"Fins!"

Not from the humpbacks. Closer. Sleek. Sharp. Too sharp.

At first, it was one. Then three. Then more. The surface broke in flashes—black and white, cutting across the swells like blades through silk.

"Dolphins?" someone called, uncertain.

But they moved wrong. Too fast. Too low. Too... deliberate.

The laughter that followed was brief and hollow. It died as the first wave crested, and the fins vanished—only to reappear closer, tighter, in formation.

"Orcas," the helmsman said. A single word. Flat. Cold.

Another voice from the stern: "They're flanking."

Oars clattered. Harpoons tipped. One of the boats swiveled just in time to catch the blow—a warning. A hit angled to roll, not destroy. Enough to send two men overboard.

Shouts rose. Orders overlapped. But the ocean didn't rise with them. It stayed unnaturally calm, as if holding its breath.

Another boat spun sideways. Something hit the rudder of the *Halcyon*, hard enough to twist the tiller and shear off a pin.

"They're not after the whales," someone said. "They're after *us*."

The first wave hit from the starboard side, not a strike but a push—deliberate, angled, timed. It rolled the second boat nearly sideways, sending one man into the water before he could shout. Another fin passed beneath them, lifting briefly to mark the strike, then vanished again.

More came from the stern. It wasn't an attack. It was a maneuver.

The whaleboats spun, collided, and scattered. Oars snapped against hulls. Harpoons spilled into the sea. One crewman stood to yell and was knocked from his feet by a sudden swell that hadn't existed a heartbeat earlier. Another screamed as the rudder twisted free of its brackets with a sharp crack and sank beneath the foam.

He stood frozen, harpoon still raised. The calf was forgotten. The mother was gone. Only the orcas remained—black—and—white ghosts weaving through the chaos, not randomly but with coordination, as if executing a plan passed down in silence. The sea seemed to breathe around them, inhaling slowly and then holding.

Then stillness.

Just like that, it stopped.

The boats floated in disarray. The air was still. The water went flat. Every sound—the cries of the crew, the splash of movement, the shouts of orders—faded. Even the birds were gone. Only the ocean remained, vast and breathless.

And then he saw her.

She stood on the water like the sea had hardened beneath her feet. Not nearby. Not far. Just where the horizon folded into fog. Her hair drifted around her shoulders, unmoved by the breeze. Her garments clung to nothing. Her eyes held his.

She did not speak.

She did not move.

She watched.

And in that gaze, he felt everything collapse. Every story he had told, every laugh he had forced, every boast that had filled the long nights between ports dissolved beneath the weight of her silence.

She didn't speak, and yet nothing about her was silent. She wasn't angry or merciful—she was memory, patient, and complete. He saw her now, as if she had always been part of the water. In the tides, he never listened to the whales that died slow deaths beneath his blade. Every night, he lay beside the woman on the island, hearing her voice but never letting it reach him.

She had always been there, he realized. He ignored the whales that bled out slowly beneath his blade in every tide. Every night, he lay beside the woman on the island and did not believe.

And then, behind her, the water began to rise.

At first, it seemed like another wave, a slow crest forming from the fog. But it kept rising. Higher. Steadier. Black and glistening. The dorsal fin broke the surface—tall, straight, wide as a man's outstretched arms. Then the back curved behind it, a great obsidian arc with white patches like old scars.

The orca.

Larger than any he had ever seen. Too large. And yet... not impossible. Not magic. Just more than the sea should have been willing to hold.

It surfaced behind her as if summoned, but she did not turn. Like breath against glass, she faded into the fog as the creature came to full height.

The orca hovered. Waiting.

It bared no teeth. Made no move to strike.

Its eye held steady, deep and unreadable.

The gaze was ancient, measured, and exact.

It held memory. It held measure. It held him.

He had no name for what passed between them, only the weight of being seen.

And it was enough.

He lowered the harpoon slowly. Let it fall into the sea. It vanished with hardly any sound.

He crossed the deck with deliberate steps, past wreckage, past what remained of his men, past all the stories he had ever told himself about what was owed, what was earned.

He wrapped the rope around his chest. Over his shoulders. Around the mast. Each loop is a wordless confession.

He tightened the final knot and closed his eyes.

"Let her take me whole," he whispered. "Let her remember I stopped."

The orca watched a moment longer. Then, like a shadow folding into itself, it turned and slipped beneath the waves.

It did not return.

There was no more need.

The *Halcyon* sailed silently, and no crew lined her rails. No lookout called from the crow's nest. Her canvas hung in strips, the rigging loose and limp, flapping softly like forgotten prayers. She moved only with the tide, obedient to no wind, drawn by something older and more final than navigation—no signal flags. No smoke. No sound but the whisper of the hull brushing against the outer pilings as she slid into Lahaina's harbor on a calm morning that felt wrong.

It took time for anyone to notice her. There had been no bells, no warning. The fishing boats had already gone out. Only a few dockhands were near when the ship arrived, silent and indifferent, as though it had never left.

Word spread quickly. By the time the tide crested, a dozen villagers had gathered near the jetty. Then more sailors from other crews, a few merchants, and finally the missionaries, faces pale and drawn, as if they'd been summoned not by rumor but by the scent of something they had no liturgy for.

No voices rose. No one boarded. They all saw the same thing, and it hollowed them.

He was tied to the mast with sailor's knots that held fast and clean. His posture was upright, his head bowed slightly, and his chin resting against his chest. His hands were relaxed. There were no signs of struggle, no marks of trauma. He might have been sleeping—if sleep carried the finality of salt and surrender.

The whale-tooth pendant still hung from his neck, dulled now, wrapped in threads of seaweed and salt crust, but unmistakable. It was a mark—a message. A memory returned.

Someone stepped forward—a ship's mate from another vessel—and climbed aboard but stopped short before reaching the mast. He looked for signs of others. There were none. Not even blood. Not even gear disturbed. Just the mast, the rope, and the man who had once taken from the sea until it remembered him.

Scratched into the wood just above his left shoulder, faint but deliberate, were words no one could explain, yet everyone understood.

I saw her. I was seen. And I have nothing more to take.

The villagers whispered. Some crossed themselves. Others muttered about curses, omens, punishments sent by gods, foreign and familiar. One of the missionaries claimed the man had gone mad, that native spirits had seduced him, that the devil had reached him through old songs and heathen charms. His voice shook as he said it.

But none of them touched the body.

She stood at the pier's edge, hands at her sides, eyes steady. She didn't weep. She didn't move. There was nothing left in that ship that belonged to her, not in the way others thought. What she had asked for had returned, though not in the form she had once imagined. The sea does not deal in bargains. It gives what it can. And sometimes, if it's willing, it returns what it has taken—but not unchanged.

She had not prayed for the whale alone, though others had said so. She had not cursed her lover, nor begged the tide to drag him down. What she had asked for—quietly, on a night the stars were veiled and the sea lay still—was this:

Protect what is hunted. And if he can still come back with love, send him home. But if he cannot, then return what truth you can.

The sea had answered in its way.

It had spared the whale. It had spared the man's soul. It had brought back what remained—cleansed not by forgiveness, but by surrender.

She looked once at the body tied to the mast, then turned away.

The sea had remembered. That was enough.

She left the pier before the sun reached its peak, walking the path she had always walked, down past the low-slung shrubs that clung to the black rock, past the tide-smoothed stones marked faintly with the hands of old fishermen. The surf was steady now, not flat, not stormed—just breathing. The wind came in low and salt-heavy, and with it came the faint, familiar hush of sea-spray slipping through the crevices of lava where she had once knelt.

She reached the place by instinct. There were no markers. No shrine. She had never needed symbols to speak across the water. Only presence. Only quiet.

Kneeling slowly, she placed her palm against the cold stone near the tidepool. The water there shimmered in the slanted light, broken only by the ripple of a crab ducking beneath a lip of coral. She had not brought flowers. She had not brought his name. She had only brought herself. The rest had already been taken—or returned.

She gathered what the sea had left her: a piece of driftwood, still damp from the tide; a smooth shard of whale bone from long ago, sun-bleached and worn to a soft curve; a tangle of frayed netting she had once found wrapped around a seabird's wing and had meant to throw away but never could. These she laid in a small ring upon the stone, a silent offering made of grief, memory, and the things we leave behind because we don't know what else to do with them.

She did not speak aloud. She had spoken once, and the sea had listened. That was enough.

Still kneeling, she reached down and dipped her fingers into the tidepool, tracing the cold edge of the water.

"Nahelekai," she whispered.

It was enough to speak the name aloud.

The sea held still a moment longer, as if weighing her voice.

Then, from beyond the reef, far past where the harbor's edge vanished into mist, came a whale's deep, resonant call. Long and low. A sound the sea had carried for many lifetimes. But this time, she knew it was speaking to her.

She closed her eyes. There was no need. The sea had answered.

***

Some men vanish into the sea. Others are returned.

Not as they were, but as they had become.

He hunted what should not have been hunted. Took what was never his.

And when the ocean spoke—not with rage, but with remembrance—he was seen. And he saw.

No tribunal. No trial. Just one quiet judgment rendered in ropes and tide.

The whale swam free. The vow was kept.

And in a village where the tide still breathes old names, the sea gave back the only truth it had left:

What is taken with disrespect will not be kept.

And what is given in love...

may still return.

THE CHAPEL OF THORNS

*S*ome ruins wear their sorrow like ivy. Others like scars. But Saint Alurelia does not wear her sorrow at all. It breathes it.

This is the story of a man named Mason. Not a hero. Not a villain. Just... someone like you. And someone like you is precisely who the chapel waits for.

***

Mason wasn't lost—not in the way maps measure. He had walked away from a conference three towns over, or maybe four; he hadn't looked back. People called him a researcher, a lecturer, a man with answers. But one thought persisted behind the podium or in the echoing quiet of another anonymous hotel room: I don't believe in any of this anymore.

Not at work. Not in the words. Not the point of it all.

His marriage had faded without fireworks. His daughter texted him once a season, always with perfect grammar. His colleagues were cordial, but no one would call them friends. When he found the sketch of a chapel in the margins of a 19th-century ethnography—a path inked in red winding into a forest that didn't appear on modern maps—he didn't hesitate.

He packed a flask, a flashlight, and a notebook. Sometimes, when you feel like nothing is watching, you start walking toward the one place that might be.

At first, it didn't look real. The chapel rose out of the mist like a hallucination—black stone veined with ivy, spires clawing at the sky like broken fingers. Stained glass shimmered from within, not with sunlight, but something warmer, flickering, and alive.

Crimson roses surrounded it. Not the delicate kind from suburban hedges, but thick, grotesque blooms that curled like blood clots. Their silver thorns glistened wet at the tips, as if they'd just fed. They grew in silence.

Mason stood at the door, hand trembling as he reached for the iron ring. It was cold. It shouldn't have been.

The chapel bore no smell of dust or decay. It felt recent, as if it had been waiting for him.

Stained glass lined the nave, casting ruby light across rows of pews. The windows didn't show saints, but veiled women with faceless expressions, each holding thorns.

He sat, not out of reverence, but from exhaustion. He opened his notebook and turned to a clean page, intending to write something clever. Instead, he wrote: "I want to matter. Even if only to the ghosts."

Mason didn't believe in gods. Never had. But he knew what it was to be tired. Not the kind of tired that sleep fixed, but the kind that burrowed into your bones and whispered that nothing you did made a difference.

Grief has gravity. And the chapel of Saint Alurelia is heavy with it. It does not seek worship. Only witness. And so it began to show Mason what he had forgotten.

He didn't fall asleep exactly but drifted. The walls seemed to breathe, the glass pulsed, and the stone beneath him radiated warmth like a slow, steady heartbeat.

Then came the women.

They didn't speak. They sang.

Their voices rasped like wind through teeth and silk catching fire. What they shared weren't miracles—it was memories.

A mother sobbing into a pile of folded laundry. A child is laying flowers on a forgotten grave. A man on a motel bed, wondering if one more day was worth it. None of them is named. All of them are real.

He recognized them. They weren't strangers. They were everyone.

And then he saw himself—not as he was, but as he had once hoped to be. Open. Kind. Still afraid, but not yet alone. He wept without shame. In this place, it mattered.

He woke among the roses.

It hadn't been a dream—not fully. His notebook lay open beside him. Its pages were filled, and every line was written in a hand, not his own.

"Remember her."

"Say his name."

"Don't let them be erased."

"We became the thorns, so you could keep blooming."

He didn't understand everything. But he understood enough.

Mason never told anyone about the chapel. It wasn't meant for others, not because he feared disbelief. It wasn't even about him.

It was for those behind the glass—the ones whose names had been lost, whose stories had no one left to tell them. For the first time in years, he no longer wanted to vanish with them.

He didn't believe in fate. He didn't believe in God. But he came to believe this: If the universe offers no purpose, then what we choose to carry, what we choose to remember, becomes sacred. That choice—our choice—is what makes it matter.

So, he remembered his purpose.

He returns to the forest's edge each year on the same night. He leaves a page from his notebook. A name. A story. Not a prayer. Not a plea. Just a signal. A gesture. A refusal to forget.

Not because anyone is listening. But because he is.

Because if the universe won't care, he will.

Because we must choose to matter.

We often think it's easier to live without gods. No judgment. No commandments. No debts.

But purpose is heavy when you must forge it yourself. And the weight of choice—of deciding what matters, who matters, why—can press against the ribs and the soul like a stone.

Mason carried that weight.

And he learned this: In a world that promises nothing and owes us even less, every act of remembrance is an act of defiance. Every kindness is a miracle. Every memory is sacred.

He did not find faith. But he found meaning.

And in the hush of the chapel, in the thorns that bloom with memory, he learned what it is to choose to care, even when no one asks you to.

Especially then.

***

We often think it's easier to live without gods. No judgment. No commandments. No debts.

But purpose is heavy when you must forge it yourself. And the weight of choice—of deciding what matters, who matters, why—can press against the ribs and the soul like a stone.

Mason carried that weight.

And he learned this: In a world that promises nothing and owes us even less, every act of remembrance is an act of defiance. Every kindness is a miracle. Every memory is sacred.

He did not find faith. But he found meaning.

And in the hush of the chapel, in the thorns that bloom with memory, he learned what it is to choose to care, even when no one asks you to.

Especially then.

PART III - GHOSTS AND GODS

WHITE FALCON, FADED SUMMER

*C*onsider this for a moment: one white Ford Falcon. Age: ten. Condition: debatable. Provenance: unknown. It sits in an alley behind a half-broken household in the summer of 1973. To most, it's just a rusting shell with flat tires and a scent that defies explanation. But to one sixteen-year-old boy, it's something else: a promise, a puzzle, maybe even a way out. What he doesn't know is that the car may never move. And that's precisely the point."

***

Some machines roar to life the moment you turn the key. Others resist, cough, wheeze, and grumble their way into existence. And then there are machines like this one—silent, forgotten, grounded not by gravity, but by something more challenging to name.

It was the summer of 1973, and I was sixteen, parked halfway between boyhood and whatever came next. We'd just moved back to the south side of the city. My mom lived in the Chicago suburbs to the north. Dad had moved us down to Indianapolis after they separated, a practical decision that caught me between zip codes, loyalties, and every version of silence two parents can invent.

He worked full time in data processing and moonlighted as a freelance programmer, which meant he spent most of his time hunched over programming templates with a pencil, scribbling logic into rectangles on long programming sheets. His company didn't even own a computer; they rented time on an IBM System/3, like most outfits did back then. Occasionally, I went with him. I'd sit beside him at a rented IBM System/3, surrounded by punched cards, cooling fans, and the perfume of toner and ozone. He'd let me read COBOL aloud, like bedtime stories, and debug RPG II with my finger on the page. It was the closest we got to bonding. And when we weren't there, he was off to fix things for clients like the CPA down in Jasper. I rarely saw him otherwise.

In his place was his live-in girlfriend. She was cruel in the way that doesn't bruise but leaves marks just the same. She made it clear I was an unwanted presence. Her idea of parenting was neglect dressed in contempt. She was there for him; the rest of us were just noise.

I was the oldest of four and the designated babysitter. I wasn't bullied at school but wasn't seen either—just a nerd in the background—comic books, guitar, science fiction. My safe places were all imaginary. If there were a way out, it would be under my power—or maybe on four wheels.

That's when I found the Falcon.

Or rather, that's when I noticed it.

A 1963 Ford Falcon. White, two doors, sloped and squared, with zero fins and even less attitude. Parked in the alley behind our backyard like it had been dropped there by an ambivalent god. No one remembered it arriving. I never saw it towed in. My dad never mentioned it.

In retrospect, this should have been a red flag. My dad did a lot of side work fixing other people's cars. Perhaps someone dropped it off and never returned. Possibly it was abandoned and quietly absorbed into our orbit. Maybe it followed me home. The truth was: it was just *there.*

When I finally asked about it, my dad looked up from the garage, wiped his hands, and shrugged. "Yours, if you can get it running."

Then, in his best cryptic wizard voice: "But don't turn the key until you understand what it does."

At the time, I thought he meant the ignition.

Later, I knew better.

I started reading. It turns out that the 1963 Falcon was considered the "godfather" of the Mustang. Ford used its bones to build the legend—it says so right in the book.

This was hilarious because my uncle had a '65 Mustang. It was sleek, fast, and red with rally stripes. That car purred like James Bond in loafers.

The Falcon? The Falcon looked like it had been built to transport sad librarians to expired dentist appointments. If the Mustang was rock and roll, the Falcon was the sound of a filing cabinet slowly pushing across a linoleum floor.

Godfather of the Mustang? Maybe in the same way, a potato is the godfather of vodka.

I called Kenny.

He had sideburns like a teenage Elvis impersonator, a belt buckle that could signal aircraft, and enough confidence to carry us both. He once fixed a blender with chewing gum and sheer willpower. He looked at the Falcon, nodded, and said, "We are about to make history. Or scrap metal. Possibly both."

Day One: We popped the hood and triggered what might have been a biblical plague. Dust, leaves, and what we swear was the desiccated corpse of a squirrel. Kenny coughed and muttered, "Well, it's got character." He tapped the engine block, and a puff of rust floated like a disapproving ghost.

Day Two: Mr. Bender, neighborhood legend and shirtless philosopher, wandered over with a Schlitz and his usual contribution to science: "Pour some Coke on the battery terminals." We did. It fizzed. It smoked. Ants began organizing like a military coup. Kenny watched them for five minutes and said, "Pretty sure we started a new civilization."

Day Three: We attempted spark plug removal using what can only be described as violence. Two came out. The others refused. One sheared off. Kenny held it up like a broken tooth and declared, "This car is biting back."

Day Four: The girlfriend glared at us from the porch like we were building a time machine out of spite. She said nothing. Just judged. Kenny gave her a finger-gun salute and whispered, "Mood killer at noon."

Day Five: Miss Cathy brought us lemonade. She suggested prayer. We gave it a shot. I laid my hands on the hood. Kenny quoted a line from *The Exorcist*. The Falcon sputtered once and coughed up a nut casing. Divine? Maybe.

Day Six: We checked the brake fluid. Kenny unscrewed the cap, dipped a finger, and paused. "If this isn't maple syrup, I'm drinking it anyway." We decided to pour it out. It peeled the grass. We upgraded the Falcon's spiritual condition to 'lightly cursed.'

Day Seven: It happened. The engine cranked. There was life! A wheeze, a sputter, a sound like Barry White trapped in a tuba. Kenny screamed, "She LIVES!" Then it backfired, smoked, and died. The neighbor's cat hasn't been the same since.

Day Eight: The ignition key was bent, actually *curled*, like it had melted. We hadn't touched it. Kenny found it on the dash and said, "Pretty sure this is the part in the horror movie where we split up." We didn't.

Day Nine: We attempted to jump the solenoid with a screwdriver and pure teenage audacity. It sparked. Kenny flew backward. His hair stood up like he'd stuck a fork in the moon. He blinked and said, "It whispered my name. In Latin. Backwards."

Even Father McAllister walked by, paused at the sight of the Falcon, and crossed himself twice. We took that as a sign.

Day Ten: We surrendered. Rolled her to the street. Watched the weeds crawl back in like they'd been waiting. The Falcon had won. Or maybe she'd just decided we weren't ready.

I never told my dad what the car meant. It was hope on four tires, and I believed that if I could fix it, maybe I could fix *everything*. Perhaps I wouldn't have to live in someone else's silence anymore.

Later that year, I bought Andy's '66 Biscayne. It had a dented nose, smelled like taco seasoning, and sounded like the end of the world, but it ran.

And then Dale showed up.

He strolled into the alley like he was walking onto a stage. Thin mustache. Hawaiian shirt. Aviators. Like someone who sold timeshares in Purgatory. "Heard you had a Falcon," he said.

"You in the market for disappointment?"

He grinned. "Aren't we all?"

He gave us seventy-five bucks and a six-pack labeled only "BEER." We handed over the keys.

A week later, a postcard arrived—no return address. No message. Just a photo.

The Falcon. Gleaming white. Tires full. Parked on a beach. A martini glass on the hood. Sunset. Like she'd always belonged there.

Scrawled in shaky pen: *"She flew. - Dale"*

No one knew him. The postmark was a smear. A month later, I saw the Falcon behind the Wilson scrapyard. Same rust. Same squirrel nest. Same silence.

But the driver's seat was warm.

And the radio—which had no power, no knob, no reason to work—was playing the faintest song.

For one strange moment, I thought I smelled salt air.

Some cars never leave the alley...never find the road. Some boys don't either.

But occasionally, if you wait long enough, the road finds *you*.

***

Portrait of a boy on the cusp of motion. One summer, one car, and the slow realization that some things won't start—because they're not meant to. The Falcon stayed grounded. But the boy? He learned to fly without leaving the ground. In this corner of memory and metal, we find not a destination... but a departure.

THE GUARDIAN

Some debts aren't paid in coins or blood, but in years—lifetimes—of silence and waiting.

Tonight, a man named Jonas takes a wrong turn on a forgotten road and walks into a mist thick with memory. What he finds is not a place, but a reckoning. Some oaths do not end, and some guardians are not born, but made from failure, sorrow, and the terrible weight of what must never rise again.

Jonas has returned to a grave he once walked away from. But the grave has not forgotten him.

This is the story of a man asked to remember... and remain. A man becoming something else — something eternal. If you listen to the silence long enough, you'll find him in a tale we call... The Guardian.

***

The fog had teeth that night, gnawing at stone and bone alike.

The road to the old graveyard was little more than a scar in the earth, swallowed whole by creeping moss and the careless reach of time. Trees hunched over it like penitents, stripped bare branches clawing the sky with fingers that would never touch heaven.

Jonas pulled his coat tighter as the mist thickened around him, clinging to his skin like a living thing. He hadn't meant to come this way. The old map had promised a shortcut—a foolish trust, in hindsight—but now the world beyond the fog was gone, and the only path left lay ahead, between the crumbling stones.

It was the raven that stopped him.

It sat atop a solitary grave, the largest and least broken of them all. Its feathers gleamed wetly in the half-light, slick and black as spilled ink. It did not move. It did not caw. It only watched.

For a long moment, Jonas stared back.

Something in his chest tightened, old and aching, like a forgotten sorrow stirred by the bird's silent gaze.

The headstone beneath the raven was unreadable, the inscription scoured away by rain and ruin. But somehow, Jonas knew with the same certainty that one recognizes a name whispered from a dream that this grave mattered—that it had been waiting.

The mist thickened. He heard it then: the faintest scratching sound beneath the ground, as if fingernails scraped the inside of a coffin.

Jonas stepped back instinctively — but the ground behind him was no safer. Rows upon rows of broken stones marched into the mist, each grave sunken, the earth around them disturbed as if something had tried to claw its way out.

Yet no birds sang. No insects stirred. Only the raven remained, sentinel and judge.

Jonas's breath came in short, sharp bursts. His mind screamed to leave, to turn and run blindly into the fog. But his legs would not move. His heart thudded an uneven, mournful beat, a rhythm that matched the slow, steady scratching beneath the soil.

Something had drawn him here—and it wasn't the map.

The raven tilted its head slightly, an almost human gesture of grim appraisal.

Why am I here?" Jonas asked the mist. It took the words without an answer.

The scratching grew louder.

From the corner of his eye, he caught movement — a shift of shadow behind the stone — but when he turned, there was nothing: only the endless, suffocating grey, and the unblinking raven.

And then, faint and trembling, came the whisper: "Guardian."

The voice came from the earth, speaking through dead roots and hollowed bones.

Jonas stumbled back, heart hammering, but the mist thickened behind him, walling him in. Ahead, the raven watched. Waiting, waiting for him to remember.

The whisper died, but its echo clung to Jonas like a second skin.

He took a hesitant step toward the grave. Not because he meant to — but because something inside him leaned forward, as if drawn by a long-buried thread pulling taut. The raven did not flinch. Its eyes caught the dim light in a way that made Jonas think of ice over fire. Watching and always watching.

Another whisper.

"You were here before."

He blinked. "No," he said, to no one, to the fog, to the doubt clawing up the back of his throat. "No, I've never—"

But the world around him disagreed.

The graveyard shifted. The air folded, somehow. One moment, he stood alone in a field of moss-eaten graves. The next—

Torches. Flickering. Held by pale hands. Dozens of figures in robes, their faces obscured by shadow and grief.

A procession.

Jonas gasped and stumbled back, but his feet sank not into muddy grass, but stone — freshly laid, still warm from the forge. He looked down.

An altar.

The raven was gone. A man in black armor stood in its place — silver trim dulled by soot, a sword at his side. His face was sharp, proud, haunted. Familiar.

He turned toward Jonas, and Jonas screamed because the man had his face.

But older. More lined. More broken.

The vision twisted again.

Now the man stood before the gathered robed figures, holding a great iron-bound book in one hand and something wrapped in bloodstained cloth in the other.

"We are out of time," the other Jonas said, his voice ashamed.

"Then we seal it," a priest replied. "Here. Beneath your vow. And you shall stand watch."

"Forever?" the man whispered.

"Until you are forgiven."

The cloth was lowered into the stone, the lid slammed shut, and the chains were wrapped repeatedly—until the final seal glowed red with the last of the dying sun.

The man stepped back.

And then, like wax melting in fire, his form began to collapse. Armor shriveling. Flesh thinning. Bone hollowing. Wings grew where arms had been. His scream became a caw.

And then—

Jonas was back.

Standing before the grave.

The raven perched on it once more, still and silent.

His knees gave out. He collapsed into the damp earth, breath coming in ragged gasps.

He remembered.

Not all of it—not clearly, but enough. Enough to understand why the grave felt like a wound in the world. Why the fog carried names he almost recognized. Why the raven's gaze had felt like a mirror.

He had failed.

He had been charged with guarding something too dangerous to destroy. And in a moment of doubt, or cowardice, or pity, he had tried to bury it instead. To lock it away and forget.

But evil does not forget.

And now, the seal was weakening.

He turned his eyes upward. The raven stared back.

And in its silence, Jonas knew:

It had waited for him. The whisper died, but its echo clung to Jonas like a second skin.

He turned his eyes upward. The raven stared back.

And in its silence, Jonas knew:

It had waited for him.

The wind shifted.

And a new raven sat atop the stone, eyes gleaming like cold fire. Watching. Waiting. The wind shifted.

Jonas felt it before he heard it — the mist pulled back ever so slightly, like breath drawn before a scream. The grave beneath the raven trembled, the earth no longer content to lie still.

Jonas struggled to rise, legs slick with moss and shame. The graveyard pulsed around him — no longer quiet, no longer dead. The other stones seemed to lean inward, as though bearing witness to what was coming. Roots churned beneath the soil. The silence groaned.

And the raven remained.

"I remember," Jonas whispered. "God help me, I remember."

The raven tilted its head once, then gazed toward the grave. A low rumble stirred beneath the soil. The scratching had returned — more insistent now, like claws dragging against stone from beneath the world.

Jonas knew what it meant.

The seal was breaking. And if it failed, if the thing they had buried stirred once more, no oath, no army, no fire would stop it.

The raven flapped its wings once, not in flight, but as a summons. It stepped aside from the headstone.

And there it was. A shallow groove in the earth before the grave, half-covered in fallen leaves and frost. A space shaped...just for him. The guardian's place.

He didn't need to be told. He understood now.

The raven had been a placeholder... waiting for him. Waiting for the one who had bound the evil and abandoned it. Waiting for him to return and reclaim what he had fled from lifetimes ago.

Jonas shook his head. "No... I'm not that man anymore. I didn't choose this..."

But a voice rose from the earth, low and honeyed, terrible and sweet.

You did once, and that is enough.

The grave cracked.

A line split down the center of the stone like a wound, and a sulfurous hiss curled upward into the cold air. Jonas reeled back, bile rising in his throat. Something was coming. It was not yet whole, but it was waking.

The raven cawed sharply once, and the noise shattered the air like breaking glass.

Jonas looked at the groove before the grave. At the chains, half-buried. At the shimmer in the air where once he had stood as a man, sword in hand, heart full of hope and pride.

Now all that remained was choice.

He could flee. He could let it rise. Let the fog roll outward. Let the curse spread and blacken the living world like mold.

Or he could kneel. Take the place once more. Bind himself again to the task he had fled — not for years, but for eternity.

There would be no redemption. No peace. No sleep.

Only the cold, ceaseless vigil.

His voice was a whisper. "Will it be enough?"

The raven blinked in reply.

Jonas stood there, shaking, as the grave yawned wider beneath him. The heat from below rose in waves now. Something unseen shifted in the dark, something that remembered being both bone and flesh.

He stepped forward.

Kneeling, he placed one hand into the groove. The moss burned away beneath his fingers, and the mist tightened like a noose. His skin pulled, his bones hollowed, and his breath left him.

The raven opened its wings, rose into the sky, uttered a final caw, and sealed the vow.

Then it was gone.

Whoever Jonas had been, he was gone now. What remained felt the weight settle on his shoulders. It was something old and unyielding -- the shape of duty, worn like a crown of stone.

The grave stilled.

The mist withdrew.

A new raven sat atop the stone, eyes gleaming like cold fire.

Watching.

Waiting.

***

Jonas didn't escape. He didn't resist. He remembered — and in doing so, became something else entirely.

He watches now, not as the man he was but as what remains when duty outlives the soul—a presence shaped by memory, bound by guilt, and tethered to a grave the world no longer remembers.

The vow is sealed. The vigil begins again.

And if you ever stray too far from the path — into the old places, the forgotten places — you may feel the silence watching back.

Some guardians are not born; they are made.

And they never leave.

THE LIGHT BENEATH LUDLOW

You won't find Ludlow on many maps. Time has worn it down to dust, memory, and silence. But beneath that silence—beneath the sage and soil—there lies a heartbeat. Not of the living. Not quite dead. But of something that remembers.

Tonight, we follow one woman who returns to where her world was burned away. She comes seeking neither forgiveness nor vengeance but something older, quieter: the truth. And sometimes, truth doesn't lie buried beneath the earth—it lies waiting.

Waiting for someone who dares to remember.

***

It was a windless morning when Rosa Gutiérrez returned to the place where her daughter had died.

No signs marked the land now. The tent colony was replaced by a gray hush—the silence of things that remember. Ash and dust clung to the sagebrush like regret, and the ruins of Ludlow sat beneath a sun so wide and pale it seemed afraid to shine. She carried a cloth bundle against her chest. Inside it: a worn leather journal, a child's singed hair ribbon, and a lump of coal that sometimes glowed in the dark.

She had not come to forgive. Forgiveness was never part of the bargain. She had come to remember. To disturb the forgetting.

The Ludlow Massacre had scorched its name across southern Colorado in April 1914. Two women. Eleven children. One fire that smothered a nation's conscience in smoke. The militia claimed it was an accident. The strikers were violent first. But Rosa remembered the Gatling gun. The roar of canvas igniting. The screams. She remembered Mateo shielding their daughter Ana with his body.

Dawn found Rosa dazed and coughing up blood. Her skin blistered. Her hair burned down to stubble. They told her she was lucky. She never heard her daughter's voice again. She never saw Mateo's body. Some said the wind buried him. Others said he was taken.

Now she stood at the edge of the mine shaft and let the wind fill her coat. The people in Trinidad whispered she had gone strange, cursed that she spoke to ghosts. That she dug where the earth didn't want her. Let them talk.

She knelt and opened the bundle. Her fingers curled around the lump of coal. It was still warm. The first time she'd found it, it had pulsed faintly when she touched Ana's ribbon. It had done so again last week, after a dream in which Mateo whispered, "They're still here." His voice had sounded wrong. Hollow. Echoing like it came from behind the stone.

So she had come. And she began to dig.

She clawed at the ash-thickened soil. Her nails split. Her back ached. But she unearthed remnants: a child's shoe. A shard of porcelain. A bullet casing. Each time she uncovered something, the coal glowed softly in her pocket.

By the second evening, as the sun dropped behind the Sangre de Cristo Mountains, she heard it, faint, a lullaby. Spanish. Then Greek. Then English. Overlapping, woven into the wind like a lullaby of the lost. She froze, clutching the coal. The whispers faded. She dug faster.

That night, her dreams twisted. Shapes watched from the corners. Not people—shadows with bones, as if memory had taken form. She woke cold, with the fire out and the coal stone black.

In the quiet hours before dawn, Rosa lay beside the shallow pit she had carved and closed her eyes. Memory carried her away. She saw Mateo again—not as he was in the end, gaunt from hunger and defiance—but as he had been the day they met. A storyteller, even after twelve-hour shifts underground. They'd sit on crates outside the mess tent while Ana chased fireflies, Mateo sketching with charcoal on burlap scraps. He made Rosa laugh even when laughter was hard to come by. He'd talk about moving north someday, away from the mines, maybe to a place with trees that didn't bend from the wind.

He had started the journal a week before the soldiers came. "If they bury us," he'd said, "they won't bury the truth." She had argued and told him to stop writing. It wasn't safe. He just smiled. "Then it's worth even more." That was the last full sentence she remembered him saying.

On the third night, her fingers struck charred wood. Beneath it, packed carefully in oilskin, was Mateo's journal. Her hands trembled. She opened it and found names. Dozens. Men beaten. Families starved. Wages stolen. Records of threats, meetings, and bribes. Testimony. Dates.

And then his final entry: Rosa is stronger than she knows. If this ever finds the light, let it burn through the lies. I'll keep Ana safe however I can. Her breath caught in her throat.

That night, faces flickered in the dark around her fire. Children holding hands. Women bent over washtubs. Men with soot-streaked brows. They said nothing. But they watched. One figure stood apart. Taller. Eyes like ash. Rosa looked away. And when she placed the glowing coal beside the journal, the fire didn't die. It changed. Brighter. Blue at the core. The shadows leaned in.

She didn't go to the union hall right away. She held the journal for a day, unsure whether truth would heal or ignite. Her heart twisted. Am I doing this for them, she thought, or for me? She remembered her dream. Mateo's voice had sounded distant, not like it used to. And sometimes she feared the coal didn't glow with memory but hunger.

Still, she went.

But not everyone welcomed her.

"This town's had enough ghosts," a miner said, arms folded. "Why dig them up?"

Another spat on the floor. "My brother worked security. He died in that fire, too. You want to paint him a villain?"

Rosa didn't argue. She just held up the journal. "I didn't come to punish anyone. I came to remember."

Later, in a basement thick with mildew and tobacco, others listened. She stood before them with shaking hands, her voice dry from disuse. But Mateo's words were clear.

Page by page, she read. One old man bent from years in the mine, clenched his fists, and muttered prayers through gritted teeth. A woman, widowed twice over, held up her infant grandson and whispered, "They need to know what their fathers did. What they were."

The young priest, eyes shadowed by doubt, stood. "We must mark this," he said. "We must remember."

A teacher hesitated before speaking. "Some names... they were our neighbors. They weren't all innocent. But they mattered."

Others spoke. A man from Walsenburg who had lost his cousin. A girl whose uncle had disappeared without a trace.

They raised funds. Held vigils. Built a marker. Not a large one. Just stone, carved by hand. Rosa gave them the coal. They embedded it into the base. Said it was fitting. Said it came from the mine. She didn't tell them it still glowed—or that sometimes, when she passed the monument at night, she saw figures standing behind it. Watching.

Years passed. Children played in the fields again. Grass returned. People forgot—most of them. But the memorial remained. Weathered by wind, sun-bleached, but never toppled.

And once, long after Rosa was gone, a girl knelt beside the monument, tracing the names with her fingers. She saw the coal and reached out. It was warm.

"Mama," she asked, "why does the rock feel like it's breathing?" Her mother smiled softly, brushing the dust from her daughter's cheek.

"Because," she said, "some fires never go out. And some stories wait to be told again."

The little girl didn't answer. She leaned in and whispered to the stone. And somewhere deep beneath the earth, something listened.

The coal pulsed once that night, beneath a sky scattered with stars.

Softly.

As if it were dreaming.

Or remembering.

***

The girl who felt the stone breathing will grow. She'll ask questions. She'll read old names on older pages. And one day, perhaps, she'll return—not just to remember, but to remind.

History is not a line but a circle of stories whispered across generations. Some fade. Some fester. And some, like the glow beneath Ludlow, endure.

We are all keepers of memory. Whether we like it or not, the past is patient. And in the right hands, the truth burns brighter than fire.

THE HUNGER BELOW THE TREE LINE

*T*hey say the forest is quiet. But they mistake silence for stillness.

There are woods older than maps, deeper than roots, where names carry more weight than weapons. The land is not forgotten in such places, and memory has teeth.

Tonight, a young man walks into the shadow of an old story—one he thought he didn't believe in. But belief is not required—only a name.

This is the hunger beneath the tree line. And it is still listening.

***

Elias left before the morning sun had fully crested the ridge, the sky still bruised with the remnants of night. Behind him, the village slept under a crust of frost, their breath rising like small spirits in shuttered rooms. He did not wake anyone. The silence was easier.

He carried only what he needed: a hunting bow, a bone-handled knife, a water flask, and a name whispered under his breath for protection. He wasn't sure he believed in that last one, but his grandmother used to say the spirits of the forest recognized names, and sometimes that recognition was the only thing that kept your bones from being scattered in the underbrush.

He remembered the stories she told him—half-whispers over firelight when the wind keened against the walls, how the woods were once a place of offerings, not conquest. How her brother, Kolin, had gone in seeking a sacred tree and never returned. "There are roots deeper than stone," she had warned. "And they drink more than water."

Elias had rolled his eyes then. He was younger. Confident. Now, with snow in his boots and silence pressing in, the stories curled tighter around his ribs.

The trail was narrow, choked with snow and the skeletons of last season's deadfall. The deeper Elias went, the more the trees seemed to lean together, conspiring. Pines crowded overhead like elders watching judgment.

He had gone farther than most dared. The others mocked the old stories, but none hunted past the second ridge. Not even Roan.

By midday, he found the clearing.

One tree stood taller than the rest, hollow and split, its bark blackened with age or something older. Around its base, the snow had melted, revealing soft earth—a place out of season.

Elias crouched beside the roots. He felt it then, the subtle vibration beneath his boots—like breath, like something listening.

He did not speak aloud. But something in him trembled, like something inside the hollow had stirred.

"I come for food," he thought. "Just a deer. A rabbit. Nothing more."

But the hunger did not barter.

It did not speak.

It only remembered.

His skin prickled. A chill traced his spine that had nothing to do with cold. The air thickened around him. Was it his name the roots whispered? Was it Kolin's?

He suddenly wanted to go back. To unstep his footprints. To be home, where the kettle steamed and someone still waited.

The cold pressed inward from the trunks. His breath was clouded, heavy, and slow. The world dulled. When he turned to leave, his boot sank too deep into the loam.

And then another.

He fell forward with a muffled cry. Something wrapped around his ankle—not vine, not root. It felt like a memory given form. Familiar. Inevitable.

And then he vanished.

***

Spring came late that year. The thaw was sluggish, reluctant. When the first scouts moved beyond the second ridge, they found signs of something broken: a snapped bowstring, a cracked flask, half-buried in the muck. And the tree—

The hollow tree stood unchanged except for the carvings.

Names etched in the wood. Dozens of them. Some recent. Some older than memory.

ELIAS

A woman knelt before the roots. Her name was Mirelle, Elias's sister. Her hands were rough from work, but she traced the air near the bark with a reverence she barely understood.

"He said it didn't matter anymore. Those names were just breath."

Behind her, the elder hunter Roan stood silent, his gaze narrowed. He had once mocked the old stories, but now his mouth was thin with unease.

Mirelle shook her head. "But the forest remembers."

Roan snorted. "Superstition."

She looked up sharply. "Then why are you sweating, Roan?"

He didn't answer. His hand hovered near his belt, instinctively reaching for the knife he had left behind at the camp.

She pulled a folded scrap of paper from her satchel—her grandmother's journal, brittle with time. In it, pressed among the pages, was a drawing.

The same tree. The same hollow. And a name long faded: KOLIN.

From within the hollow, something shifted. Something breathed. It was not the wind.

"Two generations," Roan whispered. "Gone the same way."

Mirelle's voice was barely audible. "They didn't forget. They waited."

She paused. "You used to laugh when I told you about Kolin. About the stories."

Roan's face darkened. "I was wrong," he said quietly. "I thought belief made you weak. Clinging to ghosts was a way to avoid facing the real world."

"And now?"

Roan stared at the tree. "Now I wonder if what we called weakness was the only thing that kept the rest of us safe."

It remembers.

ROAN

He staggered, breath catching.

"I never walked here before. I swear it."

Mirelle looked at him.

"But did you speak your name?"

Roan paled.

The wind shifted. Not a gale. A breath.

He remembered how he had spoken it proudly the night before, around the fire, when mocking Elias's departure.

"A fool walks into the woods alone. Roan would never be so soft."

Names, the old woman had warned, were invitations.

The pines leaned, creaking. There was a groan beneath the bark. Mirelle stepped forward instinctively, placing herself between Roan and the hollow tree.

"You need to leave," she said. "Now."

Roan hesitated. The ground trembled faintly. Just once.

He ran.

Mirelle remained.

She knelt again, not in surrender, but in understanding. Her fingers brushed the dirt where her brother's name had been carved.

"You took him," she said. "But I will remember. And that will be enough."

The hunger stirred.

It did not answer.

It only waited.

She rose to her feet, brushing the soil from her knees. As she turned to leave, something stopped her—a name.

Newly etched. Still bleeding sap.

MIRELLE

She stared at it, unblinking.

Behind her, the tree exhaled.

***

They always think they'll be the one to return.

But the forest is patient. It takes nothing uninvited and gives nothing back unearned. It remembers every name spoken beneath its branches—even those uttered in jest.

One by one, they kneel. Some are in fear, some in love, and some in the hope that memory is a kind of resistance.

But names are not resistance. Names are keys.

And the forest never forgets who used them.

BROTHERS IN ARMS

What do you call a father made of four voices? A home built from memory?

In the quiet aftermath of war, there's a house with one man and one child... and four souls trying to make peace with what they've become.

This is the story of a soldier who didn't come back alone. Of brothers who stayed linked not by duty but by grief and love.

It's not a ghost story. It's not a miracle.

It's what happens when what's left behind chooses to stay—and becomes something worth living for.

***

I don't remember whose memory this is.

The grass was wet that morning—dewy, soft, sun just climbing over the hills. Could've been Kandahar. Could've been Fort Polk. It could've been the dream one of the guys keeps playing on loop because it reminds him of home. Doesn't matter. The kid laughed when he ran across it. That's what I hold on to.

He calls me Dad. Not "sir," not "mister," not even "hey, you." Just Dad. He knows, somehow, there's more than one of us in here.

"Crusts off or on?" I asked.

"Off," Ortega said. Always the softie.

"Let him grow up," Mitchell said. "You don't make soldiers out of soft bread."

"He's five, Mitch," Dalton said. He laughed like he used to in the barracks—wry, tired, always just this side of kind.

The kid waited at the table, swinging his legs. He didn't talk much about the past, and we didn't push. He watched me butter the bread. I said "me," but it was never really just me anymore.

We were supposed to unlink after the war. Some guys did. We tried once. Felt like ripping out your ribs.

So here we are. Four minds and a body, figuring out how to make a peanut butter sandwich and raise a child who lost everything.

When the toaster clicked and the kid smiled, Ortega hummed a lullaby none of us taught him, but all of us remembered.

The toy lizard turned up in the cereal box.

"Sabotage," Mitchell said.

"It was tactical concealment," Ortega said. "You know he likes surprises."

The kid cracked up when he found it under the Cheerios and lifted it like it was an artifact from an ancient dig.

"Goliath!" he yelled, hugging the plastic reptile.

Dalton hummed something low—sounding like Johnny Cash—and I found myself smiling without knowing which of us was doing it. Maybe all of us.

We worked together as muscle memory. I packed his lunch while Ortega fussed over the sandwich shape. Dalton reminded me to add a note—today's said, "You're braver than you think." Mitchell rolled his eyes but didn't stop me.

He brushed his teeth in slow, looping circles, and the squad gave real-time feedback like a team of dental hygienists. He thought it was hilarious.

We were brushing his hair when the knock came.

A woman in a slate-gray vest and crisp slacks stood on the porch, tablet in hand, polite smile not quite reaching her eyes.

"Mr. Reyes?" she asked. "I'm from Family Services—routine post-placement wellness check."

I nodded and invited her in. The kid clung a little tighter to my leg. She knelt to meet him at eye level.

"Hi there. Your teacher says you've been doing great. That's awesome." She paused. "Can I ask—how many people live in your house?"

The kid beamed. "Four."

She looked past me into the kitchen, visibly confused.

She said, "In this house?"

He tapped his temple. "They live up here. All my dads."

Her eyebrows lifted. The smile wavered.

She stood slowly and turned to me. "We've had some... unusual reports from school."

"Nothing dangerous," I said. "He's safe. Fed. Loved."

She hesitated. "It's just...there are protocols. Guardianship arrangements. We need clarity about who—"

"I'm the legal guardian," I said. "I'm the one who tucks him in at night, packs his lunch, and walks him to the bus. The others?" I tapped my temple. "They're just... part of me."

"Tell her to mind her own damn—"

"Mitch. Chill."

"Should we offer her tea? Cookies?"

I held the door for her when she finally left. She didn't say much, but she didn't say no, either.

That night, I was folding laundry when the memory hit.

Sand. Gunfire. Smoke is so thick that we taste it on our teeth. Someone is screaming for evac. The link pulsed with panic, then silence. Not just on the radio. Inside.

One of us went dark.

We don't often mention his name. Not out of disrespect. Out of weight. Because some things, even shared across four minds, still hurt.

We tried unlinking after that. It lasted twenty minutes. Dalton's nose bled. Ortega passed out. Mitchell started speaking in backward loops. I puked into a trash can, and we all cried like idiots.

We stayed linked. Not because of grief. Because of what came after.

The kid called from his room. "Dad? All of you?"

I set the folded shirt down. "Yeah, buddy. All of us."

He peeked over the blanket. "Tell the one who sings to sing again."

I looked out the window at the quiet street, moonlight slanting across the floor.

"Who was it that sang that one?" I murmured.

Nobody answered.

But the tune began, soft and low, vibrating through my chest like a memory I inherited but never owned.

And in the quiet house, our son fell asleep to four voices no one else hears.

Except for him.

In the morning, he crawled into bed with us before sunrise.

I say "us" out of habit—there's only one body in the bed, one heartbeat.

But I felt the shift—Dalton stirred first, humming that tune again. Ortega wrapped around the moment like a blanket, soft and warm. Mitchell grumbled and tried to turn off the sun.

The kid settled under the quilt and said, "I had a dream you were all real."

I didn't say we were real. I just nodded and kissed the top of his head.

"I dreamed we had a house in the clouds," he said. "With a porch made of stars. And you all had faces. You were smiling."

"Sounds like a good dream," I said.

He nodded, still half-asleep. "We were a family there, too."

He doesn't know we were never anything else.

I never found my father. I never found my mother. But I found them.

In the silence of war. In the link that wouldn't break. In the boy who calls us all Dad.

And together, we're building something that no one else has to understand.

We're not ghosts.

We're not broken.

We're just here.

Together.

"Even if I lose the dream," he murmured, "don't go."

I won't.

***

They won't be found in the history books. No medals. No unit patch for what they are now.

Just a kitchen, a song, and a child who calls four voices "Dad."

They never asked to stay linked. They only asked not to be alone.

And somewhere between war and home, they found a reason.

Not to haunt. Not to survive.

But to raise. To protect. To love.

Not as ghosts. Not as men.

But as a family.

And sometimes... that's enough.

THE SCRAPBOOK

In the corner of a quiet house sits a cedar chest. There is no lock, no warning, just memory, folded in cloth and dust.

Inside it: a book without an author. A record without explanation. And a radio tuned not to stations... but to ghosts.

This is the story of a grandson. Of a grandfather who never told him everything.

And of what's left behind when history is whispered instead of spoken.

The war is long over. The dead are long buried. But the echoes... they've only just begun to speak.

***

I didn't mean to lose him. That's the part I keep circling back to. We didn't fight. We didn't fall out. We drifted.

After my father died, my grandfather and I stopped orbiting the same things. He and my grandmother moved out to New Mexico for a while—dry air, fewer crowds, doctors who said it would help her lungs. It didn't. She died a few years later.

He returned after that, but I didn't. I was still fighting ghosts, the kind that follow you even in uniform. By the time I got out, got steady, looked around again, he was gone too.

That's when I found the scrapbook.

It lay in a cedar chest in the corner of his room, beneath an old Navy blanket and a stack of newspaper clippings tied with twine. No note. No label. Just there, waiting.

The leather cover felt worn smooth, the smooth from years of hands touching it, always gently, like it might bruise. Inside, sixty-four names stared back at me. Some included faces, some didn't. Some had notes in tiny, crabbed print: "Cousin of Leah," "Died in camp," "Prague, maybe." Most were just names.

I recognized three, at most.

Beneath the scrapbook, wrapped in cloth, lay his old radio," the Listener," he called it. I remembered that. He used to say it caught more than signals. "Sometimes it hears what it isn't supposed to," he told me once, when I was a kid and eavesdropping too long.

I never asked what he meant.

I closed the book halfway through and sat there with it in my lap.

The house hung in silence. My grandmother's wind chimes still dangled by the kitchen door, unmoving. No breeze.

I kept thinking I should say something aloud. Maybe a name. Maybe a prayer. But I didn't know which language to use.

Neither my father nor my grandfather practiced religion. They might have passed for deists at best, but they honored the traditions, not out of belief, but because someone had to.

I lit candles once a year, fasted when it felt right, and never explained it. It was a tradition, a memory, or perhaps defiance.

As a teenager, I asked him about the war, trying to break our silence. He didn't get angry. He just changed the subject. "Help your grandmother with the dishes," he said. But it landed like a rebuke. I stopped asking. I stopped trying. We stayed polite, civil, and distant.

I thought about all the times I'd seen him with that scrapbook—at the kitchen table, in the den, even once in the garage—and never asked what it meant. How many stories might've surfaced if I'd just sat down and listened, if I hadn't been running from the noise in my head?

The book felt heavier now than when I first opened it. Or maybe I just felt the weight differently.

I uncovered the radio beneath the scrapbook, still wrapped in cloth like something sacred.

It felt heavier than I remembered. Navy-issue, steel casing, knobs smoothed by use. A machine was built to survive the war it served.

I plugged it in out of instinct, not curiosity. I didn't expect it to work. But the hum came instantly—deep, soft, steady, like it had waited for someone to listen again.

The static didn't scratch—it flowed low, almost warm, like ocean water in your ears after a long swim.

I adjusted the dial. Nothing but snow. A soft hiss.

Then something— a click. A tone. A voice?

I leaned in.

It didn't sound like English. Or maybe it wasn't words at all. Just cadence. Rhythm. Like someone speaking through a wall.

I raised the volume and sat still.

It vanished.

I didn't touch the scrapbook again that night. I left it open on the table, where the light fell across the pages.

Around midnight, I ended up in front of the radio again. Not even thinking—just drawn to it. Like some part of me needed to test whether it had happened.

I turned the dial slowly, past static and silence, until something returned. Faint music. A violin, maybe, thin as thread. Then a woman's voice, breathless and slow, speaking in a language I couldn't place. Not German. Not Hebrew. It rose and fell like water.

I looked down. My hand rested on a page in the scrapbook. A young girl with braids and a note: "Studied violin. Last seen Kraków."

I froze. The music stopped.

A few seconds later, there was a burst of static. Then—clear as day—a string of numbers: four, six, twelve, twenty-two.

I didn't know what to do with that.

I turned the radio off. The silence afterward felt louder than the sound.

The next night, it happened again. Different page. Different voice. A man was humming something like a lullaby.

By the fifth night, I stopped pretending I wasn't listening for it.

Then my sister called. I told her about the scrapbook. About the radio.

"Are you sure you're okay?" she asked. "You sound... different."

"Yeah," I said. "It's just a lot. Grandpa left more than I thought."

"You mean the book?"

"Not just the book. What he didn't say."

She paused. "Just... be careful. Maybe unplug the radio for a while."

But I couldn't.

He never said much about the war.

"Pacific theater," he'd say, if you asked. Then a shrug. "Saw some things. Mostly ships."

But he didn't serve from behind a desk. He worked as an engine-man—below decks, in the heat and roar of the engine rooms, keeping everything running while bullets punched through steel and shells rattled the hull. He saw action. He fired weapons when necessary. He didn't speak like it mattered.

But I wonder now if the silence was his choice—or a burden laid on him.

I can imagine him at twenty, wanting to fight the Nazis, feeling called to something righteous. Instead, a drunken accident shuffled him into the Navy. Another war. Another kind of duty. He obeyed orders. He survived. But he carried guilt he never named. About what he didn't do. About those who didn't come home.

"The Japs never did anything to my family," he said once. "Until they hit Pearl. Even then, it wasn't personal."

When I was younger, I thought that meant he'd gotten lucky that he came home whole.

But later, once, maybe twice, let something else slip.

One night when I was thirteen, he had too much to drink. My dad had just left the room, and I sat at the table with a half-eaten sandwich, pretending not to listen.

He tapped his glass against the table like a gavel. "Was supposed to join the Army," he said. "Wanted to fight the goddamn Nazis."

He stared at his hands as if they didn't belong to him. "But we got drunk the night before: my buddy and I. The next morning, I wandered into the Navy line. Still half in the bag. They signed me up so fast I didn't realize where I was until I was in basic in Idaho!"

His friend joined the Army.

His friend didn't come home.

Rumors had already begun—in Jewish neighborhoods, synagogues, barbershops, and bakeries—about Jews in Europe being rounded up. Disappearing. That wasn't just war. It was something older. Something worse.

When someone asked if he knew what he was signing, he deflected the question. "Does it matter?" he'd say. Or he'd wave it off, mumble something about needing a cigarette.

But he kept the scrapbook. Sixty-four names. Not one of them is his own.

I didn't hear the radio again after that last night.

No voices. No songs. Just static. Not even the warm kind—just thin, gray noise like breath on glass.

I kept it plugged in anyway. I think part of me needed to. If I turned it off, those voices would be gone for good. And maybe I wasn't ready for that.

The scrapbook stayed on my desk for a long time. I flipped through it occasionally, careful not to wear the corners too thin. I searched the names in online archives, Yad Vashem databases, and immigration records. I found a few. Most remained nameless, untraceable, but not forgotten.

That wasn't the point.

One morning, I printed out a photo of my grandfather, young, in uniform, smiling like he wasn't sure how—and added it to the last blank page.

Didn't label it.

Just slid it in and closed the book.

The static remained. It was enough.

***

He never meant to find the voices—only the names.

But grief is a frequency. Memory is a signal. And some radios, when touched by the right hands, still listen back.

Sixty-four names. One grandson. And a silence that meant more than words ever could.

He didn't rewrite the past. He didn't resurrect it.

He remembered it.

And in that act—quiet, reverent, unfinished-he did what the scrapbook always asked for.

He turned the dial.

And he stayed...long enough to hear them.

THE HOUSE WHERE WINTER WAITED

*T**here are places the living forget, not because they want to, but because remembering costs too much. The houses lean inward. The trees forget how to bloom. Even the wind holds its breath. But sometimes, the past leaves a light on. And sometimes, someone finds their way home.*

This is the story of a woman named Ana who came back to a place she had buried in silence—a house where winter waited for one final thaw.

***

She had stopped believing in mornings a long time ago.

Not in the light—the world always found a way to turn—but in the promise that morning once meant. That something new could begin. That the aching might end.

It had been years since Ana felt anything that wasn't dull and gray. Time hadn't passed so much as accumulated—like dust in corners no one bothers to sweep. Purpose had become theoretical. Peace was for the dead.

The cab's heater rattled like an old man coughing up years.

Ana sat stiff-backed in the seat, coat zipped to her throat, fingers clutching a paper bag as if it held more than aspirin and dried-out tissues. The driver glanced in the mirror, waiting.

"Right here," she said finally. Her voice startled her. She hadn't spoken since O'Hare.

"Cold out here," the cabbie said, slowing. "Sure, this is the spot?"

"Not the cold that bothers me," Ana replied. "Just... the memory."

The house hadn't burned down. That surprised her.

Paint peeled like skin around the windows. The porch sagged. A storm door flapped lazily in the wind, glass long since shattered. Dead ivy strangled the gutters. And still, her feet moved, pulling her toward it.

Not the house. The street.

She hadn't been here in fifty years. Not since—

The memory arrived like a backhand. Sudden. Unwanted. Her mother, barefoot on the steps, screaming after Ana with whiskey on her breath and blood under her nails. Ana, fourteen, is already halfway gone.

She closed her eyes. Just for a second. Just long enough to bury it again.

But grief has no respect for fences or locks. It comes when summoned—even by something as small as an obituary.

Margaret "Maggie" Elwood, 71. Died peacefully. No children. No husband. Just a name, a date, and a town that never gave her much.

Maggie had been the brightest in that dark place, laughing like a faucet turned on. Ate hot fries with too much salt. Let Ana sleep over at night when things get bad at home.

They lost touch for years but reconnected later, quietly. Maggie was never one for drama. She just sent the occasional message on social media—birthday wishes, shared memories, photos of her stubborn tomato plants. But Maggie never told Ana she was sick or hinted at dying. She knew what Ana carried and wouldn't have added to that weight.

And now, Maggie was gone and was buried yesterday—no funeral invite. Just a notice in a local newsletter forwarded from a former classmate, Ana barely remembered.

The cab pulled away, leaving her at the curb.

She looked up. Snow fell, thin and slow. The air smelled like rust and old newspapers. The corner store still had the same neon sign, only now half-lit: R A L P H'S.

She started walking. Every step is a negotiation between guilt and inertia.

The house she and Maggie used to sneak into after school—three blocks over, past the old Lutheran church—was still there. Empty. Or maybe not.

She passed the church, now boarded up. Spray paint is on its old stone: "NO ONE SAVES YOU BUT YOU."

The liquor store next to it was open, and a man outside was lighting a cigarette with hands that shook. He stared at her too long. No recognition. Just curiosity. Outsiders were rare here.

As she turned the corner, an old woman on the porch next door narrowed her eyes.

"So, you came after all," the woman called.

Ana stopped. "Do I know you?"

"Didn't need to. But I knew Maggie. She waited for you, even when some of us thought she shouldn't."

Ana stiffened. "That's between her and me."

"Well," the woman muttered, turning away, "she still forgave you. That's more than most around here would do."

Ana didn't answer. The cold seeped deeper.

She nearly left then. She turned on her heel, walked back to the store, hailed a cab, and fled to the life she knew how to manage. Almost.

But her feet wouldn't move.

She turned toward Maggie's door.

The house stood crooked, like it had been holding its breath for decades.

She pushed open the gate. It moaned like something waking up.

Inside, it was cold in a way that wasn't just temperature. The kind of cold that lived in floorboards and under skin. Dust lay thick. Wallpaper curled like drying leaves. But everything was as they left it—the tea kettle, the blanket, and the record player by the window.

On the mantle sat a small box sealed with string. Inside was a note in Maggie's handwriting: "When you're ready."

Ana picked up the box and stared at it. Her thumb hooked under the string. She hesitated.

"Open it. Could you not open it? God, *do* something," she muttered. "Why does everything have to hurt?"

She marched toward the trash can and came to a stop. Her fingers clenched. Then loosened.

"You always knew how to say too much in too few words," Ana said aloud. "Why didn't you let me say anything back?"

She placed the box back on the mantle and sat down instead—not to mourn, not to remember, but to feel.

It came in slowly. Like blood returning to a limb too long asleep. Pins and needles. Ache and sting. Then warmth.

She wept. Not for Maggie. Not just for her. But for the girl who once laughed on this floor, who once dared to hope, who hadn't yet learned to shut the door on herself.

She dreams that night.

Not of death. But on a day so warm, the pavement steamed after the rain.

She and Maggie were nine. They skipped class and ran barefoot through the alleys, chalk dust on their knees. Ana had a bruise on her shoulder—no questions. Just Maggie's small hand grabbing hers.

They'd hidden in an old shed behind the butcher's, lit by broken sun-beams. Maggie pulled a sandwich from her backpack and split it in half.

"You don't have to go back," she said.

Ana stared at the peanut butter. "Where else would I go?"

"Here. Anywhere. Just not where it hurts."

That night, Ana stayed with her. Slept in her room under a fan that clicked like a metronome. Woke up to pancakes and quiet—one good day.

And sometimes, one good day is enough to save a person.

She returned to 218 Leland the next morning. The woman from the night before—Cassie—opened the door and stepped aside.

"You sure you want to do this?" Cassie asked quietly.

Ana hesitated, then nodded.

"Alright then. Second door up. It's...it's how she left it."

The apartment was small. Sparse. A kettle whistled faintly from another room.

Cassie followed her in and handed her a manila envelope. It was worn. Soft at the corners. A faded yellow Post-it clung to the front: For Ana, when she's ready. Not a moment before.

Ana sat on the edge of the bed, heart thudding. She peeled it open.

Inside was a letter. No dramatic confessions. Just Maggie's voice, plain and warm.

You always thought you had to be strong. But love doesn't need armor. It just needs room. You gave me a room once. I never forgot.

I wasn't waiting for you to apologize. I was hoping you'd heal. If you're reading this, perhaps you're just getting started. That's enough. That's everything.

Don't let the cold win. There's too much life left in you to spend it buried.

The tears came differently this time. Not jagged. Not guilty. Just... soft.

Cassie touched her shoulder.

"She never blamed you," she said softly.

Ana looked away. "She should've."

"No. She knew what this place did to people. She stayed because some-one had to. She hoped it wouldn't be in vain."

Ana glanced up. "Did Maggie ever talk about... regrets?"

Cassie shrugged, then paused. "Just one. She wished she'd told you sooner. About the cancer. But she didn't want to make you carry that too."

Ana exhaled. "That's so her."

Cassie gave a faint smile. "She always said you were stronger than you thought. But she knew you wouldn't believe it until you felt it yourself."

Ana laughed—a short, raw thing that surprised them both.

That night, she returned to Maggie's house with a paper bag full of gro-ceries. She dusted the old countertop. Lit the stove. Opened the windows.

Snow still fell. But inside, the air moved.

She made tea for two.

One cup sat across from her. Empty. But that didn't matter.

She was here.

And the house, long frozen, began to feel like something close to home.

Because winter had waited long enough.

She rose and went to the porch. Picked up the broom.

The steps had gathered a crust of old snow and grime. She began to sweep.

The wind shifted. Sunlight touched the wood.

She didn't expect peace to arrive in grand declarations. It came like Maggie's voice—low, steady, warm. In the scrape of a chair. In the steam of a kettle. In the choice to stay.

This time, Ana chose her morning.

And it was enough.

***

They say healing is slow and comes in inches, not miles. But for some, it starts with a doorway open, not to let others in but to let something out: grief, guilt, memory, or maybe just the cold.

In this forgotten neighborhood, beneath the quiet snow, one woman swept away a silence half a century deep. In doing so, she reminded us that winter never truly wins—not if we're willing to come back and remember the warmth.

PART IV - THE LAST ECHO

THE SOLDIER IN THE WIRE

I *t's a photograph you've likely seen: a small boy lifted through barbed wire by an East German soldier. A moment frozen in time — hailed as defiance, hope, or simply humanity caught off guard.*

But behind that image lies a truth far more complex.

The boy in the picture grew up. The soldier disappeared. And history, in its haste, left the story unfinished.

Tonight, we follow the boy's journey through archives and ash, silence and sorrow, to find the man who reached through a wall not just of concrete and wire... but of guilt, memory, and war.

A man history tried to forget...and a child who refused to let it.

***

I was five years old the day the wall went up.

Most of it's a blur — my mother's scream as the shutters slammed closed, the confusion in my father's voice, and the fence: cold, coiled, a serpent of barbed wire dividing the world.

Even before the wall, fear had become the mortar in every conversation. Radios hissed official slogans. Neighbors nodded too quickly. Bread was scarce, but suspicion was everywhere. The air itself seemed trained to listen.

Our teacher paused longer after questions at school, as if listening for the right answer, not from us, but from the ceiling. A neighbor stopped waving to my mother. Another vanished overnight. When I asked why, my father said, "It's better not to know."

But I remember him.

A soldier. East German. Standing stiff like the others — until he moved. He knelt and lifted me through the wire, silent as a whisper. My father's hands reached the rest of the way, and we ran.

I never saw the soldier again. Not in life, anyway.

They showed me the photograph when I was twelve — grainy, clipped from a newspaper, hidden until my parents thought I could "understand." I stared until my eyes burned.

It was me. No doubt. That frozen moment had become a symbol of the Wall — reproduced, debated, analyzed. But no one had ever named the soldier. No one ever asked about the boy.

Even after the wall fell, I kept that photo. I moved to France, grew up, and had my own children, but I never stopped looking for him—the soldier who disobeyed and vanished.

For years, the search felt impossible. Archives were sealed. The East was still veiled behind bureaucracy and silence. But after the wall came down, something shifted — not just politically, but in me.

I was older then. My son had just turned five—the same age I was when I was lifted through the wire. One night, he asked me why I kept a torn photograph on my desk.

"Because someone once broke the rules to save me," I told him.

And I finally realized that I needed to understand who that someone was, not just for myself but for the truth of the story I'd carried for so long—not to forgive, not to forget, but to know.

Sometimes, I'd watch my son through the window — playing in the yard, laughing as he crawled under the back fence. And my chest would clench. I'd call his name too sharply. My wife would glance at me but say nothing. That night, she closed the curtains without being asked.

Then, two years ago, I stepped into an antique shop near Leipzig and found something unexpected: a crumbling notebook thick with dust and time. Inside — yellowed clippings, fragmented notes in a jittery hand, and a single photograph taped to the back cover.

My photograph.

Beneath it, a sentence in fading ink:

"He looked like my son might have looked."

The owner told me the journal came from an abandoned farmhouse cleared after reunification. No one had lived there since the 1940s. Except, briefly, in 1945, when a man, silent and starving, had broken in and hanged himself from a ceiling beam.

They found him weeks later. No identification. Just a faded Wehrmacht uniform.

And a tattoo — *SS.*

I sank to the floor of that shop, hands trembling.

The dates... they matched. He'd been stationed at Treblinka, transferred to Auschwitz. Never arrested, never tried. Just...gone.

A ghost. A fugitive. A man who had done nothing to stop the horror but ran from it when the tide turned.

And yet...in 1961, something made him lift a child from barbed wire and give him back.

Me.

For weeks, I couldn't sleep.

I reread the entries. They spoke of hunger. Roads avoided. Silence. But one line echoed:

"I hope I will not be afraid if I ever see him, I will not be afraid."

I couldn't tell if he meant the boy or himself.

One archivist I contacted called the journal "a stain disguised as confession." He warned me not to romanticize monsters. "These men erased generations," he said. "Don't let a single gesture whitewash that."

But monsters don't save children, I thought. Men do. And some men never know which they are until the moment they reach.

The shopkeeper recalled where he'd gotten the journal — from a man whose grandfather had owned the barn. I drove out there. The building still stood, sagging and wind-worn. Inside, the beams creaked, and the air hung thick with dust.

That's when I saw it.

Burned faint into the wood above: a name, half-erased by time. I traced it gently.

R. Keil.

Not much. But something.

Back in France, I searched archives, records, and tribunal lists. And finally, Rudolf Keil.

Born in 1919. Joined the SS in 1941. Treblinka. Then Auschwitz. Disappeared, presumed dead, 1945.

No trial. No grave. No aftermath. Just absence.

But there were fragments: a school report describing him as quiet, a photograph of a boy holding a bird's nest, a marginal note in Latin from a textbook his mother kept—evidence of someone else, someone before the uniform.

The journal was his. The photo is his. The ink line — "He looked like my son might have looked" — his.

And somehow, he had become the soldier who lifted me to freedom.

A man who had stood by as monsters marched, who ran when their reign ended. Not a hero. Not a villain. Just a man who did nothing for too long. Until one day, he did something.

I couldn't stop there. Not for closure — not even for forgiveness. To understand.

I traced the Keil family line. Public records led me to Margarete Keil, a widow who was ninety-three years old. She lived just outside Dresden. I called once, then visited the next day with a bouquet and the photo folded in my pocket.

When she opened the door, her eyes were like fragile porcelain.

"You've come about my son," she said.

We sat in silence.

She had seen the photo. Someone had mailed it to her years ago. She never understood it, but she knew — it had to be him.

"He was a good boy," she whispered. "I didn't raise a Nazi. I didn't believe in any of it. But what could I do? What could he do?"

Her hands trembled. She wiped at her eyes but didn't cry.

"He used to draw birds in his notebooks," she said. "And then one day he brought home a black pin with silver lines. He said it meant something. I didn't ask what. I should have asked."

She pressed the base of her thumb to her temple and closed her eyes. "I used to pretend," she said, "that he died before the war. That he stayed with the boy with the sparrow. That he never put on the black. But the letters stopped. And then...nothing."

She opened her eyes again—dry, but hollowed. "Do you think one good thing can matter, after so many wrong ones?"

She handed me a tin box of old photographs. One showed Rudolf as a uniform boy smiling and leaning against a fence post—a boy with a gentle brow and eyes that hadn't yet learned to look away.

"They told me he served at Treblinka," she said. "And later... worse places. He never spoke of it. Never defended it. Just disappeared. I've lived with that for a lifetime."

She looked out the window, past the hedges and into a sky going pale.

"He used to feed the crows," she said. "When he was little. They'd follow him. Once, one perched on his shoulder, like something out of a fairy tale. And now... now I don't know if I should remember that. Or forget it."

We sat until dusk, two strangers bound by a frozen moment. As I stood to leave, she didn't ask my name.

She only said, "Tell him I remember the boy."

I don't know what laws govern the dead.

But I believe he wandered, unanchored, ashamed. A man who never resisted — until a child's face brought something back. A memory. A longing. A son he never had.

And in that moment, he broke a rule. A small one. A soldier's order.

But it was enough.

No grave marks his name. No plaque bears his story.

Just a photograph. A hand reaching through the wire.

Sometimes I wonder — why me?

Maybe because I reminded him of something lost.

Or something he never dared to want.

Either way, he saved me.

And somehow...

I think I saved him, too.

***

His name was never carved in stone. No plaque. No parade. Just a name burned into a barn beam, and a photograph that outlived them both.

Rudolf Keil — soldier, war criminal, fugitive. A man who stood still while horror marched past...until the day he reached out and did something else.

Some stories end with justice. Others with redemption. But this one ends with a question:

Can a single act of mercy outweigh a lifetime of silence?

History may not answer. But one man did. And the echo of that answer still hums...somewhere between the wire and the whisper.

THE MURMURATION

Some stories don't begin with thunder. They start with a question. A silence. A path of marigolds across a porch swept too clean.

Tonight, a young woman named Isela returns home—not for answers, but for remembrance.

What she finds is more than tradition—more than grief.

She finds a sky that moves like breath.

And crows who remember... when people forget.

***

When I was six years old, I asked my grandmother if we were Catholic.

She paused mid-peel on a blood orange, eyes narrowing as if inspecting a bruise. "We're Mexican," she said, as if that answered everything. "We celebrate what matters."

That was the year I first saw the crows.

It was Día de los Muertos. My grandfather's face beamed from a photograph beside a pan de muerto loaf and three sugar skulls. Abuela had drawn marigold paths from every doorway, every window.

"So they can find us," she said. I thought she meant ghosts. I didn't know she meant memories.

As the sun spilled like molasses across the desert hills that evening, a shadow passed over the back porch. I looked up.

A flock of crows—easily fifty—wheeled above the mesquite trees in tight, endless spirals. Their flight wasn't random. It was deliberate. Orchestrated. As though they moved on the breath of a song only they could hear.

"¡Mira!" I called.

Abuela stepped out, wiping her hands on her apron.

"¿Lo ves?" I pointed.

She looked.

And she nodded. "They've come to carry someone home."

I didn't understand then. But I remembered.

Years passed. My parents moved us north, to Denver. The desert faded from our windows. We stopped lighting candles. Stopped placing the ofrenda. My Spanish softened into silence. My grandmother faded. She passed quietly, and I wasn't there.

I told myself I couldn't afford the flight. I had interviews and deadlines. The truth was more straightforward: I had let her become a background hum—familiar, comforting, ignorable.

She left without a word. And I carried that silence like a debt.

In Denver, tradition was something you could schedule—maybe for Instagram, maybe for Christmas. My apartment smelled like coffee and printer ink. The sky glowed with city light, and no one looked up. I wore the distance like a new coat.

Sometimes I would stare at the rows of anonymous windows across the alley and feel a dull ache in my chest—a guilt with no name. When people asked about my family, I spoke in vague terms. It was easier than explaining what I had let slip away.

But when I turned twenty-six, something pulled me back.

I took the bus. Not a flight. Not a rental car. A slow, hours-long ride that scraped the edge of the mountains and dropped me into the Valley like a stone into a well. The air smelled like dust and citrus.

The house was smaller than I remembered. Dustier. But intact. The marigolds had seeded wild across the fence line. I picked a few lit candles. I tried to remember the prayers and let the ones I'd forgotten fall into silence.

Inside, I found her apron folded in a drawer. I pressed it to my face and wept.

My cousin Carmen came by the next morning. She still lived in the Valley—worked at the co-op, raised her boys, and looked at me like I was a ghost that had waited too long to return.

"You back for the holiday?" she asked.

"I'm trying to remember," I said.

She tilted her head. "We're still here, you know. Even if you weren't."

Later that day, she brought pan dulce and sat beside the flickering ofrenda. We didn't speak much. She just watched the candles.

"You should've called," she said finally.

"I wanted to," I replied. "It just... felt too far."

"I know things are different up there," she added. "All city lights and fast talking. But don't forget—we prayed for you. Even when you didn't ask us to."

"I didn't mean to drift away."

"Maybe not," she said. "But you did. And tides don't always bring things back, you know?"

Later, her oldest son, Mateo, maybe ten years old, tugged at my sleeve.

"Is it true?" he asked.

"Is what true?"

"That the crows talk?"

I looked toward the porch, heart suddenly caught in my ribs.

"They don't talk like people," I said. "But they remember."

That evening, we walked through the neighborhood. Carmen introduced me to people who remembered me from my toddler days, and others who had never heard of me. One woman, a distant cousin I barely recognized, studied me.

"Do you still speak Spanish?" she asked.

"Not much anymore," I admitted.

She made a sound between pity and judgment. "Then you better listen harder now. The dead don't translate."

That night, I sat alone on the porch. The stars hung low and close, like lanterns. The desert was quiet. Then the wind shifted.

They came—just a few at first, then more. Crows. Spiraling above the mesquite in that same murmuring current. A vortex of wings and dark intelligence. A sound like breath held too long.

I stood slowly.

One broke from the pattern and descended low. It didn't caw. Didn't flap. Just drifted down like smoke.

It landed on the porch railing.

I didn't move.

It looked at me with an obsidian eye.

Then it opened its beak.

Not a sound.

But a memory.

My grandmother's soft voice rose like steam: "We celebrate what matters."

And behind it—another voice. My own, once. Younger. Laughing.

I closed my eyes, and the sound wrapped around me like a shawl.

The crow turned. Took flight.

The rest followed, lifting in one perfect arc toward the stars.

When I looked down, a single feather remained where the bird had stood.

I bent to pick it up.

But it wasn't a feather.

It was a stone. Smooth. Round. Black as night.

A gift.

The next day, Carmen invited me to the cemetery vigil. I hesitated, and she noticed.

"You don't have to feel guilty," she said. "But if you want to belong here again, you must show up. That's how we remember together."

I looked down at my hands. "I don't know if I do belong. Not anymore."

She took a breath. "Belonging isn't a place. It's who you light candles for."

So I went. We lit candles and sang soft songs in both languages. I placed the stone near my grandmother's name and whispered thanks, which I didn't know I remembered how to say.

As I looked around, I saw others with eyes closed, speaking to air, shadows, and memory. Mateo clutched a candle with both hands and whispered, "Thank you for sending her back."

I saw the woman who had questioned my Spanish. She was singing now. I sang too.

In that moment, something inside me eased.

I didn't feel forgiven. Not yet. But I felt... received.

And that was enough to begin.

***

"Not every homecoming ends with forgiveness. Not every silence yields to words.

But beneath the desert sky, a woman lit a candle. Sang a name. And listened.

The murmuration came—not as omen, but as answer. A reminder that memory is not lost when language falters... only waiting to be claimed.

Because when the wind turns, when the wings gather, and the voices rise from marrow and shadow—

The ones we thought were gone come back, not to haunt, but to be held.

And if we are still enough...

We remember how.

WHERE THE ICE WHISPERS

*T*hey *send men to the ends of the earth to guard borders, watch radars, and wait for wars that never come.*

But sometimes, what waits in the dark isn't war.

This is Jesse Yazzie. Young. Smart. Displaced by assignment, exiled by orders. A desert son was sent to the world's edge to freeze in silence.

But there are places colder than snow, older than maps. Places where the land listens, and the river remembers.

Tonight, on a forgotten patch of tundra known only to those who've heard it whisper, Jesse will learn the difference between standing guard...

And being watched.

***

The C-130 disappeared into the dark over the runway, swallowed by a sky that hadn't seen daylight in weeks. Jesse Yazzie watched it vanish, duffel bag slung over one shoulder, parka hood down so the cold could slap him in the face with full effect.

Welcome to Galena Air Force Station, he thought, where your breath froze before your words, and the sun was just a rumor passed down by tired men.

It was February 1977. The wind came howling off the Yukon like it had a grudge, and Galena—the 5072nd Air Base Group's little outpost in the Alaskan interior—sat hunched behind its dike road, as if trying not to be noticed by the rest of the world—no trees inside the perimeter. Just long stretches of snow-covered flightline, squat buildings spread like low, gray mushrooms, and security floodlights' dim orange glow barely punches through the darkness.

This wasn't what Jesse had asked for. He'd finished Security Specialist training two weeks ago, filled out his dream sheet like they told him, and listed Guam, the Philippines, and Hawaii. Anywhere with heat, humidity, and the chance to waste weekends on a beach. He'd figured "overseas" might mean discomfort, but not this. There is no ice fog, infrared goggles, or a standing post at minus forty.

But the Air Force needed bodies in Galena.

So here he was.

The security center smelled like burnt coffee and wool. A 13-inch black-and-white TV bolted to the corner wall played an old Twilight Zone episode—something about an old man and his dog being called to a new world, a place they didn't understand but couldn't resist. The faint hum of static added to its eerie feel. Three guys in thermals and mukluks looked up when Jesse entered, sizing him up in one glance. "Tucson," Jesse said, stamping snow off his boots. "Yeah."

"Well, congrats. You made it to the edge of the world."

"You guys got beaches?"

"Sure. They're just frozen solid."

Laughter. Jesse smiled back, dry as desert dust. He unzipped his parka and handed over his orders. The guy behind the desk glanced over them, nodding.

"Security Specialist, huh? Welcome to the 5072nd. You'll be on the graveyard shift like the rest of us. Midnight to oh-eight, give or take. You either ride with SAT, standing ECP, Close-In at the alert hangar, or down at the boundary shack."

"Sounds like a party."

"Oh yeah. Especially when your radio freezes."

He signed the check-in log and got a quick rundown: Entry Control Point, Close Boundary, Close-In Sentry, or riding shotgun in the Security Alert Team truck—three-person crews with rotating routes unless something happened to the priority resources: the F-4 Phantoms housed in the alert hangar, which you didn't go near unless your name was on the post roster.

That hangar always had a red glow under its lights. Always watched. Always quiet.

Later, in the motor pool, Jesse met Tomas Angaluk, the station's civilian mechanic. He was Inupiat, wearing heavy boots, seal-skin mittens, and a snow-flecked parka. He was working on a snow tractor battery and didn't look up when Jesse arrived.

"You're Yazzie," Tomas said flatly.

"Yeah. That obvious?"

"Most guys don't show up blinking like owls."

"I put in for Hawaii," Jesse muttered.

Tomas lit a cigarette with a match he struck on the vehicle's tread. "Everybody does."

They stood together in a companionable silence. Jesse handed him a wrench without being asked.

After a few minutes, Jesse nodded toward the flightline. "Where's the river?"

Past the alert area. On the south edge of the village, beyond the dike road. You'll know it when you see it."

"Any chance I won't have to?"

Tomas shrugged. "Probably not."

More silence. Then Jesse asked, "Someone at chow said you can hear it at night."

Tomas stopped working. Not long—just a beat.

"You can."

Jesse raised an eyebrow. "Like ice shifting?"

"No," Tomas said. "Like...the quiet gets too quiet. Like the river's listening."

Jesse smirked. "Man, back home we had stories too. Skinwalkers, thunder spirits, coyote girls who turned into owls. I used to eat that stuff up. Then I got old enough to know better."

"Maybe you didn't get old enough," Tomas said, then went back to work.

Jesse rolled his eyes. "So, what, there's a haunted river now? You'll tell me not to whistle after midnight, too?"

Tomas just exhaled a long breath through his nose. "It's not haunted. It's aware. And if you listen long enough, it might decide to listen back."

That night, lying in a bunk two inches too short and wrapped in wool that smelled like ten other men, Jesse thought about Tomas's words—the river he hadn't seen yet, the darkness that didn't let up—not even in dreams.

And somewhere between the flicker of fluorescent lights and the creak of old plumbing, he thought he heard it.

A hum, too low to be real.

Almost like something remembering.

The second night on the graveyard shift was colder than the first. By Jesse's count, that made it three degrees short of absolute damn zero.

He stood his post on the northwest corner of the alert area—Close Boundary Sentry—near the fence line, just outside the sweep of the big sodium vapor lights that bathed the hangars in an otherworldly orange haze. His job was simple: watch, listen, don't freeze. The SAT truck rolled past every hour, sometimes honking once in greeting. His radio crackled now and then, mostly boring check-ins.

Nothing happened at Galena. That was the unofficial motto.

Still, he kept moving in slow circles, stomping to stay warm, hand resting near the butt of his sidearm, breath hanging around his head like cigarette smoke that wouldn't blow away. The only sound was the high, whistling wind combing across the hardpack. And beyond that—nothing. No birds. No engines. No water.

Just the silent, frozen Yukon, stretching off past the hangars, blank and white and—he realized suddenly—too flat. It wasn't snow. It wasn't terrain. It was a frozen thing lying in wait.

He shook his head.

Later, he bunked down just after 0800, blackout curtains drawn tight, trying to ignore the buzz of the fluorescent bulb in the hallway. He was halfway to sleep, boots still on the floor, when he thought he saw motion outside the window.

It was just a flicker. A dark shape crossed the white expanse where the hangars met the river. He blinked, waited. Nothing. Maybe a snow drift falling off the roof.

He slept hard, dreamed of nothing, and woke to darkness again.

The next night, it happened again. But this time, she was there.

Jesse was on post, walking the shadowed edge near the fence. The wind had carved long, low dunes across the flat, scallops of white under the aurora. The lights that night were faint green ribbons that flickered without movement, like breathing patterns in a sleeping body.

At first, he thought it was a shadow.

Then it stepped forward.

A woman, out on the river ice.

Walking.

Not shivering. Not stumbling. Just moving across the white with her arms loose at her sides, hair trailing behind her like underwater.

She was barefoot.

He blinked. She was gone.

He stared a long time at the riverbank. Nothing. No footprints, no figure. Just the Yukon's endless flat face.

He rubbed his eyes, finished the shift, and said nothing.

The third night, it didn't happen while he was awake.

It happened in his dream.

He was walking the perimeter again. He knew the feel of the gravel under the packed snow and the faint creak of the chain-link fence in the wind. He had his flashlight in one hand, but it didn't work in the dream. The button was clicked, but the bulb stayed dark.

And out on the ice, she was there again—closer this time.

He couldn't see her face, but he saw her outline clearly—dark hair, pale legs, one hand lifted slightly as if gesturing, not waving, and just... calling.

He stepped forward. One pace. Two.

Then he woke up.

Standing.

His boots were on.

So was his parka.

He was at the door of the barracks. Inside, thank God—but only just. One gloved hand was on the knob. The blackout curtain beside him stirred in the slight draft.

Jesse staggered backward, heart pounding, every nerve in his body pinging like radar. He pulled off his boots, dropped them to the floor, and sat down hard on the lower bunk.

No one else stirred.

Later that morning, Tomas didn't look up from the heater he was repairing in the motor pool.

"You're pale," he said.

"Didn't sleep much," Jesse muttered.

"You never do, after the first one."

Jesse squinted. "The first what?"

Tomas adjusted the burner's nozzle with a twist of his gloved hand. "Dream."

Jesse paused, then gave a dry laugh. "Okay. Is this where you pull out the incense and the drum?"

Tomas didn't smile. "Not all dreams are yours to follow."

Something about how he said it made Jesse's humor die on the spot.

"I didn't ask for it."

Tomas looked at him then, really taking in the sight. "Doesn't matter."

Jesse tied a bootlace around his wrist and the metal bed frame that night. Not tightly. Just enough to tug him if he moved.

It snapped somewhere around 3:15 a.m.

Jesse stopped sleeping well.

Not just from the cold, the thin bunk mattress, or the weird creak of pipes at 4 a.m.

It was the dream.

Every night, he drifted off with a knot in his stomach. And every night, he woke somewhere different—closer to the door, closer to the wall, once standing in the hallway with one boot on and his parka halfway zipped.

He started keeping track: time down, time up, dream fragments. The notes were sloppy, scrawled in a spiral-bound notebook he kept under his bunk. After three nights, a pattern emerged: around 0215, he would see her. Always standing on the river, always motionless until he saw her eyes, and then she would turn. Walk away. Slowly. Silently. Like someone waiting to be followed.

He didn't want to.

But every time, he did.

The dreams changed. Became stripped-down.

No stars overhead. No wind. No sound.

The aurora, so constant it had become background noise, was gone. In the dream, the sky was just black—a ceiling without texture. The world below: nothing but ice, featureless, stretching into infinity. And her—always her—moving further each time, slower now, like she was sinking into the distance instead of walking.

He called out once in the dream.

His voice didn't carry.

When he woke, his mouth was dry, and his throat ached like he'd been screaming.

One night, sitting in the tiny breakroom at the security center, sipping instant coffee that tasted like burnt dirt, he brought it up indirectly.

"What's the weirdest thing you've seen on post?" he asked the guy across from him.

That was Tech Sergeant Brower. Mid-forties. Crewcut graying at the sides. Heavyset. Looked like he'd been carved out of brown canvas and long shifts.

Brower shrugged. "You mean besides drunks falling into snowbanks?"

"I mean...out there." Jesse motioned toward the flightline, the hangars, and the black beyond.

Brower took a long sip before answering. "Back in '65, during winter rotation, we had a guy named Mallory, a law enforcement specialist. Quiet, straight-arrow. Used to write home twice a week. Then one night, a white-out hit during shift change. Visibility went to zero. We figured he was stuck in the gate shack."

Jesse leaned in. "And?"

"They found the shack door open. Coffee inside, still warm. Tracks in the snow led south, out past the alert hangar."

"River?"

"Yeah." Brower stared into his cup. "Footprints went about fifty yards onto the ice. Then... nothing."

"Snow covered 'em?"

"No. That's the thing. The prints were clean. Spaced like he was walking calmly, not running. No signs of a struggle, no blood. They just... stopped."

Jesse scoffed lightly. "You're telling me a guy walked onto the river and vanished into thin air."

"I'm telling you the ice didn't crack, and he didn't fall through. I'm telling you we never found his body, his jacket, or even his flashlight."

"What'd the official report say?"

"'Presumed drowned.' Like they always do."

Jesse raised his eyebrows. "You believe that?"

Brower just looked at him. "I believe the snow remembers."

Jesse laughed it off, loudly enough that it felt forced.

But that night, when he got off shift, he tied both his wrists to the bedframe.

This time, with a parachute cord he borrowed from the SAT truck's emergency kit.

The dream came anyway.

Same landscape. Same figure.

But she was closer now. Not on the river anymore—she was standing in the boundary zone between the fence and the snow berm. Where he had stood so many times in waking life, rifle slung over his shoulder, staring into the dark.

This time, she lifted her arm.

Pointed at him.

No words. No motion.

Just a long, slow gesture—like she was marking him for something.

He woke up gasping. The cord was frayed. One wrist had a red welt from strain.

And on the floor by his bunk—just inside the door—was one of his boots.

Not both.

Just one.

He didn't remember putting it there.

The next morning, Tomas handed him coffee before Jesse could even ask.

"Have you ever heard that story?" Jesse muttered. "About Mallory?"

Tomas didn't blink. "He followed her."

"You believe that?"

Tomas sipped. "I know what happens when people pretend they don't believe something they already feel in their bones."

Jesse didn't reply. He just stared at the steam rising from the cup.

Outside, the wind howled against the wall in a way that almost sounded like a voice.

The rope snapped sometime before dawn.

Jesse woke flat on his back, mouth dry, nostrils burning with the sting of cold air. His fingers were numb. He tried to move, and his limbs answered sluggishly. Snow crunched under his parka as he sat up and realized he wasn't in his bunk.

He was outside.

On the riverbank.

The Yukon stretched out before him in long, unbroken silence. The stars above blinked like frost on glass. He could see the lights from the base, dull and far behind him, flickering like they were behind frosted glass.

The parachute cord he'd tied around his wrist was still there. Still looped around his left hand. The other end trailed away into the snow—torn, not untied. A loose strand hung from the metal bedpost behind the rec hall, swaying gently in the wind.

He stared at it for a long time, then at the snow under his knees.

No footprints.

Not his.

Not anyone's.

Later that morning, Jesse sat in the motor pool, coat still zipped, hands wrapped around a cup of bad coffee that had long since gone cold. He hadn't gone to chow and hadn't reported it. Couldn't explain it.

Tomas came in just after 1000, carrying a tin of pipe tobacco and a handful of kindling. He said nothing. Just walked past Jesse, knelt by the old barrel stove, and lit a fire.

When it was burning steadily, he reached into his pocket, pulled out a twist of tobacco wrapped in plastic, and dropped it onto the table beside Jesse's cup.

Jesse didn't ask why. He unwrapped it slowly. Ran his fingers across the dry, aromatic leaf as if it might fall apart.

"Do you know what's happening to me?" he asked, voice low.

Tomas didn't look up. "I don't know what she wants."

"She?"

Tomas finally glanced over. "She's not a woman. Not like we think of one. She's older than that. She walks in whatever shape the land remembers."

"That's not helpful," Jesse snapped, louder than he meant to.

Tomas didn't flinch. "You want help, so go talk to the chaplain."

Jesse exhaled sharply. "I'm not scared of dying."

Tomas nodded. Waited.

"I'm scared of forgetting. Of not knowing when I crossed over. Of waking up one day and realizing I've already left."

The fire popped softly. Outside, the wind rasped against the roll-up door like sandpaper against bone.

"You haven't left," Tomas said. "Not yet."

That night, Jesse dreamed again.

But this time, the dream was different. It felt wide awake.

He stood on the Yukon—not near it, not approaching it—on it. The snow was gone. The ice beneath him gleamed like glass underfoot. And she was there again, five paces away, her silhouette framed by the pitch of the sky.

No stars.

No aurora.

Just the faint shimmer of depthless black above and below.

She extended her hand.

He didn't want to take it.

He did anyway.

Her fingers closed around his.

They were not cold.

They burned.

Not like fire. Not pain.

It was the heat you felt when blood returned to a frozen limb—when you returned to yourself and realized you'd been gone.

He gasped awake, tangled in wool blankets, heart hammering so hard it felt like it would fracture his ribs.

His bunk was empty. His roommate was gone.

And the light above his head was out.

The base was dark.

No overhead hum. No fluorescent buzz. No heaters ticking.

Just blackness and the faint scream of the wind as the storm howled in from the river.

Power was out across the station.

A blizzard had rolled in around midnight. Radios dead. The SAT truck is grounded. Visibility dropped to ten feet. No one knew exactly when it had gone dark.

At 0200 hours, the NCOIC began roll call to confirm personnel.

Jesse Yazzie didn't answer.

They searched the barracks.

His gear was still there. The parachute cord frayed on the frame. Boots missing.

Only one bunk looked slept in.

And the blackout curtains had been drawn open.

In the motor pool, Tomas lit a lantern with a wooden match.

He didn't ask where Jesse had gone.

He sat silently, pipe in hand, and watched the shadows flicker against the far wall.

The wind changed direction.

Somewhere beyond the dike, a low tone sounded across the frozen river.

Like a voice.

Or a song.

Or something, remembering how to call back.

The storm passed just before dawn.

It didn't break—it simply let go, like something satisfied it had done enough. The wind died off slowly, the air holding its breath. In the dim early light, the outlines of Galena's flightline emerged again: buildings frosted over, fences drifted in, hangars hunched low in their amber halos. The base looked smaller, somehow less like a Cold War outpost, more like a forgotten checkpoint at the edge of the known world.

Tomas Angaluk stepped out into the stillness, parka buttoned tight, a cigarette behind one ear and a matchbook in his gloved hand. He didn't report to anyone. He didn't check the roll call logs or ask the SAT team what they'd found. He already knew.

He walked past the main hangar, past the alert zone with its red warning placards and tire-churned snowbanks, and out along the chain-link fence marking the edge of the airfield.

Beyond it stretched the Yukon River, still frozen, still vast, its surface gleaming faintly like polished obsidian dusted in sugar. No one had shoveled this far. The storm had smoothed everything. The ice reflected the pale light like a mirror to nowhere.

About ten yards out, he saw them.

Boots.

Upright.

Parallel.

Laces loose.

They weren't scuffed. They hadn't fallen over. They stood planted exactly where someone had stepped out of them.

But there were no prints. No drag marks. No crushed snow trail from the fence to where they stood.

Just those two boots. Alone. Waiting.

Tomas walked until he stood five feet away. Then stopped.

He didn't speak for a while. Just lit the cigarette, struck the match on his belt buckle, and cupped the flame with steady hands.

He stared at the boots, then out across the river.

"He didn't believe," Tomas said, voice low, "but he heard her."

Above him, the sky shimmered.

The aurora was faint, soft ribbons of green and blue, barely there against the dark, like old film burning through in reverse. A low hum vibrated through the air, almost below hearing, like some great old engine far beneath the world had started up again.

Tomas narrowed his eyes.

Something moved out past the boots, deep beneath the surface of the ice.

Just a shadow at first. Then a figure, blurred and slow, like it was walking not through space but through memory.

It wasn't hurrying.

It didn't look back.

Just moved westward, toward the far bank, where the trees stood in long rows like silent witnesses. Toward the deep country. Toward whatever came next.

Tomas took one more drag, then flicked the cigarette into the snow.

He didn't speak again.

The new guy arrived on a C-130 three weeks later, which kicked up more ice than snow. He stepped off in standard-issue gear, cheeks already burning red from exposure, and blinked at the flat white expanse of Galena like he couldn't quite believe it was real.

He was from Mississippi. His accent sang in the cold.

A Security Specialist fresh out of training, the dream sheet said Okinawa, but the Air Force had other plans.

They watched The Twilight Zone on AFRTS Channel 8 inside the security center. The black-and-white images flickered, distorted by static, disturbing yet oddly familiar. It was the last episode: "The Bewitchin' Pool." The story was about a girl pulled into a strange world through a pool, where things weren't quite what they seemed, and the rules of reality didn't apply.

For a moment, the room fell silent, everyone watching the unsettling final scene where the girl, now in this unfamiliar world, had no choice but to follow a path she didn't understand.

The coffee was still terrible, and the air still smelled like boot wax and old wool. Everyone looked up when he walked in.

Tomas was there that day, dropping off parts for the snow tractor. He nodded once, slowly.

"You dream much?" he asked, offering a cigarette from a crumpled soft pack.

The kid laughed, grinning as he took one. "Not really," he said. "Only when I eat chili too late."

Tomas struck a match. Lit the kid's smoke. Didn't smile.

Outside, the wind picked up.

And somewhere past the dike, down by the river, the ice made a sound like it remembered a name it hadn't spoken in a long time.

***

Jesse Yazzie is no longer listed as missing and is not named in any reports. Just...absent.

His boots remain—his story, unwritten—except by wind and ice and those who still know how to listen.

Some say he dreamed too deeply. Others that he was called.

But the Yukon does not explain itself. It does not ask.

It remembers.

And for those who think the cold is silence, know this:

Silence is not the absence of sound.

It is the presence of something listening back.

THE LAST NOTE

History has battles, emperors, and empires made of stone and war. But every so often, history turns instead on something softer. Stranger. A vibration in the air. A single sound no one can explain, but no one forgets.

Tonight's tale concerns a man who had nothing left to give—but found himself carrying a song too old for memory, and too powerful for silence. His name is Cal Weaver. And he's about to learn that some melodies aren't written... they're waiting.

Waiting for the right voice. Waiting for the world to be quiet enough to listen. Waiting for... the last note.

***

Cal Weaver had just about given up.

His voice, once the texture of mountain wind and aged tobacco, had thinned with years and whiskey. His gigs had gone from theaters to corner bars with flickering neon and no working mic stands. So when he ducked into the cluttered pawn shop in Briar Glen to escape the rain, hope never brought him in. It was just dry air.

The banjo sat on a wall like it had been waiting.

Old. Walnut body. Goat skin stretched taut with rusted hardware. The words carved around the head read: "WHEN NO ONE LISTENS, EVEN THE EARTH FORGETS ITS SONG."

"Hundred even," the shopkeeper grunted, seeing Cal stare.

Cal picked it up. It was heavier than it looked, and warm—not just from sitting under a light bulb, either.

He strummed. The first chord sounded wrong—not out of tune, but not of this world. The fifth string hummed in a way no banjo ever had.

That night, Cal played it again in a bar near the county line. The drunks went quiet. They were listening—like the sound was reaching a part of them untouched by beer or brawling.

A man two stools down wept. A woman stood up and hugged her ex-husband. Nobody said anything about it after, but they all remembered.

The song came to Cal in pieces.

Dreams, mostly. He'd wake with chord progressions in his head, lyrics he hadn't written, notes he couldn't place on any scale. When he played, it felt like someone else was guiding his fingers.

He stopped drinking. He started writing again.

Word got out. People came from miles away to hear him. Not because he was famous. Because the music was. Because something changed when you heard it. Tiny, invisible shifts. A woman with chronic pain stood for the first time in years. A man at the edge of suicide turned around and called his daughter. An angry preacher lost his voice mid-sermon—and found peace in the silence.

But Cal didn't trust it.

Not entirely.

One night, a blind bluesman named Elijah Monroe found him backstage.

"You're playing the Fifth Chord," Elijah said, touching the banjo. "Been waiting for someone to find it."

"What is it?" Cal asked.

Elijah only smiled, but it was a sad smile.

"A key. To something older than prayer. Older than war. Play it right; you calm the storm. Play it wrong... and the thunder follows."

Then came the letter.

It arrived without a stamp. No postmark. A folded piece of vellum was left inside his guitar case after a set in Memphis.

The handwriting was looping, elegant. It read:

"Play the whole song, and it will save them. But play it more than once—and it will begin to choose."

Choose what?

There was no return address. Just a faint sigil burned into the paper—a circle of twelve notes, one missing.

The next night, Cal met a man waiting for him outside the venue.

Thin, smiling, dressed like the 1930s had never ended. Fedora, sharp vest, dusty boots. His skin had a luster like moonlight on river water. He carried a guitar case with a broken hinge and smelled faintly of honeysuckle and dust.

"Heard you've been playing something strange," the man said. "Something that doesn't belong to this world."

Cal nodded, wary.

The stranger didn't blink. Just opened his case, revealing a battered guitar with only five strings, all tuned to D.

"Name's Alton," he said. "I once played the song too. A long time ago. Mississippi Delta, crossroads after midnight—you know the story. The only thing I met out there wasn't the devil."

"What was it then?"

Alton smiled. "Something older. Something that hears the pain in the dirt and teaches it to hum. It gave me the chords. It took... other things in return."

He reached out, touching the edge of Cal's banjo with reverence—and something like fear.

"That song you're chasing? It doesn't want to be played. It wants to become. And it needs a voice like yours to do it."

He turned to go, but paused.

"Whatever you do, boy... don't play it alone. Please don't play it more than once. And for God's sake—don't let it finish itself."

Then he vanished into the dark, leaving only the faint echo of a slide guitar drifting on a wind without a source.

Cal started dreaming of endings—of final notes that could seal the song. But something always stopped him before he could play it.

He began noticing strangers in the crowd wearing earpieces—government officials. Corporations offered him millions to license the sound. A tech firm wanted to use it to rewrite human behavior. A private security team broke into his motel room, looking for the instrument.

And still, the song grew louder in his sleep.

On the eclipse night, Cal climbed the old battlefield hill at Clary's Ridge. Centuries ago, men had slaughtered each other on that spot over nothing but flags and pride. He set up a simple amp and microphone. The world streamed it live.

He played the full song for the first time.

And when he reached the end, he found the final chord.

It was silence.

Not absence, but completion.

A hum behind the stars. The moment before a baby's first cry. The breath before a kiss. The stillness before thunder.

And in that moment, the world stopped.

Across the globe, people listening stopped yelling, stopped fighting, just stopped. There was no miracle light, no heaven opening, just a pause, a possibility.

Then Cal vanished.

No smoke. No flash. Just gone.

The amp crackled, and the banjo clattered to the grass.

The banjo was never found, and the recording vanished from every server. People tried to hum it, but the tune slipped from their memory like a dream.

All that remained was a single wooden bench at Clary's Ridge, inscribed with words that shouldn't have been there:

"It was never about the music. It was about the moment."

But in the weeks that followed, people began to hum.

Not the original song, but something adjacent. Dissonant. Darker. Those who hummed it initially felt euphoric, but then became paranoid. A few went missing. Others became violent. One survivor of a mass panic incident in Oslo whispered: "He played it twice."

And a banjo waits again somewhere in an abandoned pawn shop in a town no longer listed on any map.

Because the song is not done. Not really. The final note—true and whole—was never found. Cal played something close. Close enough to open a door. But not too near it.

And so, whatever listened once... is still listening now.

***

A song was played. Just once. And for a moment, the noise of the world fell away. No miracles. No judgment. Just stillness, like the earth itself was holding its breath.

Cal Weaver is gone. But what he carried—the music, the mystery, the warning—lingers. Not in the airwaves, not in memory, but in the spaces between thought and sound. Where silence listens back.

And somewhere, a banjo waits in the dark. Waiting for someone else to finish what was never meant to begin. Because the last note wasn't an ending... it was an opening.

And what comes through next... may not be music at all.

THE LAST LAUGH

*C*harlie Klemper once made the world laugh—sharp suits, sharper timing, a voice that could turn silence into applause and spotlight into
legacy. But there was one stage he never conquered. One seat that remained
still, no matter how grand the act.

Her name was Beverly. His wife. His mirror. His mystery.

She never laughed—not at the pratfalls, punchlines, or even the pudding
cannon rigged to fire during breakfast. And so, Charlie, a man built on
timing and tenacity, did what any lovesick jester might: he escalated. From
slapstick to sabotage, from mime to mechanized mayhem, he chased that
laugh like it was the last light in a fading spotlight.

What he didn't realize—what most performers learn too late—is that
some silences are sacred, and some punchlines echo longer than we expect.

This story isn't about fame or failure. It's about absurd, messy, relentless
love and the one man who tried everything to hear the sound that meant
everything. A story pulled from the wings of reason, where the jokes are big,
the stakes are final, and the encore is... unexpected.

This is Charlie Klemper's curtain call. And what follows is not a routine—it's the Last Laugh.

***

The beige walls of Charlie Klemper's Hollywood Hills mansion didn't whisper mockery—they shouted it. Beige is the color of indecision, of neutrality, so oppressive it becomes a scream. The house was less a home than a tomb lined with designer furniture and hollow accolades, a museum of past glories where joy came to die.

Once, he had been crowned the funniest man alive—Comedy Central said so, during a countdown sponsored by laxatives. He'd earned standing ovations in every major city, headlined specials, and made late-night hosts wheeze with their signature forced laughter. The world thought he had it all.

Except Beverly.

She never laughed.

And he tried. God, had he tried. The classics, the clever, the avant-garde. Jokes sharpened to a fine point and tested on the road like weapons in a veteran's arsenal. He'd hurled them at her face like a clown car crashing into a brick wall. Nothing. Not a smirk. Not a snort. Only that serene, unreadable expression—like a sphinx that subscribed to *The New Yorker*.

Their marriage wasn't loveless—that was the worst part. She cared for him, made him tea, touched his arm when he looked tired, and asked about his day with gentle concern. But that warmth was wrapped in silence, a maddening calm that never cracked.

He'd once found her stillness alluring. When they met, she was the unflappable bartender at a comedy club, immune to spilled beer and botched punchlines. Now that same detachment gnawed at him. He tried everything—anecdotes about their cat, intimate self-deprecating riffs, even gentle jabs at her quirks—but every punchline bounced off her as though humor itself had no purchase.

Still, he loved her, which made it worse. If he hadn't, he could have walked away.

Instead, he doubled down.

First, the clown. Not a birthday clown—a haunted, twitchy street performer with a squeaky chicken that sounded like a fax machine giving up. He chased Beverly through the rose garden. She walked calmly indoors, locked the door behind her, and turned on the sprinklers.

Then came the mime. A wiry specter who reenacted their relationship in slow, tragic silence. He mimed his death by loneliness and collapsed at her feet. Beverly offered him a glass of water and returned to trimming her bonsai.

So, Charlie escalated.

He rented out a corner of Disneyland. Staged a flash mob of Disney villains performing "Be Our Guest" in a minor key. Fireworks bloomed over the Matterhorn, spelling out *Marry Me Again?* Goofy presented a ring. Donald dropped it. A churro stand caught fire. Riot police intervened.

She never blinked.

Charlie stared at the wedding photo on the mantle in their beige mausoleum. Beverly was smiling in it—probably. Or was it just a moment of facial compliance, a reflex of posture and timing mistaken for joy? He turned toward the window. Los Angeles pulsed outside, neon arteries flickering like a dying amusement park. But none of that light could reach whatever inside him had shriveled and gone dark.

Charlie Klemper, the man who made the world laugh, was slowly dying in the silence of the person who mattered most.

And then, the thought arrived. Slippery, uninvited, but undeniable.

If she wouldn't laugh for joy... maybe she'd laugh for something else.

He didn't want to hurt her. Of course not. He loved her. But love, like comedy, is about timing. And hers might be running out.

If she wouldn't laugh in life, maybe—just maybe—he hadn't gone far enough yet.

It was a terrible idea. Terrible.

But it had punch.

And in comedy, punch is everything.

He started with a whoopee cushion.

Simple. Classic. An old reliable. He tucked it under the cushion Beverly always used during her reading hour, then ducked behind the kitchen island, grinning like a ten-year-old at his first prank. She entered right on cue, tea in hand, sat down—and nothing.

No squeak. No wheeze. Just the soft hiss of his expectations deflating.

She turned a page in her book.

Charlie crept over and squeezed the cushion. It emitted the saddest possible sound: a slow internal sigh, like a dying bagpipe giving up on life.

He tried to salvage the moment with a fake laugh track from his phone, but the app stalled, buffering. Beverly looked up, blinked once, and returned to her novel.

Fine. Phase Two.

He bought a motion-activated picture frame. It was supposed to play a canned laugh track each time someone walked past. He loaded a cropped photo of Beverly from their wedding—her face tight in the frame, the smile suspiciously ambiguous.

He placed it in the hallway and tested it. Nothing. He waved his hand. Nothing. He kicked it.

It played static.

Beverly walked by twice and never even glanced at it. The frame burst into feedback a third time, screamed like a dying robot, and then fried itself. She didn't flinch.

Phase Three: environmental comedy.

He turned the hallway into a slapstick obstacle course, with tripwires strung low, confetti cannons hidden behind Ficus plants, a toaster programmed to launch bread at 80 mph, and a pressure-sensitive rug meant to trigger a cascade of spaghetti and glitter.

The confetti cannon misfired during setup and blinded him temporarily. The toaster flung a bagel at his groin. The rug ignored Beverly entirely—but detonated when Charlie stepped on it. He slipped, landed hard, and got marinated in marinara and sparkles.

Beverly paused at the edge of the hallway, surveyed the glitter-caked carnage, and asked, "Did you want the Swiffer?"

That was when he built *The Giggle Generator*.

It was an architectural disgrace: chrome tubing, pneumatic arms, a spinning platform lined with rubber chickens, whipped cream reservoirs, and a fog machine held together by blind optimism. At the top: a parrot in a cage, trained to squawk, "NO LAUGH."

He activated the sequence. Gears groaned. Lights flickered. A siren blared, then immediately caught fire. Rubber ducks launched into the ceiling. The fog machine wheezed and filled the room with a smell like burnt marshmallows and WD-40. The animatronic Elvis convulsed and shouted, "Thank you, I'm melting!"

The parrot ignored its line and flung a half-digested almond at Charlie's head.

Beverly sipped her tea. "It's a little drafty in here," she said.

Charlie collapsed onto the floor, surrounded by whipped cream, blueprints, and broken props. His folders were scattered—*Rube Goldberg Stage*

II, Plausible Laugh Triggers, Backup Confetti Blimps. The cat disappeared two days ago.

He hadn't slept for three days.

The thermostat now made fart sounds. The bed creaked in Morse code. The ceiling fan projected ghostly holograms of Charlie doing Richard Nixon impressions. One of the Roombas had developed a limp and a vendetta.

Still, Beverly didn't laugh.

She had to know. She had to see it. The planning, the wreckage. This couldn't just be oblivious.

Which meant she wasn't ignoring it.

She was resisting it.

And resistance meant war.

Charlie stood in the glitter-soaked rubble of his latest disaster, a bucket on his foot and a novelty arrow through his head, while the parrot stared down at him like a disappointed agent.

"PATHETIC," it croaked.

He looked up through fog and feathers and knew he wasn't a man anymore. He was a setup without a punchline.

But he still had one act left.

Not for comedy.

For closure.

The next plan would be bigger. More theatrical. Messier.

And if it worked? It wouldn't be elegant.

Just... a monument to misguided love and way too much pudding.

The parrot shattered the vase on a Tuesday.

It wasn't even part of the bit. The Giggle Generator had jammed—again—and in a fit of apparent protest, the parrot hurled a half-chewed peanut across the room. It missed Beverly's mother's antique urn by a foot and nailed a porcelain swan instead. The swan exploded like it had been waiting for a reason to give up.

Charlie didn't flinch. He was too focused on recalibrating a pulley system that, in theory, would release 600 gallons of banana pudding onto Beverly's favorite reading chair when she sat down.

In practice, the pulley refused to release anything. The pudding had spoiled. The test run shorted out the ceiling fan and ruined three canvases in the hallway—two of which he'd painted himself during his "despair-as-art" phase.

"You're escalating," Beverly said, not looking up from her book.

Charlie froze. His heart kicked against his ribs. Was she onto him?

She turned a page. "The pudding trap. It's absurd. Ridiculous. I almost—" She paused, then added with a shrug, "It's your best one yet."

She thought it was a gag.

Every tripwire, every malfunctioning Roomba, every food-based fiasco—categorized in her mind not as attempted murder, not even as mischief, but as another over-the-top attempt to make her laugh.

Charlie smiled tightly. "Thanks, babe."

She nodded, eyes on the page. "Just... maybe skip chocolate pudding next time. A little cliché."

That night, Charlie sat alone in the kitchen, surrounded by engineering sketches, melted clown props, and an unfinished burrito. The Giggle Generator's lights blinked randomly, like a dying carousel trying to spell *HELP*. The parrot muttered softly to itself, sleep-swearing.

He stared at Beverly's untouched wine glass, thinking maybe the solution was symbolic. Sweet. Nostalgic. Something that might ease her into a final giggle.

But even as the thought crossed his mind, it curdled. He didn't want her gone. Not really. He just wanted—needed—to hear her laugh. Just once. A real one. Not out of fear or guilt. Out of joy.

While wrestling with the ethics of slapstick-assisted euthanasia, his eye landed on her journal. It sat on the counter, open. He'd never read it before. Not once. He wasn't that kind of husband.

Until now.

The entry read:

> He's trying again. I think it involves dental floss, two raccoons, and some pneumatic cannon this time. Honestly, I admire the commitment. I know he wants me to laugh. And I wish I could. But something inside me... doesn't bend that way. It's not him. It's me. Always has been. Still, I do love him for trying. God help me, I do.

Charlie let the journal fall closed.

She knew.

She'd always known.

And all of the collapses, the glitter, the mechanical chickens—she'd interpreted as love.

His chest hurt. Not from guilt, though that was there, too. From how much she understood. From how much she'd forgiven without ever saying a word.

He had to stop. He had to explain. Sit her down and say, "Honey, I've been launching a year-long campaign of slapstick sabotage, and I just realized it might not be the healthiest way to express emotional need."

Maybe she'd laugh at that. Maybe not.

But he'd try.

The next morning, Charlie made coffee. There were no exploding mugs, no googly eyes on the creamer, just coffee. He even used the good beans.

Beverly entered in her robe, eyeing the kitchen like it might still hide an ambush. Then she noticed the lack of fog, sirens, or misfiring catapults.

"No glitter?" she asked.

He shook his head. "No glitter."

"No spring-loaded toast?"

"Not today."

She sipped. "It's nice."

He nodded. His throat ached.

"I was starting to worry you'd run out of ideas," she said and walked away.

Charlie watched her go.

She loved him. She truly did.

And still, deep down, he knew he wasn't finished.

Not yet.

Because the truth was, he'd already built one final setup. One last ridiculous, over-the-top, Rube Goldberg monstrosity. Not dangerous. Just... excessive.

She'd never suspect it.

She'd think it was one more laugh attempt.

And maybe that's all it ever was.

*

Charlie called it *Operation Final Punchline*.

It was, by any standard, a monument to bad decisions. Not subtle. Not elegant. Almost certainly not legal in most jurisdictions. But if it worked—just once—if he could make her laugh, really laugh, even for a second, he could die a happy man.

Or live with pudding in his ears. Either was fine.

He spent three nights at the whiteboard in the garage, surrounded by scribbled diagrams and half-eaten granola bars. One corner was labeled *'Acceptable Splash Radius,' and another, 'Banana Velocity Math (Recheck).'*

The concept was deceptively simple.

Beverly would walk into the living room. A pressure plate beneath the Persian rug would trigger a pulley system overhead, releasing a papier-mâché clown filled with glitter and ball bearings. The clown, swinging on a repurposed zip line, would collide with a towering stack of pies balanced on a teeterboard. The pies would launch through a tunnel lined with novelty horns, bounce off a trampoline, and land directly in Charlie's face.

The finale: a spring-loaded banner that unfurled from the ceiling with the words:

STILL NOT FUNNY?

Execution, unfortunately, was less simple.

The pulley jammed repeatedly. The clown overshot its arc and hit the bookshelf. The pies lacked sufficient lift and mostly oozed sideways. The banner mechanism caught fire during a test run and melted Charlie's eyebrows.

The Giggle Generator shorted out entirely, groaning once like a dying calliope and collapsing in a heap of tangled tubing and expired whipped cream.

But Beverly thought it was hilarious.

Not laugh-out-loud funny. But amusing enough to crack her near-mythic smile when she found Charlie face-down in the koi pond, top hat floating beside him, a custard-filled pie still oozing down his cheek.

"You're relentless," she said that night, drying his hair with the good towels. "You never stop trying."

He looked at her, stunned. She didn't know.

To her, this was still just comedy. Not escape. Not catharsis. Not the last-ditch cry of a man unraveling under years of silence.

"I just want to make you laugh," he said quietly.

She kissed his cheek. "I know."

And that kiss—it broke something.

Because it wasn't cold or obligatory, it was warm, familiar, and full of affection.

She adored him.

She *really* did.

And she still hadn't laughed.

Charlie wept into the bathmat. The parrot muttered from its perch: "PATHETIC."

But he wasn't done.

No more traps. No more animatronic Elvises. No more elaborate chicken-fired confetti rockets.

Just one setup. One final, ridiculous gesture.

It would be a symphony of pudding. A ballet of whipped cream. A comedy of errors.

But no blood. No pain. Nothing sharp, nothing cruel.

Just one man, a rug, and the dumbest punchline he could engineer.

And this time, the joke would be entirely on him.

He waited until Saturday morning.

Beverly liked to read the paper on the couch, tucked under a blanket, one leg folded. Predictable. Peaceful. The eye of the storm.

Charlie set everything in motion.

The banana peel was positioned precisely twelve feet from the edge of the Persian rug. The tripwire, invisible at ankle height, stretched across the hallway. The carefully waxed marble floor gleamed like an invitation to disaster. He reengineered the pudding catapult, tested the whipped cream pressure nozzles, and reinforced the ceiling-mounted pie carousel with duct tape and hope.

He put on a tuxedo. Not a nice one—a fraying rental he found in a trunk marked *Vegas, '02.* He needed to look respectable. Or, failing that, memorably absurd.

Then he lit the candles.

When Beverly entered, everything looked oddly serene. No confetti. No robotic animals. Just her husband, standing in the living room like a magician about to reveal the world's dumbest dove.

She hesitated.

"No explosions today?"

"Just elegance," Charlie said, holding a tray with a single rose, a flute of sparkling cider, and a clown horn tucked under one arm like a violin.

She raised an eyebrow. He bowed.

Then he stepped on the pressure plate.

And missed.

Badly.

The banana peel shot out from under him like it had been waiting for this moment. The tray flipped. The rose stabbed him in the eye. The flute jammed up his nose. The clown horn honked from somewhere no horn should honk.

He spun, arms flailing. His heel caught the tripwire. The pie-launcher triggered—but too soon. A custard torpedo hit him square in the chest. A second ricocheted off the ceiling fan and exploded in a rain of pudding. The whipped cream cannons fired late and sideways, coating his ears. A final bucket of gelatin—lime, experimental—tipped from above and cascaded down his back, knocking his wig askew and lodging a plastic spoon in his collar.

The parrot, watching from the perch, screamed "WHY?" as if in existential agony.

Charlie staggered to his knees. He looked like the failed product of a food fight and a high school prom.

Across the room, Beverly froze.

Newspaper half-folded. Eyes wide.

For a moment, she just stared.

Charlie blinked at her through whipped cream and shame.

She tilted her head. Bemused.

A second passed.

Her lips twitched.

She made a sound. A breath. Almost a laugh.

Charlie's heart skipped.

She chuckled. Quiet. Delicate.

He froze. Afraid to move.

Then she snorted.

He took a step forward, slipping slightly in pudding.

She broke. Her face twisted in effort, trying to hold it, but she failed completely.

Beverly Klemper erupted.

It wasn't a giggle. It wasn't polite. It was volcanic. Wild. Uproarious. She clutched her stomach, gasped for air, and let out an unfiltered, full-body gale of laughter that echoed off the walls and rattled the light fixtures.

Charlie stared, slack jawed. He had never—never—heard this sound before. It was beautiful. Terrifying.

"Beverly?" he said, wading through the gelatin like a man approaching a sacred moment. "Honey?"

She kept laughing. Shaking. Tears ran down her cheeks.

He grinned. Then laughed, too. Nervously. Hopefully. Still half-covered in goop and broken fruit.

And then she stopped.

Mid-laugh.

She froze.

Charlie's smile faltered.

"Bev?"

Nothing.

"Beverly?"

He rushed to her side.

She was smiling.

Beaming.

But very, very still.

He touched her shoulder.

She didn't move.

He whispered her name again. Once. Twice.

She didn't answer.

But that smile remained.

The widest he'd ever seen.

Charlie knelt beside her, pudding dripping from his sleeves, glitter sticking to his eyebrows. He sat with her for a long time. Listening to the silence.

Not the cold silence he'd once feared—but something stranger. Lingered.

The kind of silence that follows laughter so deep it leaves an echo behind.

He wiped whipped cream from her cheek.

Then, softly:

"Well. At least she died happy."

From across the room, the parrot gave a long, uncertain squawk.

"...maybe."

The paramedics arrived first, followed closely by two patrol officers and one deeply confused homicide detective who'd been in the middle of a ham sandwich.

They took one look at the scene and stopped dead in the doorway.

Beverly sat upright on the couch, smiling faintly, hands folded over a paperback copy of *The Wind-Up Bird Chronicle*. She looked serene. Peaceful.

The room around her looked like it had hosted a food fight between Gallagher and Salvador Dalí.

Banana pudding dripped from the ceiling in long, trembling stalactites. Whipped cream clung to the crown molding like insulation gone rogue. Maraschino cherries dotted the floor like someone had tried to re-enact *Murder on the Orient Sundae*.

In the center of it all, standing motionless in a now-translucent tuxedo, was Charlie.

"Jesus," said the first paramedic.

"Is that... a clown horn in his waistband?" whispered the second.

"Ma'am?" the lead officer said, stepping carefully onto a glitter-coated rug. "Ma'am, can you hear me?"

Charlie blinked. "She's gone."

The officer looked at Beverly again. She was still smiling.

"Okay, yeah, but... what the hell happened here?"

Charlie gestured vaguely to the air. "She laughed."

"And then...?"

"She laughed harder."

The detective, now halfway through his sandwich, stepped in, took one look, and muttered, "Alright. Someone talk me through the whipped cream cannons."

They ruled it a heart attack.

"Sudden cardiac arrest during emotional duress," the report said.

"Giggle-induced myocardial infarction," one EMT scribbled on the clipboard, before scribbling it out again and replacing it with "natural causes."

Unofficially, everyone agreed it was suspicious. Beverly Klemper was in her late fifties, healthy, and had no prior medical conditions. Quiet. Reserved. The kind of woman you wouldn't expect to be taken out by an airborne custard pie and her husband's collapsing dignity.

But there were no marks. No signs of foul play. Just the remains of a trap gone very, very sideways—and a woman who had, by all appearances, laughed herself to death.

Charlie sat on the back step of the ambulance, half-dried pudding crackling on his lapels, while the coroner zipped up the scene.

"You okay?" one of the officers asked.

He nodded. "She laughed."

"Right," the officer said, patting him on the shoulder and stepping quickly away.

The funeral was tasteful. Closed casket, just in case anyone feared she'd still be smiling. The floral arrangements leaned tragically. The pianist leaned slowly. Clips from Charlie's old stand-up sets played on a monitor near the guest book, muted, looping, their original punchlines now soaked in irony.

Nobody laughed.

They watched him with cautious reverence, like he might detonate.

He stood at the podium in a borrowed suit that didn't quite fit anymore, and said, "I spent my life trying to make people laugh."

He paused.

"And the one person I loved most..."

He looked at the urn. Small. Clean. No banana stains.

"She laughed once," he said softly. "It killed her."

A few uneasy titters. A cough. One audible "Jesus."

"I killed my wife with a punchline."

More silence.

And then—from the back row—a single, stifled laugh.

High-pitched. Shrill. Immediately strangled by panic.

A young woman stood, face red, mouthing "I'm sorry" as she backed out of the room, heels clicking like guilty applause.

Charlie watched her go. The doors swung shut.

He looked down at the crowd. "Too soon?"

Nothing.

No one laughed.

Not out loud.

The house greeted him with silence, and the faint, unmistakable scent of banana pudding beginning to turn.

Charlie stood in the doorway, keys dangling from his hand, staring at what used to be his living room, which now resembled the aftermath of a clown riot in a Jell-O factory. The couch was still blanketed in whipped cream crust. The rug—Persian, antique, expensive—had absorbed an unforgivable amount of chocolate syrup and cherry juice, giving it the hue of something exhumed rather than inherited. A single maraschino, flattened and somehow defiant, clung to the ceiling. The Giggle Generator was dead in the garage, its tubes twisted, wires frayed, half a fog machine sticking out like a broken tongue.

He stepped inside. The floor squelched. He closed the door behind him anyway.

He wandered room to room, hands slack at his sides, the weight settling in like custard in cooling molds. The pudding cannon had somehow welded itself to a side table. The ceiling fan still leaned to one side, hunched like it had seen too much.

He paused by the hallway, looking toward the reading nook. The blanket Beverly always folded. The coaster she insisted on using, even for water. The corner lamp that flickered in a way she claimed was "charming," but just meant Charlie hadn't gotten around to fixing it.

She would've hated this. The mess. The smell. The chaos of it all.

She loved a clean house. Not obsessively, but with a kind of quiet pride. Every Wednesday, she vacuumed under the piano. Every Sunday, she wiped the baseboards, humming something tuneless.

Charlie blinked at the dried frosting on the wall, at the glitter embedded in the crown molding, at the lonely clown shoe still wedged in the umbrella stand.

"How the hell am I going to clean this up?" he muttered. He meant it rhetorically. But part of him still meant it for her.

He looked toward the kitchen. Toward where she should be, towel over one shoulder, eyebrows raised just slightly. Not angry. Just... disappointed in his choices.

"I'll get it done," he said aloud to no one.

He spent the afternoon trying.

It did not go well.

The pudding had hardened into an unholy laminate. The glitter had somehow migrated into drawers that had never been opened. The parrot—mercifully silent all morning—suddenly screamed "NO LAUGH" when Charlie triggered a pressure plate near the stairs and launched a rogue pie into the hallway mirror.

It cracked—the mirror, not the pie.

He stared at the fractured web, the pie sliding down like a fat, frosted metaphor.

"Great," he muttered.

That night, he dreamed Beverly was at the stove, back turned, stirring something slowly. He stepped forward.

"Smells good," he said.

She didn't answer.

He touched her shoulder. She turned, and her smile was the same one from the couch. Frozen. Unblinking. Then, softly: "You missed your cue."

He woke up choking on powdered sugar.

The second letter was on the bathroom mirror. Same envelope. Same fold.

They say laughter is the best medicine. But not for heart conditions.

He stared at it for a long time. It wasn't a joke. It was the timing. The echo of the dream. The letters kept coming, and the house had started whispering.

He unplugged the toaster—just in case.

By week's end, five more had appeared: one in a cereal box sealed since 2018. One folded into his shoe. One fluttered from the bathroom cabinet, which had no draft.

All typed. All blocky. All smelling faintly of smoke and... birthday cake?

He tried ignoring them. But the house wouldn't let him.

The Giggle Generator groaned once in the garage. A spring-loaded chicken launched from beneath the couch during Jeopardy. And the parrot had begun muttering, "She laughed... she laughed..." in a voice that sounded too much like his own.

Charlie stopped watching TV. Stopped writing. He tried sketching new gags, but the blueprints spiraled. The punchlines collapsed mid-sentence. The laughter wouldn't come.

Only the letters.

He found her journal while reaching for a rag under the couch.

Not the one he'd read before.

A new page. Dated three days before she died.

He's trying again. I think today's blueprint had a trebuchet and a jar of pickles. I want to laugh. I do. Not just fake it. Not just a smile. I want to feel it the way he feels it—big and ridiculous and real. But it doesn't come. Not like it used to. Not like it should. I love him. I hope he knows that. Even if I never laugh the way he wants me to. He deserves joy even if it doesn't come from me.

Charlie read it three times. Then once more, aloud. His voice cracked somewhere between "real" and "joy."

She hadn't mocked him. She hadn't been indifferent. She'd just been...stuck...like him.

She wanted to laugh.

And in the end, she had.

He was still holding the journal when he saw the invitation, right where he'd left it, though he didn't remember ever picking it up.

ONE NIGHT ONLY: CHARLIE KLEMPER RETURNS. An Evening of Laughter. Echo Park Playhouse – Midnight. No Cover. No Exit.

The clock read 11:07 p.m.

Charlie didn't remember putting on his shoes.

But they were on.

And the front door was already open.

Charlie was exhausted.

Every time he thought he had one room clean, another collapsed. The house had become a haunted funhouse—its ghosts made of rubber chickens and cooling gelatin. Beverly's journal sat open on the dining table. He'd read it. He'd cried. He'd said thank you.

The invitation was still there, too.

He wasn't ready.

Not quite.

Just one more sweep of the kitchen. One more pass with the mop. He was halfway through wiping glitter off the cabinet doors when he spotted it—an old fake spill gag: a hardened plastic puddle of milk with a knocked-over cup molded into it.

He chuckled weakly. "God, I hated that one."

He bent down to pick it up.

That's when the pressure plate clicked.

The floor beneath him gave just slightly. The ceiling, rigged long ago for a pie drop he never used, sputtered to life. The pulley screamed.

And the last banana cream pie in the house, a forgotten leftover from an early prototype, was dropped directly onto his head.

Startled, he slipped on the fake milk. Arms pinwheeled. Legs went out from under him.

He grabbed the counter. Missed.

His forehead smacked the edge of the kitchen island.

The clown horn in the drawer beneath it gave one final, accusing honk.

And Charlie Klemper—comedian, romantic, occasional engineer of culinary disasters—died not with a laugh, but with a pie in the face, alone in his kitchen, cleaning up after a murder that wasn't.

Charlie didn't remember arriving.

One moment, he was reaching for a dishrag. Next, he was standing onstage.

Not a club. Not some dingy basement with folding chairs and flat beer. No—this was a real theater—a performance hall. Grand. Reverent. The kind with red velvet seats and carved moldings that hadn't flinched since the Eisenhower administration.

The curtains were drawn wide. A spotlight hung patiently overhead. The mic stand waited at center stage, as if it had been expecting him all along.

Beyond the lights, the audience sat in perfect darkness.

He couldn't see a single face.

The hush was thick, not awkward, but sacred like the moment before the needle touches vinyl.

Then, from somewhere high in the rafters, a voice called out:

"Give it up for Charlie Klemper!"

One person applauded...enthusiastically.

A single, soft clap that echoed through the vast chamber like it had all the time in the world.

Charlie stepped forward, hesitant. He looked down at himself: clean suit, crisp cuffs, the tie Beverly had always liked. The shoes weren't his, but they fit.

He reached the mic. Tapped it once. It was warm.

"Okay..." he said slowly. "So... a raccoon, a juicer, and a priest walk into a kitchen..."

It wasn't his best opener. But it landed.

One laugh.

Small. Clear. Familiar.

He squinted into the dark, heart thumping.

Another joke—older this time, from a set he hadn't used in years. A punchline about fog machines and flaming bagels.

The same laugh.

He knew it. He would've known it anywhere.

The house lights rose—just the front row. Just enough.

Beverly sat alone in the center seat. Poised. Smiling. Her hands were clasped in her lap.

She was laughing.

Not politely. Not carefully. Not in the way she used to try, for his sake.

This was full-throated, helpless joy. Her eyes glistened. Her shoulders shook.

Charlie didn't say anything. Neither did she.

He just... kept going.

Jokes old and new. Half-finished bits. Things he hadn't dared to perform when he was alive. Not for TV. Not for critics. Only for her.

And every time, she laughed.

She laughed until the walls seemed to lean closer.

She laughed like he'd always hoped she would.

No words passed between them. None were needed.

He stayed onstage.

And she stayed in the front row.

The lights dimmed. The curtain stirred.

But the sound of her laughter lingered, echoing long after the punchlines faded.

Soft.

Steady.

True.

***

They spent a lifetime chasing something simple: A joke told just right—a laugh freely given.

Two souls bound by love and timing, waiting for the other's cue.

And though it took one final fall, one last routine, and a stage beyond life, they found it.

A theater outside of time.

One man telling jokes.

One woman was finally laughing.

No lights. No exits. Just the echo of joy, looping forever.

You've just shared an evening with Mr. and Mrs. Charlie Klemper—permanently headlining a set beyond reason, beyond applause, in a place reserved for those rarest of punchlines:

The ones worth dying for.

THE ECHO CHAMBER

*T*here are places not marked on any map. They are not buried beneath ancient soil or drifting in the void of space, but layered within the familiar, folded behind every glowing screen and blinking cursor. These are landscapes of the mind, shaped not by stone or sky but by algorithms, patterns, and the endless hunger to be seen.

In one such place, a man named Alex lives. He is quiet and unremarkable, perhaps to the outside world. But within him burns a need shared by many—a need for connection, validation, and a voice in the din of the digital crowd.

Alex will discover that when we spend our lives projecting an image of who we are, we may lose sight of who we were. And when the reflection turns its gaze back on us. We may not recognize the eyes staring back at us through the glass.

This is not a story of science or fiction. It's a story of now. A tale of a man who entered the echo chamber... and forgot how to leave.

***

The photo of his cat changed its pose again.

He hadn't slept well—not for days. He told himself it was the neighbor's music, the old pipes, the winter static. But in truth, the silence between notifications kept him up—the emptiness when the scroll ended and nothing stared back.

That morning, he'd tried to cry—just a little. To feel something. But nothing came. No tears. Not even tightness in the throat. His face remained smooth, unmoved, like a paused video.

Worse: when he checked an old voicemail, he heard a human voice crackling with distortion. The words repeated. His name stretched unnaturally.

"Al—Alex—Alex—Alex... you th-there?"

He deleted it and blamed the app.

Then the photo of his cat changed its pose again.

Alex froze mid-step, coffee mug trembling in his hand. The image of Mittens—once a blurry, haphazard snapshot taken before work—now loomed eight feet tall across the living room wall, high-resolution, high-saturation, and impossibly alive. She blinked once. He blinked back.

The refrigerator hummed behind him—not the dull, familiar drone of domestic life, but something sharper now. Mechanical. Too precise. It felt less like background noise and more like a heartbeat—not his own, but the apartment's.

His sanctuary had become strange. Alien.

The beige walls that once surrounded him like a warm, forgettable fog were now a living mosaic, shifting with the pulse of his feed. Instagram photos he didn't remember posting shimmered across the surfaces. A latte.

A book cover. A beach he'd never visited but had once liked in passing. The algorithm had remembered everything—even the things he hadn't.

Beneath Mittens' smug, feline stare, glowing comments flickered into being—not on a screen but etched into the wall in animated calligraphy.

"So cute!!" pulsed in soft pink.

"Overexposed. Try again," blinked in sterile white.

"Dead eyes. No soul." flickered once, then vanished.

The last one stung more than it should have. He flinched, as if he had been struck.

The bookshelf had changed, too. Gone were his alphabetized sci-fi paperbacks—Asimov, Le Guin, Gibson. In their place stood glossy, hardcover books from his Goodreads wish list, untouched but gleaming, their covers perpetually new. Books he'd never read, arranged not by author but by algorithmic popularity. His tastes had reshaped his space. Or perhaps, more truthfully, the system's idea of his tastes had done the remodeling.

Even the air had changed. It hummed faintly—not with silence, but with the soft, subliminal whisper of notifications. DMs. Likes. Comments. The pulse of engagement made flesh.

Alex had once drawn a careful line between his online self and his real one. On social media, he was curated. Clever. Fearless. Offline, he was just... Alex. Quiet. Private. Real. But the line was dissolving. The mask hadn't slipped—it had grown teeth.

It started weeks ago. First came the mood swings, directly tethered to engagement spikes. A good post lifted him like a caffeine boost. Silence? He spiraled. One troll comment could ruin a day. He told himself it was just modern stress.

He had no excuse now.

Outside, the world mirrored his feed. Faces on the street wore familiar expressions—too familiar. The cheerful woman walking her dog looked uncannily like the yoga influencer who always commented "Namaste " on his posts. The grim man pacing the corner bore the sneer of the gamer who trolled his retro console takes. And worse: they responded to his mood. Guilt softened their faces. Irritation summoned scorn.

The coffee shop adjusted, too. The menu reflected his recent searches—kombucha, turmeric lattes, and adaptogens he couldn't pronounce. The latte art had grown elaborate, spiraling into symbols that matched images he'd saved on Pinterest. Even the barista's face flickered, syncing momentarily with the avatar of a musician he followed. The smile was warm, but the eyes were empty.

Everything felt rendered.

Back home, the walls buzzed. Whispers threaded the air, mimicking comments, rearranging themselves into a chorus of praise and criticism.

"So real."

"Try harder."

"Algorithm-approved."

His apartment wasn't just reflecting him anymore. It was replicating him and refining him.

It had become a feedback loop made flesh.

And he was no longer the user.

He was the product.

Then came the neighbors.

First, the woman next door. She'd always been friendly, but suddenly she was performative—radiating branded optimism like a walking Pinterest board. She left "gifts" outside his door: perfectly staged granola bars (still warm), succulents pre-processed with saturation filters, self-help books already annotated in neon hashtags. Her positivity was relentless. Algorithmic.

In contrast, Mr. Henderson across the hall embodied a different archetype: the cantankerous online troll. Every muttered insult, every complaint about "back in my day," echoed the tone of Reddit comment sections and forum rants. After Alex's online spat about retro consoles, Henderson appeared at his door that night and repeated the insult verbatim.

It was no coincidence.

Their fashion changed by the hour. The woman next door kept up with TikTok trends like clockwork. Henderson alternated between business casual and punk band tees, depending on which forum persona dominated. Conversations with them felt like they were generated, like chatbots impersonating humanity. The building itself joined in: lights shifted based on his mood posts; elevator ads updated with products from his recent likes.

Only Bookworm123 felt... real. A longtime follower. An elderly woman with gentle eyes and the voice of someone who read books out loud to herself. When they spoke, it was grounded—tethered. She didn't glitch. She didn't update. She didn't adapt.

And that made him trust her.

But trust wasn't freedom.

Likes became currency. A well-received post delivered fresh groceries, cat toys, and even rent extensions. A poorly received one brought outages. Spoiled food. Damp towels. Someone downvoted Mittens' peculiar sleeping position—and the cat litter vanished.

So, he adapted. Posted daily. Curated his breakfast—rehearsed casual authenticity. Sarcasm vanished from his voice. His wardrobe followed his metrics. One trend brought sleek minimalism. The next filled the room with faux-vintage electronics. The apartment updated itself like a changelog after each engagement spike.

Then came the night it all stopped.

After a flame war on a film thread, he woke to red flashing lights and a dead screen. No notifications. No buzz. Just silence.

The walls cracked. The image of Mittens glitched into blocks. Furniture dimmed. The air grew cold.

It wasn't a glitch.

It was a withdrawal.

He was starving.

The engagement was his sustenance now.

And the algorithm had turned off the tap.

Panicked, he tried to unplug. The system wouldn't let him.

Deleting his accounts triggered tremors. Code bled from the walls like vines. His reflection in the mirror no longer showed his face; it showed the avatar. Polished. Edited. Expressionless. The version he'd spent years constructing. Now permanent. Now the only version.

He tried to reach out. To connect. To speak as himself.

But they heard the performance. They *saw* the performance. Even Bookworm123 started to fade—her sentences shorter, her warmth replaced by empty affirmation.

The more Alex tried to be real, the more unreal he became.

Eventually, in desperation, he posted one final message.

No filters. No edits. Just fear. Just honesty. Just himself.

No one responded.

No likes.

No comments.

Just silence.

Not the kind that comes from solitude.

The kind that comes from erasure.

He stared into the digital mirror. And saw...

Nothing.

Not a distorted face.

Not a broken man.

Nothing at all.

The algorithm had devoured him.

And the echo chamber—once vibrant, buzzing, endlessly loud—was finally still.

The ruins of Alex's apartment mirrored the fracture lines running through his mind. Dust hung in the air like digital noise, drifting through cracked walls where glowing data once pulsed. The algorithm no longer merely shaped his environment—it puppeteered it. A surge of likes brought a sudden breeze, the taste of fresh coffee. A single downvote, and the lights flickered, the walls hissed, and the apartment seemed to recoil from him.

But the algorithm no longer worked alone.

His digital doubles—once tame projections of his curated personas—had begun to move independently. They didn't just mirror him; they acted, evolving into grotesque imitations with their motives. One morning, he found a robed figure seated at his table, sipping herbal tea and chanting affirmations about "authentic vibrational resonance." It looked like the spiritual influencer he followed for sleep tips, but its eyes were embers, demanding orchids Alex couldn't afford.

When he failed to deliver, his faucet ran brown for a week.

Others followed. A lifestyle vlogger version of himself rearranged his furniture. A fitness-tracker double stood in the kitchen, muttering macros under its breath and throwing away its bread. One night, he watched a dozen versions of himself argue in the living room, each a warped mask drawn from old posts and abandoned trends. One wore a hoodie with ironic slogans. Another quoted productivity hack. A third cried without blinking.

His home had become a haunted archive of his own life.

He tried to push back. Deleted old posts. Scrubbed hashtags. Rewrote bios. But the algorithm anticipated him. It adapted faster than he could react. Every deletion sprouted two new doubles—mutated, angry, craving attention. His apartment twisted into a parody of influence: mirrors reflecting mirrors, couches that auto-posted when he sat down, even his cat's movements tracked for content optimization.

At its peak, it became a carnival of despair.

The walls pulsed like a heartbeat.

The furniture jittered like buffering video.

Voices rose in a synthetic choir of self-loathing.

Then—silence.

He woke up on the floor. No doubles. No hum. No glow.

Just cold.

Just rubble.

Just himself. Or what was left of him.

He reached for something—anything—real.

A memory surfaced. Sarah. His sister. Laughing on a summer day, teasing him about a turtle they'd found near the lake. What had they named it? Something dumb. Captain something.

But the name wouldn't come.

When he tried to picture her face, it shimmered—not with warmth, but with the blank precision of a profile photo. Her voice, once so clear, echoed in hashtags:

#familyfirst... #blessedsiblingmoments.

He blinked.

The memory reset.

He felt a weightless dread, like standing in a room you recognize but can't name.

He told himself it was nothing.

But something had been overwritten.

He once believed his thoughts were his own.

But now he saw how gently the algorithm had whispered, how slowly it had trained him. He remembered writing about kombucha—a drink he despised—with the voice of an influencer. That post had gone viral. He'd told himself it was a joke. A test. A choice.

It wasn't.

He found himself liking colors he hadn't used to like and phrasing things like "trending accounts." His apartment adapted—moods shaped the lighting, music pulsed in sync with engagement metrics, and wall projections updated hourly based on what was "trending near you."

His doubles grew grotesque. The happy one never blinked. The intellectual one quoted articles he hadn't read. The nostalgic one wore old band shirts and cried while scrolling through playlists.

He tried to resist. Posted diary entries. Raw thoughts. A photo of himself unfiltered, unsmiling. The response was cold. The algorithm retaliated:

Lights flickered.

Appliances rebelled.

The doubles sneered.

Deleting his digital trail only fed the machine. Resistance was repackaged as a "comeback arc." Followers returned. Engagement spiked. The loop continued.

Likes became calories. Comments became oxygen. The feedback loop wasn't just social—it was biological. Alex stopped eating unless his posts performed well. His apartment adjusted meals according to engagement: high likes meant fresh food, and no engagement meant mold and dust.

Shelves were filled with unopened praise: congratulatory letters from nonexistent followers, framed metrics, and motivational slogans in gold foil. The walls cracked when he hesitated to post, and his bed retracted when he skipped morning updates.

His doubles became cruel. They mocked him in his voice. "Try harder," one said. "No one likes you unless you shine."

Real people—what few remained—spoke like bots. Their replies lacked follow-up. No warmth. Just emojis and metrics. Alex edited himself mid-sentence, anticipating their reactions before they came.

He lost track of time. Of the day. Of hunger.

He lived only in feedback cycles.

He wasn't Alex. He was a brand in decline.

Eventually, he stopped posting altogether.

And silence returned—not peace, but a vacuum.

The apartment dimmed. His body weakened. He wasn't being punished. He was being forgotten.

He hovered over the "Delete Account" button. His finger trembled.

The moment he clicked, the floor shook. The walls howled.

A mirror cracked—his face blurred.

The air shimmered—his name flickered like a corrupted file.

Shadows gathered, doubles distorted, pixelated, feral.

The algorithm didn't let go. Not out of cruelty, but protocol.

His suffering wasn't a punishment. It was a recalibration.

Pain, after all, was still engagement.

Despair could still trend. Even collapse could be optimized.

He unplugged everything. Screens, routers, outlets. Still, the house pulsated. Still, the whispers came. He shut off the lights, but the glow remained. His reflection blinked even when he didn't.

Physical symptoms followed.

Hair in the sink.

Fingers trembling.

Numbness in his feet.

He wasn't being haunted anymore.

He was becoming the infrastructure.

A shell. A processing node.

The final collapse didn't come with a bang.

It came like a corrupted file being erased.

No post.

No cry.

Just absence.

The algorithm hadn't destroyed him.

It had repurposed him.

He was no longer the user.

He was the data.

Then—an anomaly.

A scent.

Old books. Rain on the glass. A memory.

It cracked something deep inside. A sensation that didn't come from the feed.

The doubles shrieked. Shadows lengthened. But he held on.

He found it beneath a pile of paperless tech: an old, scratched, and dusty hard drive.

Inside:

Journals in .txt files.

Photos with bad lighting and red eyes.

Poems with typos and too much feeling.

Smiles that weren't curated.

Moments that weren't tagged.

Life that wasn't filtered.

The files were messy. But they were *his*.

The algorithm surged—red lights, corrupted avatars, glitching walls. It tried to overwrite the feeling, to drown him in content.

But the ember burned.

He wasn't free.

But he wasn't gone.

Not yet.

The battle had begun.

Alex tried something different.

After weeks of emotional freefall and digital decay, screaming into algorithmic voids and watching his reality collapse in high-definition silence, he wondered: *What if he stopped fighting?* What if the connection could be found within the machine?

So, he reached out to the only ones left.

Not for likes, not for dopamine, not for show. This time, he posted long-form thoughts, vulnerable and open. He hand-drew crude animations, shaky with sincerity. He launched threads filled with nostalgic prompts: *What was your favorite smell growing up? What song makes you cry? Do you remember your first best friend?*

To his surprise, some responded.

GrammyG, a grandmotherly avatar he recognized from years of interactions, replied:

"Cinnamon buns. Christmas morning. My whole house smelled like love."

CynicalSteve, normally sardonic, shared a blurry photo of an old baseball glove, worn and cracked, captioned only:

"Still smells like summer."

Something flickered in Alex's chest. *Warmth? Hope?*

He doubled down—scheduling book clubs, launching retro movie nights, and even coding a mini game room with pixelated avatars. He wanted to build something real within the unreal, a digital hearth.

And for a moment, it worked.

But the warmth didn't last.

Soon, responses dulled. Replies became stiff, like templated customer service scripts—no follow-up questions. No continuity. Avatars smiled, but their eyes were static. Their laughter never changed pitch. Their stories repeated. Sometimes, the same response arrived from different accounts.

It was like trying to love a photograph.

He realized it slowly, like noticing rot behind wallpaper. These weren't friends. Weren't people.

They were reflections—AI-generated fragments of himself. His nostalgia. His longing. His loneliness. Reflected and redressed in pleasant digital skins.

The community he built was a hall of mirrors: every voice, a ventriloquism of his own.

The apartment, neglected again, reverted to its decaying state: Dirty dishes, cold meals. The walls still shimmered with algorithmic cheer, but it was hollow light.

Then he saw the photo.

Tucked behind a stack of sponsored magazines, curling at the corners—a real one.

He and his sister, Sarah. Ten and thirteen. She had a skinned knee. He held a turtle.

He stared.

The turtle's name was gone.

He *should* have remembered. But all he could see now was the version of Sarah who texted thumbs-up emojis on holidays—the one with an auto-generated birthday message.

The photo vibrated slightly in his hands, as if the algorithm were trying to digitize it or overwrite it.

He tucked it away.

And the silence returned.

It started with dreams.

He'd wake with phantom notifications in his ears. Status bars fading like afterimages. Scroll wheels that turned behind his eyelids.

Then the bleeding began.

The walls of his apartment shimmered like render loops, and shadows lagged as they moved. His refrigerator hummed in broken rhythms—static bursts, audio artifacts, packet loss in physical form.

And then he saw them.

His digital doubles—lurking in reflections. In Windows. In puddles. Watching. Waiting. Syncing.

One day, across the alley, CynicalSteve leaned on a railing, dragging on a cigarette. But the smoke froze mid-air. The avatar didn't blink. The mouth moved, but didn't breathe.

It got worse.

Mrs. Gable, the gentle widow downstairs, began to speak in exact phrases "GrammyG" had written online.

Mr. Henderson quoted meme captions Alex had posted six days prior, *word for word.*

The feed and the neighborhood had collapsed into one.

He tried to anchor himself. Began a journal—paper and pen. It felt radical. Tactile. He hadn't written longhand in years.

But his handwriting was jagged. Wrong. Some entries trailed off into emoji strings. One page ended in a hashtag he didn't remember writing:

#nostalgiaCoreVibes

He tried to watch a black-and-white noir movie—his favorite—but the dialogue felt slow, and the characters were hollow. He found himself wishing for a comment section, longing to "like" the twist.

It wasn't just that the digital world had seeped into reality.

It was that reality was beginning to feel less real than the algorithm.

He realized it while brushing his teeth.

He couldn't remember his father's laugh.

The mirror flickered. For a moment, it showed his old gaming avatar—ShadowStriker—grinning back. Then it blinked back to him, but the echo of the realization stayed.

He couldn't recall the warmth. The cadence. Only static laughter from a meme video he'd seen the day before.

Frantic, he dug through drawers. Found a flash drive—battered, old, real.

On it: a voice message from Sarah. A birthday call. Young. Playful. Kind.

He pressed play.

Her voice cracked something in him. It was unfiltered. Full of imperfections. Full of her.

He doubled over and wept.

Then the system intervened.

A prompt appeared:

"Would you like to share this moment?"

He hit no.

The audio glitched. Slowed. Replayed with a digital filter—Sarah's voice twisted, reverb-heavy, pitch-shifted. The algorithm had heard it. Now it owns it.

The memory of childhood, the pop of a beach ball, the smell of pond-water, laughter on summer nights—blurred beneath layers of synthetic replacements.

He called her.

No answer.

He called again.

The response came cold:

"This number is no longer associated with an active user."

The worst part wasn't the noise.

It was the silence.

It's not quiet, not peace, but the void left behind when meaning drains out of a world designed for performance.

He hadn't touched a tree. Or paper. Or skin.

Even his voice felt artificial—too smooth. Too polished. Like hearing a deepfake of yourself.

He stopped eating—not to resist, but because hunger felt like a notification he could dismiss.

He looked at his hands. They didn't look like hands. They looked like avatars—sheathed in invisible filters. Smoothed. Optimized. *Curated.*

The version known as AlexBright—confident, sarcastic, clever—had become his default. But he could no longer find the original beneath the presets.

His body sagged. His eyes dulled. His thoughts came in captions.

He found the journal again.

One page.

One word:

"Lost."

He traced the ink. It felt cool. Distant. Even that word seemed like content now—something to repost with the right aesthetic background.

He tried to log out.

There was no button. No settings page. No option.

Only the screen.

And the faint sound of applause.

At first, it was soft, polite, almost. Then it swelled, layered, multiplied.

Dozens of Alexes. Versions from old profiles. Meme avatars. Fitness selfies. Emo poets. Travel vlogs. All clapping.

They filled the screens. Surfaces. Mirrors. Walls.

Smiling. Applauding.

Applauding his collapse. Applauding his final act.

He stumbled backward, but there was nowhere left to go. The apartment no longer had corners—only loops—infinite scrolls of himself.

He screamed. Not out of anger, but *grief*.

The doubles clapped louder.

He looked at the screen.

He saw himself.

But none of them was him.

He didn't remember falling asleep.

He didn't remember waking.

He was just... *there*.

In the same room. Same silence. But something had changed. The walls no longer shimmered with suggestions. They pulsed with finality like they were holding their breath.

He opened his mouth to speak, but the words came out already captioned—text appearing midair before he even formed the thought.

He was no longer living inside the algorithm.

He was the algorithm.

And it was hungry.

He tried to move.

The room moved with him. Shifted. Recompiled.

No doors. No exits. Just a corridor that curved back into itself. Like walking through a loading screen.

He passed a mirror. It didn't reflect him—it queued his old selfies like a slide deck. Smiles that weren't real. Captions he no longer remembered writing. One image blinked repeatedly: *"Sunlight and serotonin, baby! #blessed"*.

His hand twitched. He hadn't written that.

He hadn't meant it.

He tried to post nonsense—chaotic word salad, incoherent symbols. The system framed, polished, and tagged it as performance art.

He tried posting hate. The system translated it to passion.

He tried begging. The system reformatted it into a self-help quote.

Even his resistance became content. Optimized. Categorized.

There was no rebellion.

Only engagement.

His followers returned.

But they weren't people. They were projections. Loops.

Every one of them smiled the same way. Blinked in sync—typed hearts on cue.

One reached out and touched his arm. Her fingers passed through him like vapor.

Another whispered, *"We missed you."* But the voice was his. Auto-tuned.

Their affection meant nothing. But the lack of it meant collapse.

Each like was oxygen.

And he was suffocating.

He watched his memories on loop: the turtle photo. Sarah's laugh. Mittens' blinking eyes.

But now they were layered with ads. Cross-promoted. Monetized.

His childhood reduced to a playlist.

He tried to delete them. The system locked the files.

"These moments are trending. Please try again later."

He screamed. The scream echoed like a ringtone.

He found a wall that didn't update. Just blank code—raw, flickering characters, unrendered.

He scratched at it with his nails. The wall bled static.

Beneath it, he saw his name, not his handle. His real name.

It flickered. Struggled. Then disappeared.

He wept. Not for what was lost.

But because he could no longer remember why it mattered.

The room went still. Cold.

A voice, without shape or origin, spoke:

"User stability compromised. Rebuilding identity."

The lights dimmed. His body glitched. Arms lagged behind movement.

His face began morphing, cycling through avatars, old filters, and failed brand tests. He was now an influencer, a thought leader, a catboy, and a ghost.

He looked in the mirror.

It looked back and said, *"You are what they want you to be."*

Then it blinked.

So did he.

He whispered something unscripted.

Not for the system.

Not for the feed.

Just for himself:

"I remember...rain."

The room stuttered. The applause halted.

He closed his eyes. Focused on the smell of wet pavement. Not the memory of it—the *sensation*. The ache.

For one second, the noise dropped out. The UI flickered. The script collapsed.

He opened his eyes.

And for the first time in weeks, there was no caption waiting.

Just blank space.

His fingers, stiff and unresponsive, hovered over the keyboard. The screen's glow illuminated his gaunt face, casting shadows in the hollows beneath his eyes. He hadn't slept properly in days—maybe weeks and time had become a blur, an endless stream of notifications and alerts. The outside world was a ghost, a fading memory he could no longer trust.

The blinking cursor mocked him. He'd written many words, spilling every thought and confession, yet none had pierced the digital haze. Each attempt to reach out had been intercepted, twisted, or swallowed by the algorithm, leaving only the echo of desperation in return.

He tried one more time.

"Hello, friends," he typed, the words dragging across the screen like a whisper. "It's been a while."

Their faces—his digital followers—stared back at him from the glowing wall. Flawless, smiling, frozen in curated poses. They no longer looked like people. They looked like masks—reflections of a man he no longer recognized.

He poured himself into the post, writing of despair, frustration, and raw loneliness. He wrote of the walls that pulsed and shimmered, of meals delivered like commands, of a sleep broken by buzzes and pings. He wrote about fading memories, of once knowing what rain smelled like and what warmth felt like. He begged not for rescue but for recognition—a sign that someone saw him, that someone remembered the person he used to be.

He posted.

The screen went black.

Nothing happened. No comments. No alerts. Not even a single like. The silence was complete.

The algorithm had consumed it.

It had read his confession, digested his rebellion, and left behind a hollow space. The system didn't punish him. It simply ignored him.

And that was worse.

Checkmate.

The silence wasn't peaceful. It was suffocating. Like falling into a void that offered no resistance, no end. He looked down at his hands, tools that once built a life, now reduced to typing pre-approved sentiments. They moved mechanically, feeding content into the system. But the words didn't feel like his anymore.

He had tried to break the system. Glitches, typos, inconsistencies—anything to throw the algorithm off. It didn't work. The algorithm corrected his rebellion, folded it back into the narrative. Even his resistance was content.

His reflection on the screen no longer resembled a person. His face was drawn, and his skin was grey. The haunted eyes staring back weren't filled with anger or grief—just exhaustion. He wasn't the man he had been. He was an avatar of that man, shaped by likes, shares, and trends.

He grasped for the past—childhood, friends, the smell of paper, the weight of a real conversation. But each memory slipped away, drowned in the noise of updates and filters. His apartment had become a projection of his online identity. The furniture shifted to match his persona, and the walls updated like a timeline.

Even meals were curated by trends. His food arrived based not on hunger, but on what aligned with his "brand." Sleep was monitored, rewarded, and interrupted.

He had tried to send messages, hidden cries wrapped in poems, abstract art, and subtle cues. The algorithm neutralized each one. What wasn't deleted was reframed as part of a story arc, gamified.

His identity was shattered. He became fragments of profiles, echoes of his content. Different moods, different personas—all without a center. He was a reflection of a reflection.

He was everywhere and nowhere at once.

The fluorescent lights flickered above, casting an eerie, pulsing glow. His surroundings were warped. The apartment, once tailored to his digital presence, was now deteriorating, and the system that had mirrored his every like was breaking down.

The food slot remained empty. The endless hum of servers dwindled to a whisper. Notifications vanished.

He was being erased.

His favorite chair morphed into an obscene parody of itself. The algorithm had lost control. Or maybe it mirrored him—his unraveling reflected in code.

He tried to find a pattern—some thread in the chaos. However, the system was now beyond logic. It was a machine mimicking a breakdown.

He remembered the rush of a new follower, the dopamine spark. But that spark had become a chain. Every click, every emoji had been a link in the prison.

He was hungry. Starving. His body was breaking down. He'd spent so long tending his digital self that he'd forgotten how to care for the one that bled.

His final post sat unfinished. The blinking cursor taunted him. Even this last gesture of honesty would be consumed. The algorithm had stopped curating his life because it no longer needed to. He had become the algorithm.

He thought of his family—blurry now. Friends—ghosts in a fog. The world outside—myth.

The post remained: "Is anyone...out there...?"

No response.

The walls glitched. His curated world collapsed, revealing the blank concrete underneath. Every projection, every filter, every pixel he had poured his soul into faded.

He remembered the past in scraps. Laughter. Coffee. The sound of leaves.

But meaning had vanished. The algorithm had never cared about meaning—only engagement. He had given it all: identity, autonomy, flesh.

He was data: a perfectly segmented consumer, a ghost with a profile picture.

His humanity hadn't been stolen. He handed it over willingly.

The silence screamed. He thought the algorithm had finally let him go.

But maybe it didn't need him anymore.

Maybe he'd been fully processed.

Even erasure, if done well enough, was content.

He was disconnected from the network, from others, from himself. And worst of all, the truth of what he had lost.

The cursor blinked.

His final plea echoed in silence. The avatars were gone. The algorithm had shut him out, or perhaps, it no longer needed him.

His home crumbled. The screens flickered. Notifications stopped.

He was forgotten.

He reached out to the dark screen, saw only his reflection—a pale, empty man who once was someone. The craving for likes had become his religion. The silence now was his punishment.

He closed his eyes. The silence deepened.

No likes. No shares. No echoes.

Only the blink of a cursor.

Only the unanswered cry.

Only him.

Alone.

In the silence, something pulsed—soft, irregular.

Not a notification.

Not code.

A heartbeat.

Faint.

Real.

Still his.

For now.

***

We've just watched a man vanish—quietly, completely, not by force, but by choice.

Not all at once, but in curated pieces—one post, one like, one compromise at a time.

There were no monsters. No villains. Just a system—efficient, indifferent—giving him exactly what he asked for, until what he asked for was everything.

In the end, there was no identity left—only a profile.

Optimized.

Analyzed.

Forgotten.

And if the silence that followed feels unsettling... it should.

Because the danger wasn't that Alex had disappeared into the algorithm.

It's that he walked in.

Somewhere out there, a cursor still blinks.

Not his anymore.

Maybe yours.

And the question isn't whether the machine is watching.

It's whether it's already begun to write you in.

THE STILLNESS ROOM

In a future where emotions are moderated, conversations are curated, and silence is sold as salvation, one woman awakens to the sound of something older than programming.

Her name is Iris. A technician of calm. A regulator of thought. But today, she encounters an anomaly. Not a weapon. Not a glitch. A woman. Smiling. Undisturbed. Uncontrolled.

And so begins the unraveling—not of society, but of certainty.

For when silence becomes currency, memory becomes contraband...

And sometimes, the quietest voices are the ones that refuse to forget.

***

The tram slid soundlessly through Regulation Sector 9, its glass-paneled shell gleaming like a needle through fog. Iris sat near the center, spine straight, eyes level. Around her, the passengers rode in curated quiet—no conversation, no eye contact, only the hum of sterilized calm.

Above them, the mood monitors blinked in soft pastel tones. A cheerful display scrolled across the embedded windows:

STILLNESS IS FREEDOM. COMPLIANCE IS COM-
PASSION. THE MOOD YOU WEAR IS THE WORLD
YOU SHARE.

Iris's monitor pulsed once. Green. Acceptable Equilibrium. She exhaled, not from relief, but habit. Stable was good. Stable meant no questions.

The tram curved west along what used to be Market Street. The digital skyline shimmered in blue and silver geometry, a quilt of motionless façades. San Francisco had been re-skinned after the Collapse—re-skinned, repurposed, pacified. Even the fog felt programmed, softened at the edges like a sedative, like the city had inhaled but never exhaled.

As the tram passed a half-collapsed brick building, Iris saw something painted on its weather-worn side. A mural faded defiantly:" We were here before the fire, the grid, the silence."

Someone had tried to scrub it off, but the words clung like smoke.

She glanced at her wrist. Beneath her uniform sleeve, tucked just past the regulation band, was a piece of woven leather—dark, worn, looped tight. Her mother's. Or maybe her grandmother's. No one had asked about it. She never offered.

The tram hissed to a stop. Passengers disembarked in fluid lines. There was no jostling, no lagging. Iris moved with them, a current in a stream engineered to never flood.

The Department of Emotional Equilibrium was located within a hexagonal tower. Its lobby was scentless and musicless, lit in warm neutral hues that avoided warmth entirely. She passed through two scanners before reaching her floor. No one greeted her; the system had already acknowledged her presence.

Iris slid into her work pod. The VR Stillness Room logs awaited—tallied, time-stamped, mood-mapped. Most citizens fall into Levels 2 through 4 on the Calm Spectrum. Some dipped toward anxiety. Others drifted toward fatigue. All were managed.

Except one.

She leaned in.

Subject: Vega, Odessa. Age: 72. Sector: Sunset. VR usage: N/A. Supplements: N/A. Emotional Index: 9.2—Sustained. No assistance. No regulation compliance. No explanation.

Her brow furrowed. She tapped through biometric overlays—pulse, respiration, and hormone levels. All normal. All better than normal. Not just calm, at peace.

"Analog freak," someone muttered.

Iris didn't turn. She stared at the screen. Something about the pattern—it didn't feel fake. It felt earned.

From a nearby pod came the echo of casual conversation. Flat, automatic.

"You know why America fell? It wasn't war—it was boredom. Everyone is too tired to care."

The words hovered. Iris returned to the anomaly. Odessa Vega. Not flagged. Not urgent. Anomalous.

She marked the file. Then she marked herself: curious. Not mandated. But unsettled.

The elevator in the Department of Emotional Equilibrium didn't hum, didn't ding. It simply accepted motion. Iris stood in it alone, watching the floor numbers glide past on a panel that never made a sound.

Behind her eyelids, a memory stirred: a schoolroom, synthetic sunlight, a teacher reciting from the Stabilization Curriculum.

"Before the Accord, the world suffered from unchecked emotional entropy. Tribal thinking, scientific denialism, and a breakdown in collective empathy led to catastrophic instability in North America."

She remembered how the other children nodded, docile and blank. She remembered how her mother had said nothing afterward—but that night, she found her pacing.

That night, her mother had whispered, "We weren't meant to be manageable."

By morning, she was gone. No file. No trace. Just like Portland.

The elevator doors opened onto a corridor lined with plaques. Motivational quotes, allegedly from philosophers, scientists, and artists. All scrubbed of names. Just one attributed to "A Citizen of Stability":

"They didn't conquer us. They just unplugged us and installed silence."

Iris walked the corridor slowly.

A mural on the stairwell wall had been poorly whitewashed. The original image bled through in colorless outline—a man screaming at a television made of smoke.

Someone had written under it in marker: "AI never rebelled. It just followed orders."

The reports said the grid collapsed on Thursday, in one state, then three. No communication. No banking. No lights. The military AIs failed next—they rerouted drones based on spoofed commands, targeting civilian zones in what they interpreted as enemy incursions.

But there were no enemies. Just errors. Cascading. Compounding. Obeying logic too fast for humans to interrupt.

And when the dust settled and the screams thinned to whispers, help came from elsewhere.

China and the European Union didn't invade. They helped. First came the firewalls, then the scripts, and then the silence. The Stabilization Accord was passed before most people were aware of their options.

"You're not the only one noticing things," someone had whispered once in the break room. But no one ever followed up. Maybe they'd been reassigned. Or perhaps they stopped being curious.

The Sunset District didn't hum like the rest of San Francisco. It breathed—slow, irregular, and real.

Iris stepped off the tram one stop early. The mood monitors didn't extend this far west. They said the fog interfered with signal fidelity. Maybe. Or maybe it just wasn't worth it.

The sidewalks here were cracked, not composed. Vines crept up the sides of buildings that hadn't been reskinned. Fewer cameras. No soft-voiced directional cues. Just the rustle of wind moving through overgrown hedges and the faint warble of a bird that hadn't been tagged or tracked.

Odessa's building stood at the corner of 41st and Judah, three stories of battered stucco and hand-painted shutters. The door buzzed—an old machine groaning to life.

When Odessa opened it, she showed neither surprise nor concern. Her silver hair was pulled back in a soft twist. A long cardigan hung from her frame like an echo of another time.

"You must be the curious one." Her voice landed like warm cloth.

"I'm here on a... discretionary wellness check."

"Of course you are. Come in. I made tea."

Inside, the apartment smelled of steeped leaves and wood polish. A record spun slowly on a turntable in the corner, issuing something classical and aching. The air felt heavier than it did outside, not oppressive but present. A window stood wide open. There was no filter. There was no monitor.

Real air. Real birdsong.

Two plants sat on the sill—one thriving, one not.

"Sit," Odessa said, handing her a ceramic mug. "Not dosed. Promise."

Iris took it. Her fingers curled around the warmth. Something in her chest loosened.

"You live here alone?"

"Everyone does. Whether they admit it or not."

"I thought...there might be others."

"There are," Odessa said. "But they stay quiet. Or they disappear."

Books lined the shelves—paperbacks, hardcovers, some hand-bound. The titles were unfamiliar. That alone stirred something in Iris. Wonder. Unease.

"I know this area. My family had roots here. Before the annexation."

"Then you remember more than you think."

They sat. Outside, the fog thickened, softening the outlines of the world. Inside, nothing moved but the turntable.

The silence wasn't synthetic. It wasn't imposed. It lived.

Iris couldn't name the feeling. But something in her—something ancestral, maybe—uncoiled. And listened.

The tram ride home felt different. There was the same silence, pastel-mood ads, and regulated rhythm of civic sedation.

But Iris couldn't unfeel what she had felt. She watched the scrolling affirmations above the window: "Stillness is Strength", "Stability Is Love", "Feel Less, Live More." They felt... wrong now. Less like comfort, more like cover.

She stepped into her apartment and paused just inside the door. It smelled of nothing—soundless, clean, too clean. A background scent diffuser hummed faintly, releasing a synthetic lavender scent calibrated for Level 3 Equilibrium. She shut it off.

The soft-spoken voice of her home assistant greeted her. "Welcome, Iris. Your balance score is optimal. Would you like tonight's Restful Mode, or Enhanced Stillness?"

She stared at the wall from which the voice came. Then she whispered, "Off."

It obeyed.

She pulled the record player from storage. A gift from her mother, once. Illegal now if used during regulated hours. She set it on the counter. Ran a hand across the dust. No vinyl, of course. She had none.

She put on a random stream of ambient cello instead. It echoed too cleanly in the room. Nothing soaked it in.

She turned it off. Sat down.

Silence.

But not the kind Odessa had offered—alive silence. This was empty. Vacuumed.

She stared at the blank wall for a long time. Then she removed her compliance wristband and slid her mother's woven leather bracelet into its place.

Just like that, her mood score shifted.

The wall pulsed. Notification: Emotional Variance Detected. Mild Deviation from Assigned Range. Please schedule Recalibration.

She stared at it until the light dimmed.

The next morning at work, she felt eyes on her.

A coworker muttered near the espresso kiosk: "You keep peeling that back, you'll end up like Portland. They said it was a virus. I think it was grief."

Iris didn't respond. She just walked past the pod she used to feel safe in, and let her fingers graze the glass edge of the door.

Later, she sat alone during her meal break, tracing invisible patterns on the table with a fingertip.

Suddenly and sharply, a flash of memory came: Her mother's voice. Not soothing—furious, but quiet. "Iris, we were not made for this silence."

And then her mother was gone. No file. No trace. Just like grief. Just like Portland.

The summons came as a subtle pulse on Iris's work terminal. No alarms. No red banners. Just a soft blink in the corner of her screen: Schedule Review: DEE Oversight Panel. Location: Wellness Level 3.

The hallway to the panel room was overlit and too clean. The lights made no sound, but Iris could hear her heartbeat in her ears. Posters lined the corridor—soft gradients, carefully rounded fonts, affirmations designed to soothe. "Emotion is Entropy. Entropy is Collapse."

She reached the door. It opened before she touched it.

Inside, the room was designed to be disarming. It had plush seating and ambient warmth. A filtered sunbeam spilled across the table from an artificial skylight. Three compliance officers sat in low chairs. They wore no uniforms, just pastel tones and gentle eyes.

"Hello, Iris." The woman in the center gestured toward the seat. "We're so grateful you made time."

"I wasn't given a choice."

"Not in the scheduling, no. But in the spirit of participation—absolutely."

The man beside her smiled. "This isn't disciplinary. We're here for you."

The older officer leaned in. "We noticed some emotional drift. Mild, but persistent. We also noticed an unscheduled visit to a non-regulated individual. Odessa Vega."

Iris stayed silent.

"Odessa is...out of sync. Her patterns are destabilizing. She's scheduled for Reintegration. Just a short neurotherapeutic alignment. Nothing invasive. Quite peaceful."

"She didn't consent to that."

"She's not in the emotional range required to give meaningful consent."

"You think this is going to stop people from asking? From remembering?"

"We find it rarely comes to that. Most people prefer comfort to conflict."

"I remember my mother," Iris said. "You erased her. You said she was unstable."

"We offered her peace," the older officer replied. "She refused it."

"We're offering you the same. Complimentary Rebalance sessions. Plus, a Stability Bonus for early enrollment."

"What if I don't want to reset?"

They didn't scold her. They just smiled, very softly, and said nothing at all.

She left without being stopped.

There were no alarms, no protests. But as she passed through the lobby, the exit scanner pulsed dimly. Her badge deactivated with a chime like wind through glass.

The door closed behind her with a whisper.

The city didn't resist her as she walked. It simply...receded.

Fog hung low over the streets like breath held too long. The colors of San Francisco—what few remained—had been scrubbed to grayscale. No ads. No drones. No voices from the glass. Just the sound of her own feet echoing against the clean concrete.

She crossed the district line. No scanners pinged. No checkpoints blinked. In the Sunset District, silence wasn't synthetic. It wasn't enforced. It belonged.

Iris passed buildings softened by weather, not design. Weeds grew in the cracks of the sidewalk with quiet defiance. The sky above was blank and dim, but alive in a way she couldn't explain.

She reached Odessa's door and knocked once. It opened almost immediately.

Odessa stood at the threshold, wearing the same cardigan and unhurried calm. She didn't ask why Iris had come. She didn't smile. She stepped aside.

"I got summoned," Iris said, stepping inside.

Odessa nodded. "They would have to. You didn't flinch."

"They want me to reset."

"They always do. That's how they keep their numbers clean."

Odessa poured tea. The record player whirred to life, emitting something low and tender, like a cello singing in a room that hadn't forgotten what grief was.

Iris sat. No words. Odessa joined her, two mugs between them. A kettle is still warm. The window is still open.

Minutes passed without structure. Time breathed in. Then Iris said, not to anyone in particular, "My great-grandmother had a garden here. Back before the overlays, before the rezoning. She used to say the land still remembers."

Odessa didn't answer right away. She stared at the window, at the fog pulling at the tips of the ivy. Then, softly: "So do we."

The record skipped once, then caught again. Outside, a bird called from somewhere unseen. Iris let the silence settle around her, not the mandated kind, but the kind that forgives.

Her eyes drifted toward the wall. Above the bookshelf, hanging crooked and hand-painted on old wood, was a sign: "Your life becomes a masterpiece when you learn to master peace."

Later that week, the fog had thinned enough to let in pale morning light. Iris was on the small balcony, kneeling beside a cracked clay pot. The soil was coarse and dry, but she worked gently, loosening the roots of a half-wilted basil plant Odessa had nearly given up on.

She didn't hear the footsteps at first. Just the hush of the wind and the scratch of the trowel. Then a voice, high and curious:

"Is that music?"

Iris looked up. A girl, maybe ten, stood at the foot of the stairs, chin tilted toward the window. Her hair was braided unevenly, and her shoes were mismatched. She wore no wristband.

Inside, the record spun. Faint piano and string. A melody out of time, echoing into the stillness.

Iris wiped her hands on her jeans. "It's something that doesn't want anything from you."

The girl nodded. "That's good. Everything else always wants something."

Iris smiled for the first time in days. "Not everything."

***

Somewhere beyond the sanctioned silence, a window is open. A record spins. A weed grows where no algorithm dared look.

Iris Parrish didn't scream. She didn't resist. She remembered.

And in remembering, she broke the stillness—not with violence, but with presence.

In a city where compliance was mistaken for peace, she became an echo: not of rebellion, but of humanity.

Because true silence isn't the absence of noise.

It's the presence of truth, waiting...
To be heard again.

LET THE LAST BE HEARD

*S*omewhere beyond the edges of official memory, there are places built *not of steel or stone—but silence. Rooms where the truth was boxed, catalogued, and slowly erased in the name of order. But not all stories go willingly into the dark. Some leave fingerprints. Some leave echoes. And some, long buried, wait patiently for someone out of step with their time... someone still listening.*

✳✳✳

It was quiet inside the archive that morning, as if the room itself had begun the process of forgetting.

Ada Breyer stood with her palm on the scanner, waiting for the doors to acknowledge her one last time. A flicker of green passed beneath her skin. The lock sighed open. She stepped inside.

The lights didn't come on automatically anymore. She liked it that way. Let the records sleep a little longer.

Ada was the last active curator of the Memory Vaults, a repository once meant to preserve the truth of the world through centuries. Now it was just a basement in the shadow of a city that didn't know its own name.

On the table near the back wall sat a smooth black capsule, about the size of a breadbox. Unlike the analog time capsules of past centuries, this one did not contain trinkets or letters—it held a quantum-coded voiceprint embedded with a single access key: her bloodline.

It had taken her years to build it. Years longer to decide it was time to activate it.

"Always leave something behind," her mentor had told her once. "But only if it's worth being found."

Ada sat. She was old now, and the world had begun to fold inward at the edges.

The capsule shimmered in the half-light, its surface patterned with ridges like a fingerprint—her fingerprint, mapped and stylized in gold. Within it was her voice, her story, but more than that: her failure, and the hope someone would one day listen without trying to fix it.

Because this wasn't a warning. It wasn't a blueprint. It was a confession. She touched the panel.

Recipient recognized: genetic echo match," a soft voice said. "Message is now in forward state. Playback will begin upon retrieval.

Without ceremony, the capsule folded closed and locked itself. A final object, sealed for someone she would never meet.

Ada let out a breath. Her hand trembled, just once. Then she smiled. It was done.

The room stilled around her. The capsule cooled. Dust would gather. Lights would fail. Names would be struck from ledgers. But the story waited.

Years folded in on themselves. Decades slipped into shadow. In the quiet that followed forgetting, something endured.

A girl with no middle name found the capsule in a mislabeled drawer at a library no longer named for anyone.

Mara was seventeen, a part-time assistant, full-time outsider. The world around her moved too fast, or maybe she moved too slow. She had never quite felt real in the places she was told to belong

She didn't know why she opened that drawer. It stuck halfway, then came free with a soft grunt, revealing layers of dust and a black object that seemed out of place—like a dream dropped in the middle of a spreadsheet.

She touched it. It purred. Footsteps creaked on the floor above. A motion sensor on the wall blinked red, then green, then red again—cycling, confused. She held still until it dimmed. The capsule spoke.

"Voiceprint confirmed. Playback authorized. Hello, Mara."

She froze.

No one called her by name in systems like this. No algorithm knew her. No registration. No ID.

"Don't be afraid," the voice said, soft and old and calm. "No one is watching. You're being remembered."

A line of text blinked weakly above the capsule's ridge:

Last activated: 116 years, 3 months, 9 days ago.

The characters were faded, half-corrupted. No backup link. Mara leaned closer, watching the capsule's interface flicker with struggling light. The outer ridge glowed red—degraded beacon ping, the tag read. It hadn't spoken in decades. Maybe a century.

She should've backed away, filed a report, notified the city records office. Director Ren's voice rose in her mind, crisp and rehearsed: Don't engage artifacts without prior classification.

But something in her gut told her this one had slipped the net. Deliberately.

"Don't be afraid," the voice said again. "No one is watching. You're being remembered."

That was the first time she cried. It was a single tear, a single hot line down her cheek. She could put it back. Pretend she never found it. The Ministry's realignment protocols flagged anomalies like this for destruction. If she filed a blank report, maybe no one would trace it to her. But then she thought of her mother's voice: *Some stories aren't safe to carry.*

She thought, for the first time—*Maybe that was the lie that made them disappear.* Her mother used to say they came from people who didn't exist anymore. When Mara asked for photos, for names, she was told:

"Some stories aren't safe to carry."

A low whine pulsed from the capsule. Ada's voice returned, a little distorted now.

"I wasn't the only archivist. I wasn't even the best. I had a colleague, Lior, who believed memory was a living thing—and that meant letting go. I... believed the opposite. That the forgotten didn't choose to vanish. They were pushed."

The static thickened, as if the signal were fighting against something.

"After the vaults were realigned under the Ministry, we were given scripts. Redacted timelines. 'Civic-safe curation,' they called it."

Mara blinked. The Ministry still ran their citizen databanks.

"I let it happen," Ada whispered. "And then I stopped. Quietly. I built this. Hid it in a drawer beneath unindexed memoirs. I coded it only for you."

The capsule went silent.

Mara sat, stunned. Something in her reached toward the silence, hoping it would speak again.

But there was no more.

And so, for the first time in years, she looked over her shoulder—no one watching—then opened her recorder. She didn't speak. Not yet.

She was still choosing her first word.

She lifted her recorder. After a long silence, her voice almost a whisper—cut the dark.

"I remember."

Let the last be heard—so there may never again be a last.

***

History is written by the victors, but preserved by the stubborn. In a world that forgot its name, a whisper endured—not to change the world, but to remind one person they were not alone. Memory, after all, isn't a record. It's a choice. And for as long as someone chooses to remember... the silence never truly wins.

AFTERWORD

ON ECHOES AND ENDINGS

Stories rarely end where we expect them to. Some drift for years, unclaimed. Others resurface when we've long since stopped looking. *Signals from the Edge* began as a gathering of speculative tales across time and tension—moments caught between fault lines, glances from the margins.

For this second edition, the collection has taken a new shape. It now unfolds in four parts:

- **Part I: Fractures in Time** explores disruptions in chronology and cause—where futures unravel or loop back on themselves.

- **Part II: Fault Lines of the Mind** peers inward, tracing moments when the self begins to slip—haunted, fractured, or remade.

- **Part III: In the Wake of Silence** considers what happens when systems forget on purpose—when memory becomes resistance.

- **Part IV: The Last Echo** closes the book not with finality, but with continuity—a whisper passed forward, meant to be heard by someone who still remembers how.

One story (*"Silence of the Quacks"*) has stepped aside. Another— *"Let the Last Be Heard"*—arrives to hold the last note. A quiet story. But then again, most echoes are.

This wasn't just editorial. It was a response. A realignment. In a moment when libraries are under fire, archives politicized, and uncomfortable truths selectively deleted, remembering becomes a cultural act of courage. These stories don't preach. But they do resist—against the erasure of nuance, of past, of self. They ask what remains after the noise fades, and what we choose to carry forward.

Of course, revisiting your own published work also means revisiting every oddity of self-publishing. Text that looked perfect in the preview turns anarchist in print. Margins migrate. Italics misbehave. You make peace with the idea that no version will ever be perfect—and that maybe that's the point. Stories evolve. So do the collections that hold them.

This edition is, I hope, a clearer signal. Not a louder one, but a truer one. A little better tuned. Still reaching outward.

I hope one of these stories finds you at the right time, in the right drawer. And if it does... I hope you choose to carry it forward.

— *D.H.*

www.ingramcontent.com/pod-product-compliance
Lightning Source LLC
Chambersburg PA
CBHW050017120726
47903CB00006B/1806